Magic of The Mortokai

The Third Chronicle of Daniel Welsh

I0555652

By

D G Palmer

MAGIC OF THE MORTOKAI

First edition. May 7, 2021.

Written by D G Palmer.

THE THIRD CHRONICLE OF DANIEL WELSH

MAGIC OF THE MORTOKAI

D.G. PALMER

Also By D G Palmer

The Chronicles of Daniel Welsh

Birth of The Mortokai

Rise of The Mortokai

Magic of The Mortokai

Standalone Books

The Choices of Man

Prologue

The night watchman paused and looked up at the full moon shining down on Almedia. He searched his pockets, and after finding what he was looking for, took a moment to pack tobacco into his long-stemmed pipe. He lit it from his lantern and took a few puffs to get the embers started. As the orange glow from the pipe's bowl partially illuminated his face, the watchman began his rounds once more, pleasantly puffing away.

He had barely taken a few steps when his ears twitched at the distinctive sound of a horse approaching. He raised his lantern and called out. 'Who goes there?' No reply came. The footfalls of the horse got closer and closer. The watchman drew his sword with a shaking hand and called out again, louder this time. 'Who goes there? Answer or face the consequences!' The hoof beats stopped and were replaced by approaching footsteps.

'The consequences?'

The voice from the shadows was familiar to the watchman. 'Tristan? Is that you?' He sighed with relief when he saw the swordsman step into the light. 'You had me worried there,' he laughed. 'Why didn't you say any—urk!'

Tristan grabbed the guard by the throat and began to squeeze. 'Consequences? You want to know about consequences? I'll tell you. Daniel, your Shade Slayer, will suffer the consequences for the actions of his father,' he said, his grip tightening. 'And when his beloved son is no more, then the great Eric Mondragon will know all about consequences too.'

Tristan released the lifeless body, and it slumped to the ground. The troubled swordsman crushed a pipe underfoot as he continued on his way to his destination, Hyasda's Herb and Alchemy store.

'HYASDA!' TRISTAN CRIED as he used his key to enter his elderly god-mother's closed store. 'Where are you? I would have words with you.' He was just about to make his way to her living quarters when the bricks on the back wall began to shift and move. When they finally stopped, her secret forbidden sanctum was revealed.

He stormed in, emboldened by the sense of betrayal he was feeling, which in turn fuelled his anger. 'You knew who he was all along, didn't you? And yet you said nothing!' Tristan swivelled around when he heard the voice of his guardian come from behind a curtain.

'I suspected,' Hyasda replied.

'You should have told me!'

'Who are you to make demands of me?' Each word carried with it magic power which rocked Tristan to his bones and forced him to his knees. 'You forget my interests will always take precedence. But now it seems as though our interests lay on the same path... for the moment.'

'What do you mean?'

A blackened and withered hand pulled the curtain aside, and Hyasda stepped out from behind it.

'What happened to your hand?'

'My hand?' The elderly woman held up her withered appendage and examined it. 'This was an unexpected parting gift from your brother. It's not as bad as it was. It will heal, especially now my duplicate is back, and I am once more whole. It will just take time.'

Tristan's brow creased as he tried to digest what he was hearing. He went over things in his mind several times and came to the same conclusion every time. Tristan looked up and what he saw in front of him confirmed what was going around in his head. Hyasda had dropped her disguise. 'You're — you're Sayyidah!'

The Egyptian mage, the shadow mistress, instigator of the second war, stood imperiously before him. 'That I am, dear boy.'

'You've lied to me from the beginning! Over and over again.'

'And your point is? Do not forget that it was I that saved you. Healed you. Your life belongs to me.'

'Why save me at all?'

'I watched your duel from afar. You fought well, many others would have fallen against you, but you were against Eric Mondragon. I sensed something in you, a good base to build on. I needed you in my ranks; even then, I was planning for my return. When the Athenatoi had left, I came to you. You were alive, barely, cursing the stranger you had fought and vowing revenge. The rage and hatred kept you alive, and I intended to help you direct it.'

'So, I am nothing but an instrument to you?'

'Again, I ask, what is your point is? You are but one of many tools I possess. And now the time has come to realise your goal. But you are not ready.'

'What do you mean?'

'You have seen the power Daniel commands. If you had continued with my magic tutelage, you would have been better equipped to face him, but you wanted to develop your swordsmanship, emulate your father in a way.'

The comment rankled Tristan.

'All is not lost, however,' Sayyidah continued as she cast a spell. 'We shall just have to do things the hard way – the painful way.'

Tristan's body suddenly became rigid, unable to move, his arms forced out wide. A large empty container then appeared near his right hand. A second similar-sized container near his left hand, this one, however, was filled with a black liquid.

'I am sure you are wondering what is about to happen to you. Well, in simple terms, the person you were is about to die.' She finished another spell, and blood began to pour from the fingers on Tristan's right hand. 'You are of course familiar with the exsanguination spell which I just used on Gydion. This time we will go further. A human can die from losing two-thirds of their blood, but fear not as it will be replaced with this.' She gestured towards the second container. 'The blood of a dragon. This is where the pain begins, but when it is over, you will have immense power, the power of a great wyrm!'

The draconic blood entered Tristan through the pores of his left hand. He could feel it burning through his veins like wildfire. He wanted to scream as sweat poured down his face, but couldn't because of the spell Sayyidah used to hold him. All he could do was scream in his head as the obsidian blood filled his heart. He could feel it beating faster and faster as if it were about to explode until each of its chambers had been touched by the foreign blood as it was pumped throughout his body.

As the excruciating blood transfer drew to a close, Tristan opened his eyes, now as black as the dragon blood that coursed through his body. Sayyidah smiled with great satisfaction at what she had just achieved. 'You have your Mondragon, Gydion, and now I have mine. Soon, my progeny of the champion, you shall go forth and cause the death and destruction that has been prophesied.'

Chapter One

A Recurring dream

Daniel stirred from his sleep as he heard the gentle crackle of a nearby fire. The rhythmic tapping of metal striking metal came from outside, interspersed with the baaing of sheep. It all suggested one thing to him. He opened his eyes and once again found himself in a place that was all too familiar. It was an Iron Age roundhouse, distinctive with its wattle and daub walls and conical thatched roof. For the last week, ever since the shock of Trinity's death and he had started living with Gydion in his sanctum, Daniel had experienced the same dream. He might have found it more distressing if he didn't always wake up and find the same person there.

Daniel sat up, and sure enough, there she was. Trinity. He stared at her, a smile on his face, as she knelt at the central hearth cooking. Every time his dreams brought him here, Daniel found himself watching Trinity for several minutes, taking in the sight of her, reaffirming his mental images of her, knowing that when he awoke, she wouldn't be there because she was gone from his waking life.

Trinity's head popped up. She could feel Daniel's eyes on her, and she turned to face him, pushing her fiery, red hair back from her gently perspiring forehead. 'I'll have to get used to you looking at me like that,' she smiled.

'Like what.'

'Like you can't believe I'm here,' she replied as she took the food off the heat and joined Daniel on the bed of straw covered with animal skins.

'Maybe it's because I can't.' Trinity was dead; he knew it. He had held her in his arms the day she died, struck by a spell from Sayyidah that was meant for him. She gave her life to save his. But here she was, dream or not, she was here. He could smell the floral aroma in her hair, and it evoked memories of that first day they had spoken.

'Even *now*, after all this time?' she questioned. 'I may be Aloisia, the daughter of a tribal warrior king, but I *am* here, with *you,* Daniel. You are my chosen. Nothing can change that. You make me so happy you cannot understand.'

'I think I can, because I feel the same.'

Trinity gently, slowly, ran her right hand across his forehead before cupping his cheek. Daniel repeated the gesture on her. To complete their ritual of love and companionship, they both lent in and kissed.

As they separated, Daniel heard distant singing and chanting. 'What's that?'

'No doubt it is Elginor and the other druids,' Trinity said through pursed lips.

'You don't like him much, I gather.'

'Of course not! And neither should you,' she replied sternly. 'If he had his way, I'd be with him and not you. He always had dreams of making me his high priestess. I don't trust him.'

'Then let's go and see what he wants, together,' Daniel smiled. Trinity relaxed at his response and nodded.

AS THE COUPLE STEPPED out of their roundhouse and walked through the massive hillfort of the Dobunni tribe, scenes of Iron Age life played out in front of them. Being a fan of history, Daniel enjoyed every second of it. He had read so many books about so many different ages and civilisations that he revelled at the chance to partake and experience everyday life almost two-thousand years ago.

A man with pheasants over his shoulder greeted them as he returned from a hunt with his favourite dog. A father and son played a game of chance at the entrance of their home whilst the mother used a rotary quern to grind wheat into flour. Other roundhouses had sheep bleating outside of them in pens. Some kids played, whilst others listened to a storyteller. The older boys trained to be warriors, using swords, shields and slingshots.

They passed various workshops, blacksmiths, potters, carpenters and weavers, all plying their trade, taking grain or intricately carved gold and silver coins as payment. Daniel thought that life in this age was rather idyllic and stress-free. That was until they got to the large roundhouse that King Connah used for gatherings and other official business.

DANIEL AND TRINITY entered the building where the tribal elders stood before the king. He was leaning forwards, listening intently to what they had to say. They were deep in discussion until the king's hunting dogs ran up to Trinity, tails wagging wildly, and he himself caught sight of his daughter, at which point he leapt out of his throne and brushed past his advisers.

Connah was every bit the Iron Age warrior king. Battle scared and burly, he was taller than any other man in the hillfort, and the surrounding tribes, coming in at over six feet tall. His thick moustache and braided hair, once a dark brown, was now heavily speckled with grey, which just seemed to add to the aura that surrounded him. 'My beautiful daughter and her chosen one!' King Connah bellowed as he threw his arms around them and squeezed.

'We heard the distant chanting and came straight away,' Trinity said once her father had released them from his bear hug.

He nodded his head. 'Yes, the druids are coming, but they are not the only problem we will soon face.'

'What do you mean?' Daniel asked.

'The Romans,' the king stated. 'They have returned. Claudius is trying to do what Caesar could not.'

'The Roman invasion,' Daniel whispered. As soon as he heard that bit of news, he knew that the year was 43AD, the year the Romans began their successful campaign in Britain. 'Aulus Plautius led them,' he recalled. 'They landed in Kent and swept inland, storming hillforts and destroying all those that stood against them.'

'Then the new ramparts you designed will surely be tested,' the king responded.

'And if you intend to stand and succeed against the invading Roman army, you will need the help of the druids, and we and the gods in turn will want their blessed one,' Elginor, high priest of the druids said as he strode into the meeting hall. He and the other female druids that followed were bald headed and pasted all over in chalky white paint with strange black symbols on top.

'Greetings, Elginor,' Connah said as he made his way back to his throne. 'You and your kin are welcome.'

The druid priest bowed his head slightly. Despite the pleasantries, there was a palpable tension between the two influential men. And it all stemmed from one thing. 'Aloisia, if the Dobunni tribe are to survive this invasion, you must shed your old life and step into the Druidic world that you were born to be a part of.'

'I can serve my people better by being here and fighting alongside them,' Trinity replied.

'And you shall, once you complete the rituals and pledge to walk the path of the druids. You will be reborn as an instrument of the gods.'

'I have already chosen the person in life I want to walk with,' Trinity said and squeezed Daniel's hand.

Elginor looked at their interlocked hands and then at Daniel. 'Unfortunately, it will have to be severed,' he smiled. 'You may have some abilities now, but in order to fully accept their blessings, you cannot let yourself be bound by earthly conventions.'

'Now that's not entirely true, is it.' A stranger to the Dobunni tribe had walked into the meeting, unannounced and unguarded, which prompted swords to be drawn. He appeared to be similar in age to the king. Unkempt blonde hair, lamb chop sideburns, scruffy multiple layers of different coloured cloths. He wasn't native to these isles; that much was certain. It was as if he had guessed or read a description of what people wore.

'Guards! Seize him.'

'That won't be necessary, King Connah,' the stranger stated.

'I will decide what is and isn't necessary,' replied the king. 'You sneak into my fort and think that there won't be repercussions? You have guts, I'll give you that. In a moment, I'll show just how much. What are you? A Roman spy?'

'Firstly, I didn't sneak in,' he said matter of factly, 'I simply walked in through the entrance. And I'm not a spy; I'm just a humble traveller who has an uncanny talent to find exceptional people.' He looked at Trinity and smiled. 'It seems, however, that I have found two for the price of one. Perhaps I'm not the only one that does not belong.' He looked pointedly at Daniel, forcing the young man to feel uneasy.

'What nonsense are you babbling? Just who, in the name of the gods, are you, and what do you want?'

'I'm sorry, your majesty,' he said, suddenly remembering his manners with a bow. 'My name is Penwyll, and I am here for your daughter.'

There was a hushed murmur amongst the elders. The king's guards took a step towards the strangely dressed man as Trinity tightened her grip on Daniel's hand.

Elginor smiled and rubbed his bald painted head. 'You needn't have wasted your time coming here. The girl is already destined for The Green Faith. She is a daughter of Sulis, and we will take her, instruct her, teach her that all living things are connected, that all aspects of the natural world are sacred, and under ritual, we will awaken her.'

'When I said I was here for her,' Penwyll interjected, 'what I actually meant is that I'm here to *help* her. She seems to have little interest in leaving her home. I can help her unleash her power right here. Without this man touching a hair on her head. Without any need to leave your home. That does not mean that it will be without sacrifice, however.'

'What do I have to do?' Trinity inquired.

'Do not believe this stranger! He knows not the ways of the druids.'

'I know the ways of the druids – the *true* druids. I have spoken with Cernounos, the Green Man, on many occasions. You may have some knowledge of The Green Faith, but you use that knowledge to exploit people and take advantage of them.'

'You dare accuse me of such things? I am the high priest, the spiritual mediator between nature and the people.'

'*All* the people? Yet, you only seem to accept women into your following.'

'As a female deity, Sulis calls to women,' explained Elginor.

'Then why are you it's head? Surely it should be a woman in that case.'

Elginor could feel the questioning looks upon him, even the ones that came from his own followers. Before those looks could formulate into more questions, the under-pressure druid cast a spell. 'Feel the wrath of Sulis!' He yelled as he unleashed a green globe of nature energy at his accuser.

Penwyll turned around just in time to defend against the cowardly attack and sent the destructive ball spiralling into the conical thatched roof of the roundhouse. 'As I said, you have some knowledge, but nothing to what this girl will become.' With a final look to King Connah, seeking permission to continue, Penwyll was ready to begin. 'It's time for you to go, Daniel. You have seen all you need to. Tell Gydion that he has chosen well.'

'Wait, What?' The way Penwyll had first looked at him made Daniel suspect he knew he wasn't supposed to be there. Him using his first name confirmed it. 'How do you know my who I am?'

'I know a great many things about a great many things,' Penwyll replied.

'I've heard that before.'

'And where do you think *he* got it from?'

'I thought this was just a dream?'

'It is; of sorts. But also, much more. You mean a lot to Trinity, but I'm sure Gydion will explain. Anyway, shouldn't you be getting up now? After all, it is your first day at Hartfield Mage Academy.'

Chapter Two

A revelation

Daniel opened his eyes to the soft melodic sounds of song and music. A little golden butterfly-winged figure, singing and playing a harp, fluttered above his head. 'Stop alarm,' he said, and at his command, the little musician burst into a shower of golden faerie dust.

When Daniel first arrived at Gydion's sanctum and was given his own bedroom, which was actually more like a suite compared to what he was used to, the Archmage told him that it was enchanted, like many rooms in the tower.

'Open the curtains,' he said, and they did as they were told, drawing aside to be neatly tied up to allow the first of the sun's rays to stream in even though there were no windows visible on the outside of the tower. Daniel smiled broadly, like a kid in a candy store. He couldn't help it. Seeing all the mundane things people did back on Earth being done by magic was a marvel for him to behold. He wondered what his mother would think of it all, and in that moment, Daniel came to the decision that one day he would bring her to visit Ariest.

A short time later, Daniel made his way down for breakfast, where Gydion was already waiting. 'Are you going to be giving lessons in martial arts?' He remarked, looking at the changsang the Archmage wore.

'This was a gift from sword master Haiche. It's light and comfortable, good to wear for meditation,' he explained as he demonstrated its ease of movement in the oriental clothes. 'The wardrobe probably thinks I am in need of a session, hence why it presented it to me this morning.'

The enchantment on the bedroom wardrobes allowed them to pick your outfits. Not only that, but to select items of clothing it felt you needed on any particular day. Clothes weren't the only thing the sanctum could provide to meet your needs. Food as well. Whatever food you desired would appear on the table in front of you. It wasn't a free for all, however, since it would limit the amount of "bad" food you were allowed to consume. So, no rum and raisin ice cream for breakfast, lunch and dinner, no matter how many times Daniel tried. So magical and extraordinary was Gydion's sanctum, that if someone told Daniel that it was alive, he would have no recourse but to believe it.

The teen sat down at the dinner table, noting that the room's decor had changed from the reds and browns it had yesterday to the yellows and oranges of today. This was the third time Gydion's abode had redecorated itself within the week Daniel lived there. 'It still hasn't made a decision about its new look yet, then?' Daniel asked rhetorically as a bowl of porridge, made to his favourite consistency, with blueberries and chopped banana appeared in front of him.

As the pair ate their respective breakfasts, Gydion, tucking into his beloved Lincolnshire sausages, they discussed the youngster's progression through the Archmage's personal library, which made the elder almost splutter his fruit tea. 'Just to clarify, you have read how much?'

'At a guess, I'd say roughly two thirds,' Daniel replied thoughtfully.'

'That's three hundred books. Impressive. I'll have to take you to the tower sooner than I thought.'

'The tower?'

'Yes, the Tower of Par Atreia. It is the most comprehensive library of magical text anywhere. It has some fourteen million books on its shelves, and its librarians are always adding more. Since they specialise in texts, I intend to have them go over the Book of Azul just in case I've missed something to suggest why Sayyidah wants it so badly.'

Daniel stared into space as he tried to contemplate the vast number of books. 'Fourteen million,' he repeated over and over. 'When can we go there?'

'Not so fast, young man,' Gydion began, instantly putting a stop to Daniel's enthusiasm. 'It isn't a simple case of walking into a building with a library pass. You need to be at least a High Mage to even be allowed to apply for admittance.' Gydion knew just the thing to clear Daniel's crestfallen face. 'I know it won't take you long to make it to High Mage, even though today may be your first day as an Adept. Which reminds me, I was going to add this to your wardrobe, but I thought I'd present it to you myself.'

Gydion held out his hands, and after a bright and brief light, a perfectly folded set of clothes appeared there. It was a pair of navy-blue trousers with a 3/4 length single-breasted blazer in the same colour with a stand collar and red trim. There was elaborate patterning around the collar and cuffs which were also red.

'This is your academy uniform,' Gydion explained. 'The red shows your level as an Adept. When you advance to the next level, it will change colour; purple for Initiate, gold for Novice. The inside pockets are enchanted with a "store-all" spell, so you won't need a satchel.'

'This is awesome! I wish Trinity could see it.' Daniel fixated on the uniform, gripping it tight as he held back the tears that were trying to build up, then whispered. 'I dreamt about her again.'

'The same dream?' Gydion asked, suddenly attentive to his young ward.

'Yes; the same Iron Age setting, the same Dobunni tribe, living in the same roundhouse together. Now that I think about it, each time I've had the dream, a little more is added to the "story". This was the first time the druids came for her, and someone named Penwyll, a powerful Mage by all accounts, arrived to stop them. He was about to awaken her mind when he sent me away.

Gydion chuckled. 'Penwyll, you say? Master Penwyll was the Mage that trained me.'

'That explains it then. He said that you had made a good choice, and when I asked if this was a dream, he said that you would explain it all to me. So, what does it all mean?'

'These aren't dreams,' Gydion began after a momentary pause. 'What you are experiencing is her past life. The woman you know as Trinity was actually born Aloisia in 25CE Britain. It was no accident that I chose the name Trinity. She has had several past lives but only three major ones. This the third after Aloisia and Bianca Daumier, and you are her anchor to this life, just as

Daicornog and Cassius Stewart were in her past. You will play a part in her revival.'

'What do you mean "revival"?'

'Trinity's resurrection into her final form. She has always been special; you've seen that for yourself. She has been chosen by the goddess Sulis. Now is the time for her to ascend to her rightful position, earlier than we anticipated, but needs must. I have no idea what will be expected of you, but just as the goddess has chosen her, Trinity has chosen you. The love you have for one another is a powerful bond, which is why she is subconsciously linked to you. By all accounts, you are her anchor. Only you can help her progress, so there must be some clue, some connection between her past lives that is important for you to know. Whenever you have these episodes, be sure to pay attention to everything.'

Daniel hardly heard a thing Gydion had said because one overriding thought reverberated through his mind. *Trinity is alive!*

Chapter Three

Illandor, the Imperial City

This was the first time Daniel had ever had to wear something so smart. As he admired himself in the mirror, the young Mage couldn't help but notice how good Hartfield's uniform looked on him. No matter how well the outfit suited him, he knew that Finn would tease him the moment she saw him in it. Whenever that was going to be.

He hadn't liked the way Gydion had all but whisked him away from Finn as if she didn't matter. But she was his friend. To Daniel, she mattered just as much to him as Trinity did. They had both been integral in his social growth; shown him what it was to love and be loved, beyond the familial. They had become fast friends, and he wondered if she had made it to his family estate yet.

It would have been good to have gone there with Tristan, both brothers seeing it together for the first time. But things hadn't worked that way. His older brother had revenge on his mind, and he intended to fulfil it, even if it was against his own father.

'Come on, Daniel!' Gydion called from downstairs. 'You're going to be late!'

'I wouldn't be late if you would just teach me yourself,' Daniel responded as he came running downstairs.

'And I told you, I'm busy,' the Archmage answered as he looked at Daniel in his uniform. 'It suits you very well.'

'I know, right?' replied Daniel as he admired the academy badge, a gold and red shield with a triangle overlaid with a large circle and two smaller circles, one at the point of the triangle and one below. Above the shield-shaped patch was stitched the word Hartfield Academy.

'That logo represents every student at Hartfield; the triangle is you and your thirst for knowledge, the circles are your Essence reservoirs. And there's also this. What is your name, student?' The Hartfield Academy lettering on the badge vanished to be replaced by Daniel's own name, momentarily, before it reverted back to reading Hartfield. 'I quite like that touch,' smiled Gydion. 'Anyway, we must leave before you are even later.' Gydion walked with purposeful strides to the sanctum entrance, the entrance which couldn't be seen from outside. Daniel hurried to catch up, and when he did, the door opened, and they stepped out into the city.

After several quick hand gestures from the Archmage, a gust of wind surrounded the pair, lifted them into the air and transported them over the Imperial City. Daniel was beginning to like the feeling of being airborne. But this controlled flight was a far cry from his previous experiences; falling above Almedia and riding the back of a terrifying Manticore in the Imperial City bank vaults.

The Imperial City was, in actual fact, two cities. At its epicentre, floating above, was the original elven city of Illandor. It was created millennia ago, through magic, which was easy to believe given its pristine, ethereal and otherworldly architecture. As the "Dark Times" began and a new race, humans, were brought to Ariest against their will, in most cases, so new settlements began springing up around the elven city.

By the end of the Elven War, a significant human population had been established, and the activity of non-elves around Illandor had become a metropolis in its own right and had been dubbed Imperial City. The High Bourne Elves, the supreme rulers of Ariest, were not best pleased at the predicament, believing that being in such close proximity to beings, whose lives were but a fleeting moment of their own, would affect them, invariably leave them joyless and despondent, as they would be surrounded by ageing, death and ultimately the grief associated with those mortal lives. These elves weaved magic as easily as breathing. It is as natural to them as water, air and earth are to humans. Through high magic rituals performed by these ruling elves, the city of Illandor was raised thirty metres into the air, where it remains, in a self-imposed segregation from the rest of Ariest. The crater that was created, during the passage of time, filled with water to become Illandor Lake.

Daniel thought it was an interesting history, one of many that this colourful world of Ariest seemed to have. And the more he learned, the less straightforward and harmonious things seemed to be. The High Bourne Elves separating themselves from and, literally, above the other races wasn't far removed from the mandate of the Krez, the right to rule and exert dominance over all races because they were the perfect creation of the gods, but the Krez were reviled, while the High Bourne were lauded.

They circled around Illandor and landed in the lush, green grounds of a large, walled, estate not far from the lake. Several buildings were part of the property, all of varying sizes, and the main one, which Daniel and Gydion approached, had gold flags with the same insignia as the one on Daniel's badge.

'Welcome to Hartfield Mage Academy!' Gydion said with a flourish.

'I still don't see why you can't train me,' came Daniel's reply.

'Long ago, things were like that,' Gydion explained, 'a master taking a student or two and teaching them as best he could. However, some Mages, no matter how good they are, may not be good teachers. There was no dedicated structure to their training. Some Mages even ended up teaching themselves. When the first war happened, the inadequacies of depth in the Mage talent pool were exposed by this method, and The Assembly founded the Mage Academy with a much more formal method to education. Now masters act as mentors to students during their academy years and take over their further education.'

As they walked and talked, Daniel couldn't help but notice that every student they passed bowed with respect towards Gydion. He expected that it would have been a similar situation if his dad had been there amongst a group of swordsmen.

Seeing the adoration on their faces, the same look film stars got from fans back on Earth, was something Daniel could only dream of one day receiving. He knew he would have to work hard if he ever hoped to make it a reality, and that's exactly what he intended to do, just as his father had wanted him to.

Unfortunately, in life, not everything we plan to do is achievable and if they are, they are seldom easy to obtain. That's not because of anything we ourselves do, but rather because life enjoys throwing obstacles in our way.

'Well, well, well, Mr Welsh. We meet again,' sneered Radek Zislaa.

Chapter Four

Hartfield Mage Academy

Gydion climbed the stairs and shook the hand of the Master Mage. 'Ah, you two know each other?'

'Our paths have crossed,' Radek answered, his piercing gaze stuck on Daniel.

'Radek,' Gydion said to Daniel, 'is the headmaster of the academy.'

'You mean vice-chancellor and de facto head,' said Radek, 'since you are in fact the chancellor and head of Hartfield Mage Academy.'

'You know as well as I that it is just a figurehead role. Radek is also Vice Archmage and takes the chair in my absence.'

Daniel's blood ran cold when he saw the bald head and braided sideburns of the Mage he had shouted at when he had returned to Ariest after visiting his parents back home on Earth, at the Faerie Transport Network. He didn't know what to say and just smiled weakly. It wasn't as if he regretted his outburst at the FTN station, he stood by what was said, the Mage Assembly and the Queen of Ariest *were* wrong to ignore the calls for help from their then ally, the sea-dwelling Undany, but maybe he did regret the manner of it, perhaps he could have been a tad bit more diplomatic. Especially now that he knew that this creepy Mage had such a high standing within the magical community.

Luckily, the visage of the woman that stood next to the headmaster distracted Daniel so much that he didn't have time to stress about any possible repercussions for his actions. She stared back at him with ruby coloured eyes, her long jet-black hair flowing in the gentle breeze.

There were quite a few words that Daniel could think of to describe her, astounding and extraordinary just two of them. Both words were perfect descriptors for her lustrous skin, jewel-toned eyes and beauty. She was statuesque, almost as tall as Radek but much more athletic.

She reached out her hand in introduction, and Daniel took it enthusiastically. 'I am the Proctor, Morgana Goodfellow,' she said as Daniel stared. When he didn't reply, she prompted him. 'And you must be the Shade Slayer, Daniel Welsh, son of Eric Mondragon.' Daniel nodded.

'Shade Slayer?' Repeated Gydion as he shook forearms with Morgana.

'Apparently,' she began, 'that is what they called him in Almedia after he vanquished the Shade there. With all the traders and bards, the story is slowly reaching north. I take it that this is the first time he has met a Scion of Galadrin?'

Gydion gently elbowed Daniel. 'Close your mouth, lad, you're embarrassing me. The Tower of Par Atreia is all he knows, and I only mentioned it to him today.'

'So, he knows nothing beyond Ariest? This is just more proof that he should wait until next term or even next year.'

'That would be a waste of his time, Morgana. Just give him the books he needs, and he'll surprise you.'

'We are only having this discussion because it's you, Gydion,' she admitted. 'That and the deeds he has already accomplished. But I am still not pleased with this highly irregular admission so late in the academic year.'

'Daniel is exceptional. He'll catch up in no time, trust me.'

'And if he doesn't?'

'We'll expel him,' Radek added matter of factly.

Daniel looked at Gydion, already feeling the pressure.

'Don't worry, Daniel, I believe in you, and so does Penwyll. You've read my library, so the spell knowledge is in there,' he said as he tapped the youngsters head. 'All you have to learn is how to apply that knowledge. And that's why you're here. You'll be fine, you're the Shade Slayer after all.'

Hearing Gydion's words of encouragement boosted Daniel's morale no end. His chest swelled with pride. If the Archmage believed that he could succeed, then surely, he could.

'Right, I need to go,' Gydion said. 'The quicker I get started, the quicker I'll be back.'

Before Daniel could even ask where he was going, Gydion was gone.

'Typical,' Radek said with a roll of his eyes. 'Leaving at the drop of a hat, expecting others to pick up after him. This is what he did last time, and look how long he was gone then. I swear the Mage Assembly should just make me the Archmage and be done with it.' When he realised that he was thinking out loud, he quickly changed the subject. 'Don't you have admission papers you should be taking care of, Morgana? And while you do that, I'll take the boy to his first lesson.'

THE MAGE ACADEMY'S main building looked like a grand Elizabethan prodigy estate, a palace in all but name, with its prominent examples of stone masonry and proportion exhibited in only the highest sixteenth-century architecture. It had many windows that got larger from the ground floor up to the fourth, where they were almost floor to ceiling. Some even joked that there was more glass than wall.

Daniel was excited about seeing as much of the academy as he could, but there was one thing troubling him. He understood why the creepy Radek Zislaa would be frosty towards him but what he didn't understand was what could he have done to draw the ire of Proctor Morgana. After all, she had seemed receptive towards him when she introduced herself.

'You can blame Gydion for that. She is a Scion of Galadrin, a celestial crusader, from Simaciu,' Radek answered after Daniel swallowed his pride and asked him about Morgana. 'The divine strength of will, extraordinary patience, and discipline her people possess make her ideal for her position here. The proctor is the internal Ombudsperson. She makes sure that the academy and its members adhere to its statutes. The role also incorporates student welfare and responsibility for enforcing academy discipline and sanctions; I'm sure you will become very familiar with that particular side of her role,' Radek said with a smile.

Daniel looked sideways at the headmaster for his veiled insult. There was no alternative for him but to grin and bear it. However, when they arrived at the classroom and the headmaster opened the door to Daniel's first magic lesson, to say the earthen was aghast would be an understatement. 'This can't be right,' Daniel said as he looked into the classroom of children as they practised their hand gestures. 'It must be the wrong room.'

'What do you mean? Professor Pinnywickle's class on familiar conjuration is a foundation course.'

'But they're kids!'

'Yes, ten to twelve-year-olds tend to be Adepts.'

'But I'm much older! Shouldn't I be in a class for my age group?'

'Here at Hartfield Mage Academy, your level of study isn't determined by your age. If you think you are good enough to progress and pass the Test of Succession, you can move on. For exceptional students, it's that simple.'

The words of the headmaster swirled around Daniel's mind. He couldn't bring himself to join a class of children. How humiliating would that be, he thought. 'What grade would someone my age be in?'

'Well, there's Adept, Initiate and Novice levels, and each level has a grade one and two. I'd say that your age group would be Novice. Or, *if* you were truly exceptional, you would be getting further education travelling with a master as a High Mage,' he added with a sneer.

Daniel ignored the comment. 'I want to start at the Novice level,' he stated after a moment's thought, before continuing to convince himself that he was making the correct decision. 'I've fought Shade. I've fought Sayyidah. How hard could it be?'

'Indeed,' smiled the headmaster. 'I know just the class for you.'

It wasn't far to the classroom in question, and when they arrived, Radek threw open the classroom door. 'I'm sorry to interrupt, professor Tavsan, but we have a new student starting today. This is Daniel Welsh, the Shade Slayer.' Daniel was shoved out in front so everyone could see him. There were gasps and whispers as the students saw the young hero of Almedia for the first time.

'Um, I see,' professor Tavsan replied. She cleared her throat before continuing with her lesson. 'Well, welcome to the class, Mr Welsh. We'll find you a space in just a moment. In Abjuration class, we learn and practice the different ways of protecting ourselves and others, be it barriers, wards or some other kind of effect. This term we have been learning the spell, Anti-magic Field. This field can either be personal.' Professor Tavsan cast the spell in demonstration, and a luminescent barrier appeared around her. After a moment, it expanded into a dome. 'Or it can be extended to encompass an area and protect several people. In each case, it still works in exactly the same way. Magic cannot pass its outer layer; no one within the field can cast spells, use magic abilities or magic items. It is a potent defence that can only be penetrated by a stronger Mage and is tempered by its duration. Unlike a Magic Shield, which lasts until its durability is expended, the Anti-magic Field has a duration of up to one minute before it ends.

The students hung on every word the professor said. Many had taken notes; others practised the specific hand movements.

'Now,' professor Tavsan continued, 'yesterday's homework was to practice projecting your own fields. So, what we will be doing, in turns, is to have one of you come up, project your Anti-magic Field, and another student will send an attack at it. Who wants to go first?'

'Well, since Mr Welsh is already standing, we might as well use him, don't you think?' Suggested Radek Zislaa who, up until that moment, had been quietly standing by.

'If you insist,' replied the professor.

'I do,' the headmaster said with a nod.

'Then I'll just need someone to cast the attack spell.'

'Might I make a suggestion there also? As this is the Shade Slayer and by all accounts is exceptional, we'll need someone of high standards; Philip Strath-Holm perhaps.'

Halfway up the banked seats in the lecture room, a boy with black combed back hair and gold armed rimless glasses sat reading his notes. At the sound of his name, he stood up, took his glasses off and, as he made his way down the stairs, slipped them into the pocket of his red trimmed uniform. Excited whispers and murmurs accompanied him all the way down.

Two white-haired girls, twins, that sat next to him stood and shouted out, 'Show him, Philip!'

'Cara and Mara Yacon, be quiet!' Professor Tavsan snapped.

The buzz surrounding the young man was well deserved. Many of his peers believed he had power enough to be a High Mage let alone a Novice, but he never put himself forward for the Test of Succession, and when tutors did so on his behalf, he never seemed to be able to get the job done.

When Philip Strath-Holm stood before him, Daniel saw for the first time that he had two different coloured eyes; his left was blue while his right eye was hazel. He felt some sort of affinity towards him. Perhaps because he knew if they were back on his world, then Philip would no doubt have to contend with the same stares that he would. They were like kindred spirits.

'Now,' began professor Tavsan, 'Mr Welsh, you are going to erect your anti-magic shield at my prompt and then you, Mr Strath-holm will test its strength with a spell. Got it? Good.' She turned, pointed at Daniel and said, 'Go!' At which point, Philip, with impressive hand speed, cast a spell. Daniel was like a deer in headlights when the attack came at him. It struck him in the chest, and almost immediately, pus-filled boils erupted all over his hands and face.

There were groans of disgust that reverberated around the lecture room, accompanied by the sound of several students as they retched at the sight of boils beginning to burst and release the oozing yellow viscous liquid which had been within them moments before. The pus itself was acidic, and Daniel waved his hand about in pain as the acid burnt his flesh.

Professor Tavsan and students in the front rows tripped over each other desperate to evade the offensive goo. The other students howled with laughter at the scene before them.

Daniel had flashbacks to his high school back on Earth. He thought those days of people laughing at him were behind him. But here they were again on his first day at Hartfield Mage Academy. He couldn't go through it all again; the bullying, the hiding away.

So, Daniel did what he was good at. He ran.

Radek Zislaa all but leapt out of his way before he checked his robes to make sure he hadn't any pus on him. Daniel ran into the corridor and almost into Proctor Morgana Goodfellow, who had been drawn to the commotion in her search for Daniel and the headmaster.

All sounds of laughter stopped as the proctor appeared at the door with Daniel, a stern look on her face. Students were tripping over each other, this time not to avoid projectile pus but to get back into their seats.

'Is someone going to explain what's going on here, or do I have to start cracking heads?'

The proctor was indeed an imposing and fearful figure, for students and professors alike.

Chapter Five

Daniel's first class

Daniel had been wrong about the proctor. It wasn't that she hated him at all. She was a proponent of order and hated wrongdoing; be it a student joining halfway through the term or that same student being bullied.

'What the vekt do you think you were doing taking this student to participate in a Novice class? Luckily that spell he was hit with was easily reversed. He could have been seriously injured.'

'Doubtful, I knew it was an Abjuration class. I am the headmaster, you know. Besides, it was what he wanted.'

'And since when do you give students what they want?'

'When that student comes with the word "exceptional" attached to him. Although,' Radek turned to face Daniel, 'I wouldn't call what I saw exceptional; I would say it was more... like pathetic.' With that, the tall figure of Radek Zislaa strode off and disappeared around a corner, leaving Daniel alone with the proctor.

'Don't pay any attention to him,' said Morgana. 'If Gydion says that you're exceptional, then I'm inclined to believe him. He doesn't usually take such a vested interest in students, so you must have something about you. Anyway, here we are.' They had made their way back to the first class Daniel had visited, but before she opened the classroom door, Morgana Goodfellow gave him a little origami bird.

'What is it?' Daniel asked as she gave the folded paper a quizzical look.

'It's a wayfinder. Infuse it with a bit of Essence and then ask it to show you the way. Come and see me after class. You'll need to choose what subjects to study for the year.'

Daniel nodded, and the proctor opened the door.

'Ah, you've come back,' Professor Pinnywinkle said. 'Hopefully you'll be taking part in the lesson this time.'

'He will be,' assured the proctor. 'This is Daniel Welsh. And this, Daniel, is Professor Penelope Pinnywinkle, your Summon Familiars tutor. I'll leave him in your care, Penelope.'

'So, Daniel, what do you know about familiars?' Professor Pinnywinkle asked once Morgana had left.

'Well,' began Daniel. 'Familiars are magically summoned creatures that are linked to the spellcaster.'

'That's excellent! Well done.' Pinnywinkle enthused.

'I read it in one of Gydion's books.'

She walked Daniel around the class. The animals he saw were recognisable cousins of species back on earth; dogs, cats, weasels. He noted that not every student had a familiar with them, understandable considering this was the lesson that taught you how to gain one, and the ones that did have were playing with them and doing tricks. One student seemed to be talking to himself, but the professor assured Daniel that the student's familiar could turn invisible.

'Does that mean familiars have powers too?'

'Oh yes! Familiars are not ordinary animals people would have as pets. They have a telepathic bond with their master, but they can also talk.'

'Really?' Daniel said incredulously and took another look around the class, and sure enough, the animals talked back.

'Familiars can do many things to help the spellcaster. You know that lower-level Mages have to continually recommit used spells to memory? Well, your familiar can not only memorise additional spells for you; they can also deliver spells, as in ones that need to be in touching distance. They can act as scouts, assistants, fonts of knowledge amongst other things. They will be your most loyal friend and staunchest defender, fighting by your side to the death.'

'Wow! They sound amazing.'

'Because they *are* amazing!'

'So, can you help me summon my own familiar?'

'Of course, I can! That's the name of the class.' The professor called over the three remaining students that still hadn't summoned familiars. 'Ok, let me show you the somatic.'

'The what?' a confused Daniel asked.

'The hand gestures that create the magical nexus to draw the essence from you to fuel the spell. I take it you haven't been to any of Professor Milton's Magic 101 classes?'

'No, I haven't, but I do know the hand gestures.' Daniel said and showed her what he easily recalled from Gydion's many spellbooks.

'Excellent!' Professor Pinnywinkle replied. 'Most of the students that are struggling at the moment are the ones that can't quite get the somatic right. Ok, so which Essence pool do you think we use?' A hand from each of the children in the small group shot up into the air but she pointed at Daniel.

'Personal, using arcane energies.'

'Correct, Mr Welsh. So, now we're all going to try to cast it together, slowly.'

Daniel tried to concentrate on the arcane energy of his Personal Essence pool. As they performed the gestures, he could see the magical energy flowing from the professor's head, down her arms to her hands. He saw the same happening to himself and the three students.

In all the time he had been around magic, he had never taken the time to watch it. The way his purple luminous Essence moved through his arms was almost hypnotic... beautiful.

Then the familiars began to appear. An eagle on the professor's shoulder, an artic fox around the feet of student and a large centipede on the shoulders of another. But Daniel and the final student struggled. He could see that one of her hand gestures was incorrect. A fact which was brought to the girl's attention by professor Pinnywinkle. Once the correction was made, a four-eared rabbit appeared at her feet.

Then the bell rang, signalling the end of the class. Daniel was the only one without a familiar. He was left wondering why, and he wasn't the only one.

'Don't worry about it, Daniel,' the professor said as the other students left to go to their next classes. 'Maybe it's not ready to reveal itself to you yet, that's all.'

'Not ready?'

'Yes. Sometimes —' Professor Pinnywinkle began just as her eagle familiar whispered in her ear. 'What? Are you sure? Well, Daniel, according to Ciran here, none of the familiars were able to answer your call.'

'I don't understand. What does that mean?'

'Familiars live in another realm. Our spell of summoning opens a portal to that realm. We can't pick our familiar, and likewise, the familiar can't pick its master; it's by random chance. Only the chosen one can go through the portal.'

'Maybe my portal was too far for my familiar to get to.'

'It doesn't work like that. Portals appear within a distance of every creature there. No, this can only mean one thing.'

'And what's that?'

'Your familiar is already here!'

DANIEL STOOD IN THE corridor, Professor Pinnywinkle's words reverberating around his head as he took out the origami bird that Proctor Goodfellow had given him. How could my familiar be here already, he wondered as he held out his palm and let his Essence rise in his hand and into the paper sculpture. 'Show me the way,' he said, and it immediately fluttered its wings and set off towards its destination.

He apologised as he barged his way pass the corridor of students, aimlessly milling about. Being the new boy in the academy, he didn't like drawing so much attention to himself, but the wayfinder was moving at a fair pace, and it was all he could do to keep up. Luckily, it wasn't too far to the proctor's office as the paper bird erupted into a puff of sparkles as it flew into the nameplate on the door. Daniel took a deep breath and knocked before entering.

THIS WASN'T THE FIRST time that Daniel had been inside a tutor's office. They tended to have books that reflected the tutors subject of teaching, their desk strewn with papers waiting to be marked. Proctor Goodfellow's office looked like it wouldn't be out of place in the British Museum.

The walls were lined with various antique weapons from the myriad cultures of Ariest. Different styles of armaments, long swords, short swords, axes, maces and taking pride of place, behind the proctor's desk, a red, gold and silver heraldic shield with the emblem of a female Hellenistic head on top of a sword with a pair of wings around it. Hanging crisscrossed beneath the shield were a pair of pole arms whose blade edges glinted as they caught the sunlight.

'Wow,' exclaimed Daniel as he looked around the office in wide-eyed wonder.

'Remnants of my past life,' Morgana explained. 'Take a seat, Daniel.'

Daniel could see the wistful look on the proctor's face. 'Radek mentioned that you were a celestial crusader.'

'Yes, a war priestess, a Scion of Galadrin. She is the deity of Simaciu, where I hail from. She is the goddess of valour, justice, honour and knowledge. The Tower of Par Atreia is her gift to Ariest, and the recipients of her boon, the women of Simaciu, are charged with its protection and upkeep.'

'Sounds amazing,' Daniel said with genuine interest. 'Why did you leave?'

'That is a story for another day. Today is about you, Daniel. Thanks to Radek and what happened in Abjuration class, many students will think that you're only here because of Gydion and not on merit or any ability you may have, despite the stories coming from Almedia and other western realms. You'll need to prove yourself to them and find a way to earn their respect if you want to have an easy time at Hartfield, Daniel. What we have to do now is create your curriculum by selecting the courses you wish to study. Apart from Magic 101 and Mystic Physical Education, which are compulsory, you can choose any of the other courses.'

Morgana Goodfellow slid a parchment towards Daniel. It showed a list of lessons, but he had no clue what they would involve; although their titles gave a hint. Conjuration, Divination, Illusion, Alchemy, Necromancy were just a few of the courses available. The wide selection didn't help him with his decision making.

'I'll take them all,' Daniel suddenly said.

'What? I know I said that you'll have to earn the respect of your fellow students, but you don't have to kill yourself to do it.'

'The thing is, I have so little knowledge about any of this. Everything I know has been learnt on the fly, in the real world. I knew little about these different subjects. All I know are ice spells. So, I'll take them all and drop out of any I don't like. I'll take all the books needed, and at the end of the day, I'll go back to Gydion's sanctum and study hard.'

'There must be some misunderstanding. You won't be leaving, Daniel. Adepts live in the academy. Your things are already in the dormitory.'

'Wonderful.' Daniel's response dripped with sarcasm.

The only reason he had been able to get through the teasing and malicious laughter each day at his high school on Earth, was because he only had to avoid until that final bell rang, then he could go home and not see them again until the next day. The students at Hartfield were already laughing at him. How was he supposed to avoid them if he's locked in with them 24 hours a day?

A knock on the door interrupted his thoughts. Proctor Goodfellow bid them enter and one of the white-haired girls Daniel had seen in Abjuration class walked in. Only to soon find out that it wasn't. The collar, cuff and hem of this girl's uniform was purple, signifying that she was an Initiate; the ones he had seen wore gold, meaning they were Novices.

'Perfect timing. This is Sara Yacon, one of the brightest and most gifted students here. This is Daniel Welsh. It's his first day here today,' the proctor said as she handed a parchment to her. 'I'd like you to show him where these Adept classes take place and then take him to the dormitories.'

'Yes, ma'am,' Sara replied and turned to leave.

'I'll have the books you'll need for the year sent to your room, Daniel.'

He thanked the proctor and left her office, closing the door behind him. Sara was already halfway down the corridor when he caught up to her. 'So,'

Daniel began as he awkwardly tried to drum up some conversation, 'triplets, huh? I saw your sisters in another class... well, I assume they're your sisters. It'd be kind of weird if they weren't.' He could immediately tell that she was a little agitated. 'I'm sorry for taking up your time. I didn't think that she would get a student to show me around.'

'So, it's true,' Sara said, paying no mind to Daniel's apologies. 'The Shade Slayer is here.' She came to a sudden halt, which Daniel wasn't expecting. 'But how exactly did you manage to do that if you couldn't even stop Philip's juvenile trick?'

'I had friends helping.'

'The songs say you were inside the creature alone.' She started walking again.

'The truth is I was lucky. That and something that I don't completely understand yet. I don't even really remember that first time I fought a Shade.'

'What do you mean by first time?'

'I fought three more on my home world with my dad and my friend, Finn.'

Sara tilted her head a moment and, satisfied that Daniel was telling the truth, held up the piece of parchment. 'And what's with this long list of courses? Are you trying to flaunt your greatness?'

'No! It's nothing like that at all.' It was the first time Daniel had ever been accused of acting in that manner; it wasn't in his nature. If it was, it would be a sure-fire way to get the respect he always desired. 'My knowledge is so limited I need to learn the craft. I don't know what classes I'll like and what I won't, so I wanted to try them all. And the proctor said I needed to earn respect and show that I deserve to be here.'

'Sounds reasonable, I guess,' she replied as her prickly attitude relented. 'Pleased to meet you, Daniel. So, you've met my lovely, adoring and bitchy sisters Cara and Mara. I'm sorry for questioning you like that. I had to be sure that you weren't going to be another Philip Strath-Holm. This academy doesn't need another big head. But you would have more reason than most to have one. You've done things that students at Hartfield only dream about doing. And I don't think anybody knows about that other battle against the Shade. You're a humble guy, Daniel Welsh. I like that.'

'Does everybody know about what happened in Almedia? It's just that when I was in the Summon Familiar class, they didn't react when I joined; I kind of liked it.'

'What do you expect? They're Adepts! Even your exploits can't compare with getting a familiar for the first time,' laughed Sara. 'Rest assured, they know who you are.'

They had made their way through half of the courses, seeing many wondrous things happening in those lecture rooms, and had just arrived at Necromancy. They peeped through the window and saw a girl sitting at the front facing the class. Another girl stood beside her.

They heard the professor, who was standing to one side with his arms folded, say 'Begin'.

The girl that stood, cast her spell, and ghoulish spectral figures appeared around the other girl. They began to float around her and emit their tortured ghostly moans of suffering.

'Faster,' the professor said, and the girl moved her hands faster as if she were conducting a twisted choir.

The girl in the chair fidgeted violently, as if she suffered from an invisible assault. The professor urged her to get up and move from her seat and told her the pain would stop. But she couldn't. She wept as she collapsed from her chair into a twitching heap on the floor.

'Stop, stop, stop,' sighed the professor, then pointed at a couple students sitting at the front. 'You two, help miss grimes to her seat. She'll be fine in a minute or two.'

'Well, I think you can cross Necromancy off the list,' said Daniel, shuddering from what he'd witnessed.

'Don't be so hasty. Necromancy harnesses the power of life and death. Although it can drain life, it can also give life. Of all the magical schools, this one is most balanced by its negative and positive traits. People wrongly think that its use is fundamentally evil and will lead you down a dark path. No school of magic can do that. Each Mage can pick their path.'

They began to walk to the next class when an idea suddenly came to Sara. 'You said that you were taking all these courses partly to earn respect?' Daniel nodded, and she continued laying out her plan. 'Well, a sure-fire way to get respect is to become an Altus Vex.'

'A what?'

'Altus Vex. Each grade has them. The students in that position are the liaison between the faculty and the other students. They are also their representative in meetings. All the great Archmages have held it.'

'So, how do I get the position?'

'That's simple. Everybody that applies for it must compete against each other in a knockout tournament.'

It didn't take much thinking to convince Daniel that this was something that he had to do. He said it over and over in his mind; Daniel Welsh, Altus Vex. He had to admit he did like the sound of it. Now, he just had to make it happen.

Chapter Six

Daniel makes a friend, Finn makes a deal

After the lecture rooms' tour where his classes would take place, Daniel was then taken to the dormitories. Although he wasn't sure about having a student as a guide at first, Sara turned out to be an excellent choice. She knew a lot about Hartfield Mage Academy's history, such as the fact that although it wasn't the only or oldest academy in Ariest, it had produced the greatest number of Archmages.

Hartfield was more than just the four wings and courtyard that made up the main building. There were other structures used for more advanced spell casting and end-of-year examinations and a substantial garden for the Alchemy and Herbology students, which happened to be Sara's major. Beyond that, there were three regency estates within the grounds of Hartfield. Each one housed a different student grade, and we're all painted accordingly; red for Adept, yellow for Initiate and gold for Novice.

'My hometown of Ostia is far to the north,' Sara explained to Daniel as they walked up the path leading to the Adept dormitories. 'It's on the other side of the Merexit Forest in the valleys of the Spine of The Goddess mountains.'

'I was told that there are giants in the mountains,' replied Daniel.

'There are all manner of creatures up there. Especially in the haunted forest.'

'Merexit is haunted?'

'Only the locals and the fearless travel through it. But often times the foolish venture into the dense forest never to be seen again.'

Daniel stared at Sara to see if there was any flicker of jest but found none. He was about to question her further about it when a voice from behind interrupted them.

'I've finally found you! I've been looking all over the place for you.'

'What do you want, Philip?'

'Nothing from you, Sara. Now run along before I tell your sisters that you've been harassing me again.'

'No, I haven't!' She glanced at Daniel, then back to Philip. 'Fine, you can show him the dorms. I'll see you around, Daniel Welsh.' With one last scowl at Philip Strath-Holm, Sara headed off down the path and towards the initiate dormitories.

'Look, I just wanted to apologise for what I did to you earlier,' Philip said once Sara was out of earshot. 'It wasn't personal, I can assure you of that. It's just that Zislaa has expressed an interest in continuing my education when I finish at Hartfield, and seeing him there and knowing who you are, I kind of lost myself and jumped the gun.' He offered his hand to Daniel. 'No hard feelings?'

Daniel pondered for a moment and thought about what Sara had said about Philip. He wondered what would happen if he refused. Would he find himself in another situation where he was constantly bullied as he was back on Earth? But Bobby Brinkmeyer never made any attempt to apologise.

He didn't want his academic life on Ariest to mirror the one he had on Earth, so Daniel took Philip's outstretched hand and shook it.

'Excellent,' Philip grinned with relief and patted Daniel on the back as he began to guide him through the regency styled dormitory house. 'I heard that you had some problems in Pinnywinkle's Familiar class,' he said as he heard sniggers when they passed through the common room.

'Just a bit. For some reason, no matter how hard I tried, I couldn't summon anything,' replied Daniel.

'Given what you've already done, you shouldn't be ridiculed, especially by Adepts. They should be fighting each other for the privilege of cleaning your boots. They should respect you for who you are and what you've done. Most of them won't get to do the things you have.'

At first, Daniel was taken aback by Philip's passionate reaction, but it wasn't long before he came around to his new friends' way of thinking. Especially when he made his offer.

'Let me help you get the recognition you deserve, Daniel. You were probably anxious, and that's why your spell wouldn't work. I know how to alleviate that.' When they reached the room that Daniel would be sharing, with three other students, as an Adept, Philip ran them out so that the two of them were alone. 'It's called essevate, but people in the know call it EV. It'll make you feel amazing.'

'What is it?'

'You know about Replenishment?' Philip continued the explanation when Daniel nodded. 'So, you know that it can refill your Essence and calm your mind. When your reservoirs are full, there is an excess. That extra Essence can create a visible representation of your Essence. You don't want that. You want to be at the point between having full reservoirs and having it burst out and flickering around you. All your senses are heightened; your mind is opened and freed. You'll be in euphoria, and nothing will trouble you. Your problems, your anxieties will simply melt away. Don't you want to try?'

Daniel took little time to think about it. 'Show me what to do, Philip.'

IT WAS DUSK, AND FINN was having another lonely drink at The Dirty Dog. She had planned to be in Imperial City by now, hanging out with Daniel and seeing the sights of the elven influenced city. But she was still waiting to hear from the Thieves Guild, having requested an audience with the guild head, Eamon Wolff, days ago. She was beginning to think that he had found out about her plans to leave the guild and was making her wait deliberately. She wouldn't put it past him.

She wondered how Anjunel was getting on. The Krez elf and former Shadow Dancer had stayed with her a few days before deciding to return to her lair, hoping to spend time with Tesserae before her own judgement day. She knew the punishment meted out to her would be severe, yet she still intended to do the honourable thing and face the court in Darkenville, the Krez city. Finn hoped that she didn't forget to come back and pick her up first.

The atmosphere in the tavern had changed; that was easy for the young scoundrel to see with her own eyes. People seemed on edge, and there was more hushed whispering than normal. The fact that the food wasn't up to its usual exemplary standard, due to Eveline taking time off after Tristan's murderous vow and subsequent disappearance didn't help lift the mood of the establishment or its owner, Mavis. It wasn't just The Dirty Dog that suffered from this anxiety; the whole of Almedia was feeling it. But the return of someone like Sayyidah was bound to have that effect. No one knew what she would do, but they all knew what she was capable of. The only thing they could do was wait.

'Oi! Finn shouted as a glass of mead was slammed down on her table. 'I didn't order that,' but it was too late. The person was already gone. She examined the drink more closely and determined that whoever left it didn't work behind the bar, judging by the drinks huge head. Moving the glass aside, she opened the napkin placed underneath it and read the message. It was in a code that only members of the Thieves Guild could decipher, and it was what Finn had been waiting for; the Wolff was ready to see her.

ONCE UPON A TIME, THERE had only been two ways to gain entrance to the Almedia Thieves Guild hideout; one underwater and one wading through the brown stuff. To say it hampered their recruitment would be an understatement. The disadvantages of using an abandoned sewer system as a base of operations.

But when Finn was a kid, she would always be found there. Eamon Wolff figured out that she knew another way in, which she did; the old sewer system had been expanded and improved upon by the Jesson's after all. Finn, being the precocious kid that she was, traded that information for a spot in the guild. And a fruitful friendship developed between the two. As she made her way to see him, she had to figure out how Finn would tell him that she was out.

The third way into the guild hideaway was down a stairwell behind a hidden door. As soon as they discovered its location, the guild built a facade around it. The hidden entrance was now in the back of a fortune tellers store.

Portillia Alloern, guild member, was the fortune teller in question. Although hired to fleece customers, it turned out that she was actually the real deal. Finn had yet to try it for herself, however. But each time she sat down before the woman, she was tempted. And this time was no different.

'Are you ready to hear your fortune, Finn? One gold coin is all it takes,' Portillia said.

Instead of placing a gold doubloon, though, Finn put down her gold sovereign with a fist on top of an open palm engraved on it, the insignia of the Thieves Guild. The precognitive pulled aside the curtain behind her, and Finn picked up her sovereign and entered.

The antechamber was what one would expect in a store such as this; lace and coloured scarves adorned the walls, and the air was thick with incense. A marked improvement on what was in the air of the other guild entrances. There was one thing that stood out in that room, and that was a stature of a boy, looking down at his empty outstretched hand, begging.

More guild upgrades.

Finn walked up to the boy and placed the sovereign in his hand. It was a counterweight, and it bounced up and down until it was balanced, at which point a light shone from the statue's eyes and swept over the sovereign. Once that examination was satisfied, only then would the hidden door open.

She retrieved the Thieves Guild token, then went through the door and pulled it shut behind her. Finn quickly traversed the magically illuminated stairwell and passages. Passed apprentices training, stopped now and again to greet and joke with comrades until she finally arrived at the office of the guildmaster. Finn knocked on the heavy oak door, and the deep, gruff voice of her boss bid her in.

EAMON WOLFF WAS A BIG man, tall and broad-shouldered. It always flummoxed Finn how he could have been a good thief with that build, as he gestured for her to sit down while he finished his conversation with Freddie Four-Fingers, one of his lieutenants.

'What's good, little Finn?' Eamon said after his discussion was over and Freddie had made his exit. The guildmaster lit one of his customary fat cigars and sat down.

She looked at his face, his dark skin contrasted by the white of his hair and walrus moustache, and finally figured out how she would tackle the matter at hand. 'Well, you know that I've always looked up to you as a sort of father-figure?' Finn was undeterred by the sceptical look on Eamon's face. 'And since I am the daughter-figure in this scenario, under the protective wing, so to speak. The time comes when the chick needs to spread their wings and fly the coop.'

'What?' The sceptic look had been replaced with one of confusion.

'There comes a time when you need a change, and you need to strike out on your own. Go and venture to pastures new. I feel that I have reached that point in my life. I need to grow, and to do that, I need to leave the guild.'

'Leave the guild?' Eamon let out his deep, bellowing laugh. 'So you can start a rival faction. This isn't a country club, Finn, you know that. Once you're in, you're in. There's only one form of membership when you join the guild, and that's a life member. The only way out is blood. And you know what that means.

'She did. 'I wouldn't be setting up another faction. I've been offered a job. Somewhat of an ambassadorial job.'

'You have a job here, stealing from the rich and splitting with the guild. I've got pickpockets, beggars, burglars, cutpurses, all kinds of thieves in my rogue's gallery, and you're one of the best, so no, I won't be letting my prize asset go anywhere.'

Finn loved hearing how great she was, much more than the next person, and it almost succeeded in distracting her from why she was here. 'But haven't you ever wanted a change? To try something new, something bigger?'

Eamon scrutinised her with a suspicious eye. 'What have you heard?'

'About what? Have I missed something? Should I have heard something?'

'Alright then,' Eamon said as he slowly puffed on his cigar as he decided whether to take Finn into his confidence or not. 'I do want something new. I have grand plans. I want to take the regional Thieves Guilds and combine them into one organisation. One organisation with one head. That's why we're having a guild meeting in Imperial City.'

'A crime syndicate,' whispered Finn. There was a rumour among the guild that an attempt had been made in the past to do the same thing, but it had failed. In those days, the guilds had been headed up by families, intent on keeping their individualism. Now only the Imperial City guild still had family ties. 'Do you think they'll go for it?'

'I doubt Landon Skipton will, but the others, who knows,' shrugged Eamon.

'Well, the one thing I know about thieves is if you dangle a big enough carrot in front of them, they're bound to want a bite.'

'What do you have in mind?'

'My job offer from Fungal. He has a corridor of portals to other realms. He wants me to scout out suitable ones for his new business venture. But what if I was scouting them out for you too? Who knows what kind of valuables these other realms have? I could open the way for you across multiple realms.'

'These could be a very lucrative venture for us. You may have just bought yourself an influential position in my new crime syndicate, little Finn. Unless, of course, you're still intent on leaving the guild.'

'Let's not be too hasty.' Finn grinned as she shook the proffered hand.

'That's my girl! I have these two new recruits that I'd like you to take with you when you start. Their names are Teresa Bint Ishraq and Jarl Gálvez. They're thieves from Sisoara in the Southern Lands. I'll need you to put them through their paces and teach them the way of the guild. You'll meet them soon when we all go to Imperial City and lay out our plans for the new crime syndicate. Is this the growth you were looking for, Finn? Because you and me kid are about to be catapulted to the top of the tree.

Chapter Seven

A hero's death

The last thing Daniel expected to see when he opened his eyes was Master Penwyll vigorously shaking him.

'What's going on?' Daniel asked drowsily. He gazed around and saw that he was back in the Iron Age roundhouse of the Dobunni tribe.

'You sleep like the dead, that's what,' replied Penwyll. 'I assume you spoke to Gydion about all this.'

'Yes, I did. He said I would play a part in Trinity's revival and that I should pay attention to what happens and find the connection between her past lives and her present one.'

'And so you should. The time will come when you will need to stand before the great divine tree in the druid grove, having demonstrated that you understand and speak what you have learnt to wake her.'

That was the moment that Daniel realised that the girl he loved was not sleeping beside him. 'Where is she?'

'She's in trouble.'

'What are you talking about?' Daniel said forcefully as he jumped out of bed and hastily dressed.

'Things have progressed while you have been away. The nearby tribes ruled by Caratacus and Togodumnus have both surrendered. Aloisia held off the Romans early attacks with her nature magic, but the tribe have accepted an offer from them — the girl for their freedom.'

'They betrayed her.'

'Well, people quickly forget what others have done for them.'

They heard the cries from the watchtower simultaneously... the Romans were coming. As they stepped out of the roundhouse, Daniel and Penwyll saw the tribe running in a panic; although they had made the deal, many were dubious about the Romans keeping their end of the bargain.

Daniel was both excited and terrified at seeing the Roman machine first-hand. He had read so many books about them, knew everything about their military tactics, knew the strengths and weaknesses of the legions that had been exploited by others, that he believed that given the right tools, he could defeat them. But he wasn't here for that. 'I can see Aulus Plautius leading the army, but who is that hooded person riding next to him?'

'I don't know,' Master Penwyll replied.

'What do you mean? I thought you were here when this first happened centuries ago?'

'I was, but that person was not.'

The implications of what Penwyll said weighed heavily on Daniel. Who was that shadowy figure advising the Roman general, and why were they here? And further more, how did they get here. 'This is bad. This is supposed to be Trinity's memory of her past life. How can someone just come in without an invite?'

'Don't worry about that now. You have to get your friend out of here. They have her in the grand roundhouse. Go!'

Daniel didn't waste another second and sprinted off. As he drew closer, he saw a single guard at its entrance. The guard seemed to be in a dilemma, he wasn't sure if he should stay or go. His indiscipline was because he wasn't one of King Connah's guards but one of the farmers who led the betrayal.

His indecision played directly into Daniel's hands. He picked a discarded shield and cracked it over the man's head, knocking him out cold. The young Mage blasted into the grand roundhouse, expecting to see more farmers guarding their prize, but there were none, just the king and Trinity tied up.

'Dannel!' she cried when she saw her love. 'I thought I had lost you, that they might have killed you. I should have listened to you. You told me to leave, warned me that something bad was coming. But I never thought it would come from my own people, the same people I refused to leave.'

'There's no time for regrets,' Daniel said as he released Trinity and before attending to King Connah. 'Aulus is here with his legions; we have to leave.'

'I have to stay,' the king said, 'but you must take my daughter and go north, Dannel.'

'No, father! I won't leave you!'

'You must, Aloisia, for if you don't, they will surely kill you.'

'He's right. You and the druids pose a threat to the Romans. They are a war machine, but they love health, relaxation, and their gods, just as much. Take them to the Temple of Sulis, show them the hot springs, tell them about its healing properties, and your people will be spared.'

'I will do as you say, Daniel. Now, take my daughter away from here,' the king pleaded.

Daniel nodded. 'We'll go north to Caledonia. She'll be safe there.'

Aloisia hugged her father for what would be the last time; tears filled her eyes. 'Goddess, watch over you.'

'And you.'

With their final goodbyes said, Daniel and Trinity parted ways with the king of the Dobunni tribe. The two lovers quickly moved towards the stables, desperately trying not to draw attention to themselves, an almost impossible feat when one had flaming red hair.

'Look! The princess is escaping!' A lone tribesman yelled as he tried to block their path whilst sounding the alarm. He was suddenly sent flying through the wall of a nearby roundhouse.

Daniel and Trinity looked at each other and wondered what had just happened when Master Penwyll came running up to them.

'You're welcome,' he said. 'Now get moving, this isn't the time for sweet nothings; the Romans are already entering the hillfort! Grab a horse while I make an exit for you.'

As Daniel helped Trinity mount the horse, he heard Penwyll blast down the fort's wall with a spell. He climbed up behind the princess and chanced a glance at the Roman army. The hooded figure beside Aulus Plautius leaned towards the general and pointed at them. Then the Roman archers made their way towards the escaping couple.

'Go now, Daniel,' Master Penwyll said, slapping the rump of the horse a setting it on its way.

Daniel couldn't help fretting about the Mage, even though in the back of his mind he knew that this wasn't real. It was Trinity's past. He kept reminding himself that. Besides, Daniel knew that this wasn't where Gydion's teacher died.

He geed up the horse and held Trinity tight as the first arrows from the Roman bowman rained down around them. They suffered three more waves of arrows before they were out of range and into a forest.

'I think we've made it,' Trinity sighed with relief. 'You really are my hero, aren't you?' The only response she got was a splutter, and she felt his warm blood on her shoulder and his extra weight as he slumped onto her back. 'Daniel? Daniel!' She cried and pulled the horse to a stop which caused him to slide off onto the ground.

Trinity jumped down and couldn't hold back her cries of anguish when she saw the arrows sticking out of her lovers back. She cradled his head as her tears dripped on his face like raindrops, as it dawned on her that he was using his own body to shield her. 'You should have left me,' she said as she rocked back and forth. 'What were you thinking?'

'The only thing I could. Isn't that what you're supposed to do, to protect those that you love?' Daniel took a sharp intake of breath and sighed as his last breath left his lips.

DANIEL SHOT UP IN A panic, eyes wide, gasping for breath. He reached around and checked his back. It may not have been real, it may just have been scenes from Trinity's past relived, but the dying part sure felt real enough.

Feeling no wounds, Daniel fell back on the bed and let out a deep sigh of relief. He wondered if he still had time to relax before classes began because his bed was suddenly feeling comfier than ever. He didn't remember his pillows being so fragrant, though.

He inhaled deeply, and the floral aroma ignited memories of being back at school, that fateful day when Trinity opened his eyes to magic.

'You always did have a thing for this scent. And that is why I make sure never to run out of it.'

It was a familiar female voice, and Daniel shot up in bed again, this time taking note of his surroundings. Had he somehow gone to the girl's dormitory by mistake? The comfortable bed he lay in was a four-poster with silk sheets. The room had high ceilings and was elegantly and richly furnished, decorated with exquisite paintings, ceramics and gilded wall mouldings.

Then he saw her.

Trinity, wrapped in a silk sheet from the bed, sat at an inlaid table covered with a breakfast assortment of fruits, cheeses and croissants. 'I was beginning to think that I would be breakfasting alone,' she said as she delicately picked a grape and placed it in her mouth.

Daniel stepped over the myriad clothing; a dress, ruffled underskirts and stockings, breeches, jacket, hat, that were strewn across the carpeted floor as well as the bladed weapons and pistols next to them.

He stood before his deceased girlfriend as she slid her fingers through the ample curls of her long copper-coloured hair, running them from front to back, the spring sun that shone on her skin also made her emerald eyes sparkle.

'Well, are you going to sit down or not?' she asked. Daniel took the offered seat. 'This must be a first. The great Cassius Stewart, The Dandy Rogue, standing on ceremony?'

Cassius Stewart? Daniel had heard Gydion say the name before. He was one of the anchors to her past lives, which would mean that this was Trinity as Bianca Daumier. And also meant that he should have learnt what he was supposed to from the Iron Age. A fact that Daniel was very dubious about. After all, he died in that timeline.

Bianca put her hand on Cassius's knee and leaned over to kiss him. 'I was more than happy to see you arrive from England, mon amour, and your timing could not have been more perfect. Look at this.' She handed him the latest issue of La Gazette. 'It would seem that our old friend has come out of hiding and struck again, n'est-ce pas?'

'"The noblewoman, Marie-Madeleine-Marguerite de Brinvilliers, accused of murdering, by poison, her father, one Antoine Dreux d'Aubray, and also taking the lives of her brothers, Antoine and François d'Aubray, has absconded from justice." So, you think this Madame de Brinvilliers has been killed?' Daniel asked after he finished reading the article.

'Quoi? No, no, no of course not,' Bianca replied and let out a sigh of exasperation. 'I wish you would not return to London so frequently, Cassius.

The air there seems to remove any intellectual growth you gain while being in my presence. No, she has not been killed, and neither do I believe she is the architect of these murders.'

Daniel was incredulous. 'How can you be so sure?' he asked as he poured a cup of tea for each of them.

'Have you already forgotten? We met the lady in question but five years previous at the Duchess de Cadenet's ball, shortly before her father's death. I distinctly recall you commenting that she was rather amiable.'

'And that's enough to absolve her of all suspicion?'

'It should, yes, because I agreed with you. But since you need more convincing, you should know that, while you were away, there has been a spate of other such crimes that I have been investigating. As the daughter of the former king's spymaster, I could not let such an intriguing set of circumstances pass me by.'

'And what did you find?'

'Aristocrats killing aristocrats. Usually, the mother, wife or daughter is accused of the crime, as they are the only suspect.'

'And you're telling me that they're not?'

'Oh, they did it. Every last one of them killed their fathers, husbands or brothers, but not of their own freewill.'

'I still don't understand.'

'Luckily for you, it was your wit and fashion sense that drew me to you, Cassius. That and your ability with sword and pistol. Good thing you have me to be the brains and beauty of this relationship,' she stated with a flick of her hair. 'By "not of their freewill," I mean the killer's actions were being controlled.'

'What? How did you come to that?'

'By doing research. I looked into all of their backgrounds, looking for connections, and found one commonality; each of their families made their fortunes in the slave trade. I hypothesise that these murders are either related to money or are the product of revenge.'

'Revenge?'

'Yes! L'intellect l'emporte! Are you familiar with the beliefs of voodoo?'

TIME HAD LAPSED IN the blink of an eye. No longer were they in the boudoir of the Countess Bianca Daumier but between the main streets of the centre of Paris; within its maze of narrow, winding streets, dimly lit by oil lamps, between wooden houses four and five stories high.

Night had fallen, many of the streets were closed with large chains across them, as was the custom, and it was one of these closed roads that Bianca entered with Daniel close behind. She was ready for action, dressed in dark wine-red leather pants and a three-buckle black bodice, her hair in a single tightly plaited braid. She edged down the seemingly deserted street of the slum district, knowing they were being watched, by unseen eyes, at every step, with a pistol in her left hand and her Toledo steel schiavana in her right.

'We are almost at the storehouse my contact told me about, Cassius,' Trinity reported in a whisper.

Daniel made no reply. His mind was playing catch up, trying to keep track of everything, every scrap of information he had seen. From Iron Age Britain to renaissance France, and not to mention the different names, Aloisia and Dannel, Bianca and Cassius, Trinity and Daniel, he had almost forgotten what name he was supposed to be answering to. There was one constant throughout all three lives; Trinity had always been courageous.

'So, what's the plan when we get there?' Daniel asked.

'We stop them of course. I sent my little Cour des Miracles vagrant to find some gendarmes, but in the meantime, we apprehend the mastermind, and you get to feel what it is like being on the right side of the law, for a change, mon petit coquin.'

Bianca sheathed her sword and replaced it with a second pistol. Daniel, likewise, drew the pistol that was holstered across his chest and another from his hip. There was African chanting coming from within the storehouse, and finding the door ajar, they toed it open and slipped inside.

The pair soon realised that they needn't have bothered trying to be stealthy, as inside the building they found fifteen aristocratic women waiting for them.

'Cassius, holster your guns,' Bianca said. 'I know these women. They are innocents.'

Daniel didn't hear a thing she said as his gaze was squarely focussed beyond the barrier of women to something he wasn't expecting. Beside the Voodoo priest, who was dressed in a juxtaposition of noble finery and African jewellery, was the same shadowy, hooded figure that had been beside Aulus Plautius.

'You were right, my friend,' the African man said. 'They arrive just as you said they would. Let them pass!' The women parted, and Daniel and Bianca stepped through them.

'Who are you?' Daniel demanded.

'My name is Kamba,' answered the voodoo priest, although the question was directed to his hooded accomplice.

'So, I was right,' Bianca said triumphantly, 'this is about revenge.'

'How could it not be? Your nation has decimated my home and pillaged this new world. I escaped Hispaniola intent on getting my vengeance against those that profited off the back of my family, and why not use their families to bring them down.' Kamba directed their attention to his collection of effigies. 'Each one represents one of these women, giving me power over them to do my bidding.'

'Let them go,' Bianca ordered and aimed a pistol at him to emphasise the directive. However, as soon as she drew her weapon, the women put themselves in the firing line. 'These ladies are innocent. They should not have to be punished for the deeds of their menfolk. I do not agree with the methods or actions taken with this colonisation, far from it, but there are other ways to resolve this without more bloodshed.'

'You are right. And with the guidance of my companion, things were set in motion, as soon as you entered, so that the appropriate people will be punished. All the heads of the hydra will be eliminated at once!' Kamba let out a deep laugh. 'In less than fifteen minutes, my revenge shall be complete!'

Bianca thought for a moment before she holstered her gun and sprinted out of the storehouse, Kamba's laughter ringing in her head.

Daniel caught up to her as she leapt onto her horse, and he followed suit. 'Where are you going? Are we just going to leave them?'

'We have to. He intends to attack the Palace of Versailles. The king must be warned. Kamba and his friend will keep for another day.'

They set off into the night at high speed. The trees raced past them as they galloped through the lush green scenery, intent on stopping whatever it was that Kamba had planned.

As they raced to save the king of France, Daniel's mind kept flitting back to the hooded figure. Surely it was no coincidence that he was here again, imposing himself in another of Trinity's past lives. Was this an enemy that she always had to contend with, or was it something else completely?

Lost in his thoughts, Daniel almost didn't hear Bianca calling his attention to a speeding carriage ahead of them. 'That must be it!'

They spurred their steeds on and came alongside the transport. In the back was a large chest with holes perforated in it. As the pair edged to the front, their problems escalated to another level. There was no rider, and the horse was a golden mechanical construct.

Without a second thought, Bianca deftly jumped onto the thundering carriage. 'Get in there and check out that box!'

There was no way Daniel could have made the jump; he wouldn't even have attempted it. But this was the body of Cassius Stewart, with all the skills and daring the swashbuckling, dandy, rogue possessed. Climbing on to the moving vehicle was nothing for him, but it wasn't long before he wished that he hadn't.

'There are barrels of gunpowder in here!' Daniel shouted as he checked through a couple of them.

'Whatever is in the chest must be the fuse to ignite it!'

'Give me a second to pick it; it's locked!'

'You are fast running out of seconds, my love!' Trinity shouted back as they rapidly closed on the remarkable palace.

'I got it! There's no fuse, though! It's heavily padded with bottles of an opaque liquid!'

Liquid? Poison perhaps? Blow up the gunpowder to disperse the poison. But then, where is the explosive? There must be a timed fuse somewhere, or else why mention the time I had at all?

Bianca's gaze fell upon the golden horse.

'Cassius, empty the carriage and get up here!'

He did what he was told and tossed barrel after barrel. The sturdy case was another matter, being a lot heavier than he had anticipated. But after locking it, and with all of his strength, he was finally able to slide it out of the carriage and see it land heavily on the ground as he made his way to Bianca's side.

'The horse is the bomb. I can't see any way to stop it, and every time I turn its head, it swings right back, always true towards the palace.'

'Then we just leave it. I doubt it will do much damage.'

'And I doubt that Kamba installed only a single firecracker inside his construction. To damage a building as vast as Versailles would take an explosive just as vast.'

'Perhaps together we can overpower the mechanism. Direct it toward the lake, but that would mean — '

'I had the same thought. However, I could not ask you to make such a...'

'You're not asking.'

The pair began to pull on the left side of the reins, hand over fist as if they were in a tug of war. Sure enough the golden horse automaton began to veer to the left, away from the palace and into the direction of the lake.

'At least this way I get to go out with a hero's death,' Cassius said between his grunts of exertion.

'That you will. A hero's death that no one will know about. Time must be almost up.'

'I love you, Bianca,' he said.

'And I love you, Daniel.'

'What? How did you...' His moment of confusion was swiftly cut short by the inevitability of the golden horse automaton exploding just as they reached the body of water.

Plumes of smoke rose into the air, and droplets of spray from the lake rained down. The aftermath of the bomb would be seen from the palace. King Louis XIV would despatch his musketeers to investigate. They would find debris and nothing else.

DANIEL SCREAMED HIMSELF awake and, inadvertently, the three other Adepts he shared the room with. The kids looked at each other and laughed before putting their heads back down. This was another incident that would probably go around the school in no time and put even more doubt in the other students' minds concerning Daniel's legitimacy of being at the academy. He let out a deep sigh as he envisioned his life seemingly being repeated; being in a school, teased and laughed at.

Chapter Eight

A trip to Darkenville

The tranquillity of nature is a wonder to behold. Especially within the months of renewal, when the flowers are springing up, when chicks are hatched, and animals awaken from their long slumber. The peace of hearing birds chirping and bees buzzing is enough to calm anyone's soul.

Unless, of course, the soul belongs to Finn Jesson. 'Two vekting weeks! I've been sitting here twiddling my thumbs, waiting for you for two vekting weeks! I could have gone to Imperial City and come back many times over. What took you so long?'

Her companion, Anjunel Lynsu'unara, the Krez elf, rode solemnly beside the young girl, her face a picture of contemplation as she neared her inevitable fate. 'I was spending time with Tessera,' she replied after her long silence. She had barely said a word since they had left Almedia. 'Once I am exiled from the Shadow Dancers, the next time we meet, one of us will have to die. It was best for us to say our goodbyes alone whilst we were still free to act of our own accord.'

Finn's face reddened from the sudden guilt. Anju was about to have everything stripped away from her; her home, her status among her people, her lover.

They continued the rest of the way without speaking, the silence only broken by the sound of nature and the footfalls of their horses. It wasn't long before they arrived at the scene of Daniel's rescue and Trinity's unfortunate death, the currently empty Shadow Dancer cave. The events of that night flashed through Finn's mind as she and Anju made their way through the Krez stronghold.

As they navigated the numerous passages, Finn glanced at her compatriot and wondered if the assassin had any feelings of loss, since it could be the last time she would be in these familiar surroundings. If she was, it was masked by the impassive visage on of her face.

'Do not fret for me, Finn. I am resolved to my fate,' she replied without so much as a sideways glance, as if she could sense the young thief's eyes upon her.

'Are things really that bad?'

'I have broken the edicts of the Krez. I will either have a swift death or a slow one.'

'Is there a third option? One that doesn't involve death?' Finn was of the mind that everyone should be as averse to dying as she was, which was hard to believe given the risks she was known to take in pursuit of adventure. 'I thought you would just be exiled from them. If that was the case, you would be more than welcome to join me in my new business. In fact, I insist. I'd be glad to have someone I know and trust with me,' said Finn as she briefly considered what remit Eamonn's two cronies will have when she commenced Fungal's business venture.

'If I survive the initial punishment, then I will be exiled... that is a slow death.'

Before Anju could respond to Finn's questioning look, they found themselves right back at the huge cavern with the central rock formation, which had served as the battleground between the companions and Sayyidah with the treacherous Ch'tan.

They entered the central column as before, via the secret passageway, but this time instead of going up, they went down. And down. And down.

'Quick question for you, Anju. Exactly how far is it to Darkenville?' Finn asked. She was pretty sure they were passing through the lava lake as the air was decidedly warmer than it was at the top.

'We are on the edges of The Hollow now. Darkenville is in the Lower Hollow, roughly seven or eight miles down. We won't be walking through.'

'That's good to know... hold up! Did you say The Hollow? I've heard adventurers talk about it, but I never believed any of it; you know how some of these guys are, they brag and boast and fabricate the truth.'

'What is so hard to believe about a world within a world? The Hollow was the home of the giants, not up there. There have been adventurers, some foolish enough to go beyond the upper and lower to venture into Helion.'

'There's something deeper?'

'Yes, Helion is where the remnants of creation reside, the denizens of dark, the weird and unusual that people of the surface could not fathom.'

'Sounds peachy!' Finn said, her tone dripped with sarcasm.

Anjunel led the way out of the rock column once they had reached the bottom. To Finn's surprise and disappointment, after a brief look around, realised that it was nothing more than a cave.

Then she heard a screech like nothing she had heard before.

'What the vekt was that?'

'Our ride,' replied Anju. A short passage opened into a small bestiary housing several of the two species creatures there; a blind eight-legged lizard and an equally blind leather winged animal.

As Anju proceeded to harness one of the winged animals, a puzzled Finn took a closer look. The creatures resembled species from the surface, but it was like they were distant cousins.

A sudden wind was whipped up as the avian animal exercised its wings in preparation for flight. 'These are funny looking animals you got. What are they?'

'Funny looking, maybe,' admitted Anju, 'but perfectly built for life in The Hollow. These are called Mikash, and those eight-legged reptiles are known as Octogar. They are common transport down here, equivalent to your chartered griffins and horses. Now climb aboard, and we will be in Darkenville in no time.'

THE MIKASH BEAT ITS leathery wings and propelled them through the air with tremendous speed. The cities of the goblins and dark dwarfs flashed past as they traversed the Upper Hollow. With the speed they travelled at, it wasn't long before Anjunel told Finn that they were about to enter the Lower Hollow, at which point the human pulled down the enchanted goggles, which allowed her to see in darkness, given to her by Daniel. The same pair he had worn the night Cernounos, the Green Man had been poisoned.

Finn had tried to paint a mental picture of what Darkenville would look like from the native elf's descriptions. But anything that Finn had imagined about the little-known city, paled in reality.

They flew through immense caverns, several of which had underground lakes and rivers. Huge stalactites and stalagmites were made into multi-storey abodes. Wide rope bridges spanned the gaps and crisscrossed above much like they did in the Druid Glade, but this was on a much vaster scale given the size of the Krez city.

Anju steered their avian into a spiral descent and eventually came to a gentle landing in front of a stable. An elderly Krez attendant approached and, upon recognising Anjunel, took the reins from The Shadow Dancer with an air of reverence. Among her people, Anju had a high regard that Finn was only now beginning to fathom. And which made her upcoming exile even more poignant.

'Nice landing,' the familiar voice of Tessera stated. 'You always were the best of us.'

'With an emphasis on "were",' Anju replied.

'Whatever happens, you always will be.'

'I think we both know what is to happen, my dear.'

'Those that survive are strong,' the black-haired elf said as she and Anju tenderly touched foreheads. 'And you are the strongest among us.'

Tessera glanced at Finn, who looked around and tried to be inconspicuous, not wanting to intrude on the couple's reunion. When the human caught her looking, Tessera began a discussion in elvish with Anju.

Although it didn't look like it, Finn had been eavesdropping on everything that had been said up until that point. She remained on guard in all but the most safe and comfortable of surroundings, a habit that she would never lose, and being in Darkenville with a Krez elf who, up until a couple weeks ago, would have gladly killed her, met neither of those criteria.

The elvish discussion became more heated, then it was abruptly ended when Tessera stormed off.

'Problems?' Finn asked as she and Anju slowly followed the angered elf.

'She thinks it was a mistake to bring you here. In her mind, she believes I should have pleaded with the head for clemency, that having you here only adds to my transgressions against the edicts of the Shadow Dancers.'

'Does it?'

'Irrelevant. She knows that breaking one edict is the same as breaking them all. She is just blinded by other matters. Besides, I need you. You have powerful friends. Even the name of Gydion is known down here. It is a small chance, but he may be able to save me.'

Finn couldn't believe what she was hearing. 'You're using me?'

'Yes. You and I are not dissimilar, Finn. I am sure you would do the same if you were in this situation.'

Finn thought for a moment and then shrugged with a nod as she reluctantly agreed with her companion's statement. 'So, what do you need saving from?'

'The Rising.'

WHEN THEY REACHED THE temple, stronghold of the Shadow Dancers, Tessera led them through a roughly hewn side entrance. Anjunel had whispered its name, the Cave of Sorrows, the traitor's entrance.

Countless passages led off the tunnel they followed. It spiralled down and zig-zagged until finally, they stepped out of the corridor and into a vast semi-circular chamber.

Around the cavern's circumference were several tiers of banked seats, seemingly cut out of the cave itself. They were divided into two by a passage which Finn assumed was the main way into the hall. At least six hundred Shadow Dancers sat before them and Finn could hear the muttering and unrest. She concluded, judging by the looks she garnered, that she was the subject of their whispers.

As the three crossed the open space, for the first time, Finn saw the balcony above the passage where they had entered. It stood out compared to the rest of the chamber, being lavishly decorated, complete with two statues, standing either side of a throne. They were of a four-armed woman with three-eyes, and it was those eyes that held the young thief's attention since, as far as she could tell, they were gemstones.

Tessera dragged her along to a seat in the front, which she made vacant by pushing the elves that were there further along the bench. Finn sat down, and that's when she saw that Anjunel had remained standing in the middle cavern.

Finn was just about to ask Tessera what she was doing when a hush descended over the crowd of assassins, and three more Krez elves entered. The one leading the way was a female with dusky-purple coloured skin and red pupil-less eyes; her attire showed just as much as it covered, much like the statutes on the balcony, Finn noted. The next dark elf wore a black suit of armour with wicked-looking hooked spikes. She took off her helmet and shook her black hair flow loose, all the while staring at Anjunel, who met her gaze. The third newcomer was a male Krez elf seemingly older than either of the females and dressed more conservatively in a simple grey hooded cloak; he still walked with an air of reverence surrounding him.

They came to a stop beneath the decorated balcony. As soon as they did, another elf stepped out onto the balcony, at which point all the seated Shadow Dancers stood and began to call out the mantra of the Krez. "Those that can survive are strong!" Tessera pulled Finn up as the human knew little of what was happening. He looked over all the Krez below him, his armour red like the colour of blood and draped in purple. He raised his hands, and the crowd immediately hushed. He lowered them, and they sat. 'It is the time of The Quelling, my friends,' he said. Such were the natural acoustics of the space that everyone could hear him without any need to shout. 'You have all done well for our society. Done what was needed for us to survive because we are strong. But before we can take part in the ceremony, we have a task to perform. We are gathered here to judge one of our own. She stands before you, accused of defiling the edicts of the Shadow Dancers. Anjunel Lynsu'unara, angel of death, chapter head, what are the edicts?'

Without a pause, Anjunel recited them. 'Never reveal information of the Shadow Dancers. Never fail to assist or avenge a clanmate. Never be disrespectful to your clan elders. Never place personal desires or ambitions above those of the clans. Never return having failed to execute an assignment. Never slaughter one of our own. Never succumb to the Rising.'

'Loscivia, proceed.'

'As you wish, Pharinox,' the red-eyed elf replied. 'Through the veils of magic, it was shown to me that your chapter was decimated, and many of their lives were taken by your blades. Explain.'

'Their minds were not their own. They had been taken by an Undine named Ch'tan, who in turn was controlled by Sayyidah.'

There were murmurs upon hearing the name of the harpy queen.

'Ilvaria?' Loscivia, the high priestess, handed the questioning to the military head.

'Did you fail your chapter?' she asked.

'I saved those I could.'

'But made sure that your lover, Tessera, was among them.'

'Ch'tan is dead.'

'But Sayyidah walks free.' Ilvaria paused a moment before continuing. 'Ve'assen, go ahead.'

'The contract you received was never fulfilled?' asked the chief scholar.

'It was not. I will not be controlled in doing my job. If I am to kill, it will be my own decision.'

'I see,' Ve'assen mused. 'And this human you have brought to the Temple of Na'roli?'

'She is my student,' Anju replied. Finn was just as surprised as the others at hearing that.

'That is all I have to ask,' Ve'assen said to Pharinox.

'I have heard what has been said, and you stand accused of breaching five of the sacred edicts. How do you plead?'

'Pharinox, supreme clan head, I plead —' Anju glanced at Tessera and then back up to the balcony. 'I plead guilty.'

There was a universal intake of breath among those watching. This was Anjunel Lynsu'unara. They regarded her as the best among them. Many thought that because of her status she would plead not guilty and be cleared.

But the one dubbed Angel of Death showed what type of character she was – one that would not shirk the consequences of her actions.

Holding his hands up to quiet the assassins once more, Pharinox delivered his judgement. 'I have heard what was said. You have broken several of the edicts of our clan. You revealed information of the Shadow Dancers to an outsider and even brought them here. You failed to avenge your clanmates; a pawn was killed, but the queen still lives. By saving Tessera, it could be said that you put your personal desires above those of the clan's. You did not kill the one you were tasked to kill, and finally, Shadow Dancers were killed by you.' The head of the Shadow Dancers took a moment to deliberate matters further in his mind while everyone waited.

It dawned on Finn why Tessera was not happy that Anju had brought her here. If she had known that it would be trouble, she would have refused to come. But it begged the question, why had the elf asked her in the first place? Surely, she knew what would happen.

'I have decided to absolve you of guilt regarding the following edicts,' Pharinox eventually continued. 'You failed to complete your assignment because your mind was being controlled by others. Thus, you are not guilty of breaking this edict. You displayed great strength in resisting. You saved Tessera, known to be your lover, but she is also a great asset to the Shadow Dancers, you saved other clan members also. Thus, you are not guilty of breaking this edict. Ch'tan, the pawn, is dead, and I would not expect you to kill Sayyidah alone, no matter how talented you are. Thus, you are not guilty of breaking this edict. You have brought an outsider to the Temple of Na'roli, but you say she is your student. Thus, you are not guilty of breaking this edict. You have killed clan mates, and of this, I find you guilty. Although they were not of their mind and that other members of your chapter also participated, as a chapter head, the responsibility of that chapter belongs to you Anjunel Lynsu'unara. And as you know, break one edict, and you break them all. You are hereby exiled from the Shadow Dancers.'

'I understand,' she replied.

'As is the way, with your guilty verdict comes death. The swiftness of that death is down to you; either here down in the pit, on the surface at the hand of one of your former clanmates or by succumbing to the Rising.'

'I understand and am ready.'

'Disrobe her!'

With the command issued, two elves began to disarm and undress the disgraced elf until she stood only in her leather bodysuit.

'What the vekt is going on?' Finn whispered to Tessera.

'She must fight in the pit, but she is only allowed to do so bare-fisted, no weapons. This is just to make sure that she has none concealed.'

'And what about him saying that she could be killed by you lot?'

'Since she is no longer a Shadow Dancer she is no longer protected by that edict. She is now prey. However, as her student, you are protected, meaning that no Shadow Dancer will accept a contract against you.'

'Well, that's comforting to know.'

'That only lasts as long as she does.'

'Small comforts, huh.'

The head of the Shadow Dancers addressed Anjunel once more. 'You were highly regarded among us; the most skillful and talented Shadow Dancer I have seen in a long time; your tattoos are testament to that.' Agreement rippled through the audience. 'My ruling stands, but it would be a shame to see talent as yours wasted, so I give you this caveat; if you survive the pit and if you somehow avenge your chapter and kill Sayyidah, your exile will be ended. You will be welcomed back.'

Finn listened to the hushed whispers of the crowd. Although she couldn't understand the Krez language, body language was universal. 'I take it that not many exiles get invited back,' she said to Tessera.

'None that I have heard of. It will make for interesting times for sure.'

'How so?'

'If a Shadow Dancer were to kill Anju, all that was hers would become theirs. Now that she has a chance of redemption, those that covet her things will act swiftly.' Tessera then drew Finn's attention to two male Krez. 'That is Imrathon, and he is Sadron. They are the other chapter heads. They have always thought themselves better than her. They would be glad to see her dead. Mark their faces. They could well strike sooner rather than later.'

'They don't need to worry. Do you really think that she has a chance of killing Sayyidah? Vekt! You saw her. All of us together couldn't do a thing to her.'

'Only Gydion and your friend,' the elf replied.

'Daniel. And it cost the life of another friend.' It had been a while since she had thought about her rival for Daniel's affections. She had come to like her, even if she was the complete opposite to her. She had a deep respect for Trinity, and Finn was disappointed that she never got the chance to tell her that.

'Look,' Tessera said, bringing the young girl out of her introspection, 'it is about to begin.

Finn followed her gaze and saw Loscivia step forward as Anjunel stepped back. The high priestess raised both of her hands overhead, and the stage area began to slide back beneath the tiers of seats, to reveal an enclosure below. It was just like the illegal arenas Finn had seen before.

'Are you ready to face your fate Anjunel Lynsu'unara?' Loscivia asked.

'I am.'

'Then enter the pit to be tested.'

Anju did as she was told and jumped down into the pit, landing like a feather. Everybody stood up so that they could get a better look at the upcoming procedures. Finn had no idea what to expect, but even her heart pounded in expectation.

Loscivia's hands created patterns in the air as she cast a spell. 'May the goddess Na'roli shine upon your soul and take you into her fold, Anjunel Lynsu'unara.' It didn't take long before the effects of her spell began to manifest. Anju shuddered as four wisps flew from her tattooed side and into the wall surrounding her. Four elf-like creatures then began to step out of the wall itself. Their faces were twisted by anger as tears of blood ran down from the dead elven eyes.

Finn couldn't believe her eyes. The stench of death filled her nostrils and sent a shiver down her spine. Fear rooted her to the spot. 'What are those things?' Finn asked.

'They are Herecaté. The bodies of the recent dead filled with the souls of some of those she has taken and finally animated by negative energy. These souls are unrepentant in death and filled with rage and vengeance. There is usually only one such suitable soul among the elves Hegati, their tattoos, but such was the ability of Anju; she has slain many and such was the morality of her that she tended to accept contracts of those she believed deserved to die.

Those that would welcome a chance of revenge. As Herecaté, they get that chance.'

Anju stood passively as the four undead creatures surrounded her and withdrew their maces. Once they had stopped, she readied herself and waited for their attack. Barehanded or not, Anjunel Lynsu'unara, the angel of death, was just as deadly without weapons as she was with them, but in actual fact, she had four weapons at her disposal; she just had to relinquish them from their owners.

The Herecaté attacked as one, charging at the tattooed slender form of the elf. The diabolical undead creatures swung their maces with violent intent. Anju waited until the last moment to spin away from one attack, step aside another, duck one more and use the momentum of the fourth to throw him into the wall.

Every time Finn saw Anjunel in action, she was always in awe of her, of how agile and fluid her moves were. Graceful with unseen power. She was as elusive as wind. Somersaulting and cartwheeling out of the way of the crushing mace attacks, the Herecaté couldn't lay a finger on her.

Then she was struck with a heavy blow.

Finn gasped as she saw her friend crumple to the ground. She vaguely heard Tessera say something. 'What was that?'

'I said it's over,' she repeated calmly.

'What! Are you kidding me? Anju hasn't hit any of them. She's in trouble.'

'Anju is unlike any of us. She has a mind geared for combat. If she watches someone for a while, she can see their strengths and, more importantly, their weaknesses. She learns how you fight and knows how to counter and combat it. Taking that blow from them was an assessment of their physical strength. Now she knows, this battle is over.'

Finn turned back to the action in the pit just in time to see Anjunel get to her feet and take up a stance again. She crouched low with one leg extended in front her, arms out wide, and each hand hooked over. To Finn's eye, she resembled a bird of prey, and when she struck, it was with the speed and finesse of an avian hunter.

As one Herecaté swung at her, Anju sidestepped it and rained a furious torrent of blows against the animated creature. It reeled backwards, unable to defend itself. She kept pouring on the pressure until it was forced up against a wall. Another of the undead attacked Anju from behind. She ducked it at the last moment, and the vicious spiked mace crushed the face of the elf's opponent.

As the second life it had been given was extinguished, the wisp left the animated body and returned to Anjunel's vine tattoo. Four became three, and now she was armed.

She made quick work of the remainders. They never stood a chance. They were souls of the dead inhabiting dead bodies, not their own. She, on the other hand, was a trained fighting machine that found killing as easy as breathing. Putting them to rest once more was an inevitability.

Anjunel wielded two maces with a flourish as she faced up to the last Herecaté. She blocked its overhead attack with one mace and struck its knee with the other. It buckled from the blow. Still, it tried to fight on, but another block and strike, and it had lost its arm. Defenceless to the oncoming assault, Anjunel Lynsu'unara did what she had done many times before and delivered the coup de grace.

Many of the audience clapped, having never seen the angel of death in action before, only ever hearing the stories of her exploits. Finn clapped along with them, more vigorously than most since her own head had been on the line too.

'I expected nothing less of you, Anjunel Lynsu'unara,' Pharinox declared. 'Those that can survive are strong, and you are among the strongest. Lower the ropes so she may exit.'

Anjunel had no intention of using them, however. She backed up to one side of the pit, then sprinted to the opposite wall, jumped as high as she could and planted foot. She pushed off and propelled herself higher towards the wall she had come from. It was just as Finn had seen her do in Almedia, when she was being chased, and she bounced from one side to the other between the close buildings to reach the roof. The pit was wider than the gap between those homes and yet she still made it out, as if she were striding through the air.

A statement had been made by the angel of death's display; she showed them that she was strong, and if they chose to come for her, she would be the one to survive.

The pit was covered once more, and a large brazier was brought out and placed in the middle of the stage. Loscivia sauntered towards the raised container. 'It is now time to commence with The Quelling. Rise and give your offerings to Na'roli!'

Finn watched as each of the Krez elves raised a fist overhead; some held parchment with fulfilled non-lethal assignments, which would glow and then disintegrate. The high priestess continually chanted and cast her spell until smoky, black tendrils escaped from their upraised hands and drifted towards the brazier.

The young thief looked on in wonder, positive she was witnessing an event never seen by a surface dweller before. She was about to ask Tessera a question, but then she saw the blank expression on the face of the dark-haired elf. Finn looked around and saw a similar countenance on others. It was as if everyone were in a trance except herself and the spellcaster. She was tempted to rifle through a few pockets but desperately fought the urge.

As the last bits of the smoke trails entered the brazier, it erupted and bathed the entire cavern in an eerie red glow. Finn could feel her palms warm up. Her chest rose and fell quickly, her breathing elevated. Her levels of adrenaline rose as she gazed at the spectacle before her.

Thick clouds of red mist lowly poured from the container. It spread along the ground like an ominous incoming tide until it was everywhere, swirling around the bodies of everyone present. It possessed a bitterly pungent, acrid smell, which made Finn retch and her eyes well up. The Krez, however, breathed it deeply into their lungs with great relish. She could see a faint red glow through their skins as the mysterious substance spread through them internally.

After a few minutes, the red mist had all dispersed. The Quelling was over.

With the ceremony ended, many of the Shadow Dancers were unsteady on their feet; others couldn't stand at all. Finn recognised the effects. She had seen them plenty of times before in the slums of Almedia. Those wretches couldn't deal with their demons just as the Krez, were trying to keep theirs at bay.

'Now that The Quelling is completed,' Pharinox announced, 'before we end this trial, one announcement must be made. Tessera Eidrassil, stand up.'

She did as she was told. 'You are hereby appointed to the vacated position of chapter head, with immediate effect.' It was just as Anju had predicted. 'As for you Anjunel Lynsu'unara, you are hereby decommissioned and exiled from the Shadow Dancers, with immediate effect.'

As soon as he finished, the head of the unique clan of assassins turned his back to the disgraced elf, signifying that he no longer saw her. The other Krez followed suit, each turning their back on their former comrade. Tessera was one of the last to turn. Finn thought that she wouldn't, but after one last tender kiss goodbye, Anju finally urged her to turn. The very last to show their back was Ilvaria, the military head. She gave a nod and a smile, which Anjunel returned, and then she too turned, her cloak fluttered behind.

Her whole experience in The Hollow wasn't exactly what Finn had been expecting but, to be honest, she hadn't really known what to expect. One thing was for sure, she may never return to this extraordinary underground world, but she would remember what she had seen for a long time.

'So, what happens now?' Finn asked as she helped Anju retrieve her clothes.

'I get dressed,' replied the elf matter of factly.

Finn rolled her eyes. 'Well, if you've got nothing better to do, we could always head to Imperial City and see how bored Daniel is at his little Mage Academy.'

Anjunel made to reach out and touch Tessera, but hesitated as she had second thoughts; this was going to be hard enough for both of them. 'Those that can survive are strong,' she whispered before leaving with Finn, unaware of the tears that rolled down her former lover's cheeks.

Chapter Nine

A spell learnt and a decision made

To be accepted into Hartfield Mage Academy was no easy feat. Sure, there were other academies and wizarding schools in Ariest, you could attend, even in Imperial City itself, but there hadn't been an Archmage yet that had not graduated from Hartfield.

At age ten, the parents of magically Adept children would apply to these establishments, hoping to secure their child's place when they reached eleven. Hartfield, however, first contacts parents when the child turns eight, and then only if they possess significant Essence.

A representative of the academy will give them some mental agility and dexterity exercises to practise and some basic spells to learn. They then leave and have no further contact until they return in two years. If after that time the child does not show any development and does not achieve a perfect score in the on-the-spot test they are given, then Hartfield's interest in them ends there.

Such was the academy's prestige, it was not unheard of for pushy parents, that could afford it, to hire private magic-tutors to school their kids from five years old, to give them the best chance of being accepted.

This no doubt gave rise to the notion that Hartfield was just for the wealthy elite. That couldn't have been further from the truth. Unlike other magical institutes of learning, Hartfield Mage Academy had no admission fee. It did, however, have a condition whereby graduates would donate five per cent of their future earnings. So, it didn't matter if you were the king's grandson or a street urchin; if you had the ability, you could study at Hart-field.

They prepared themselves their first classes of the day. Not one of them showed the slightest bit of consideration to the fourth person they shared their dorm room with.

The three Adepts laughed and joked whilst Daniel pretended to be asleep. He could hear them sniggering and making fun of him. Calling him a fraud, saying, "How could he have destroyed a Shade if he can't even summon up a familiar?" They laughed. "There's no way he'd get into Hartfield if it wasn't for Gydion." Another one brought up Daniel screaming awake in the middle of the night and, as the trio left, one of them mimicked it before he slammed the door shut.

Daniel was glad to hear their fast-retreating laughter and footsteps. He waited until he could hear them no more before finally getting out of bed. Such was the microcosm of school life. Daniel's reputation was in tatters after only one day.

In some ways, this was worse than it had been back in his old high school on Earth. At least there he could go home and have some respite at the end of the school day. At Hartfield, there was no escaping it.

He sighed deeply as he briefly contemplated the idea of not showing up for class, but then he thought how pissed Gydion would be if he did. That stray thought of the Archmage reminded Daniel that he needed to find a way to let Gydion know about his new dream.

'And how exactly are you supposed to do that? It's not like he left any clue as to where he was going.' Daniel was becoming frustrated with Gydion's habit of up and leaving without explaining what he was doing.

He had hoped that when he finally found the elusive Archmage that they would be spending time together, that he might be able to hear some more about his father's exploits, before he travelled to Earth realm. He always thought that he would be personally trained by Gydion, he even had lofty ideas of possibly travelling with him as he did so.

But the reality was far removed from what he had been expecting.

After Trinity's funeral, they had spent several days at Gydion's tower, and now he found himself here, palmed off at Hartfield Mage Academy. No word. No message. No nothing. He felt like he'd been abandoned. He might as well have stayed in Almedia. At least he had friends there.

As much as Daniel was angry and frustrated, he knew that feeling sorry for himself wasn't going to change anything. If he wanted things to be different, he would have to actively alter them. And that meant going to class and facing the laughs of the other students.

He imagined that Trinity would be proud of his decision. She had an unwavering belief in him, much more than he had in himself. If he could muster up just an iota of that faith, he could accomplish great things.

He knew a way; a way to feel empowered. To feel capable of doing anything. A way of feeling unstoppable, euphoric and boost his confidence.

Essevate. Or EV as Philip called it. Daniel had only done it once, but he couldn't deny that after doing it he felt energetic, focussed and alert. Maybe I can quickly do it before I go to class, he thought as he prepared for his first full day of lessons at Hartfield.

He grabbed his blazer from on top of the trunk Gydion had sent his things in, and that was when he heard a knocking coming from inside of it. Daniel hadn't even taken the time to see what was in the storage box for the simple fact that he hadn't accumulated many things in his short stay at the tower, but now he was intrigued by the knocking sound and investigated.

He tentatively flipped the latch up and lifted the top of the chest, half expecting something to jump out him. Daniel let out the breath he had unwittingly been holding when he saw what the origin of the knocking was. 'Grim?' Gydion's dark red, rune embossed spell-book lay on top of Daniel's clothes. 'What are you doing here?'

'About time! Do you know how stuffy it is in there? Grim queried. 'What do you think I'm doing here? I'm here to keep an eye on you. Make sure you keep up with your studies; give you training when you need it.'

'So, you're going to be tutoring me?' Daniel slumped onto his bed in disappointment, but then he shot up as the presence of Grim reminded him of the first time he had encountered the talking book. 'Astral projection!' he said excitedly. 'I can use astral projection to speak to Gydion!' Daniel settled himself and prepared to cast the spell.

'Yes, you could use your astral self to communicate with Gydion, but there is one slight problem with that, you need to know where he is. You could search the whole of Ariest, but what if he's not on Ariest?'

'Don't you know where he is?'

'No, I'm his grimoire, not his keeper.'

'Great! I really need to find him and tell him about the new dream I had with Trinity and about this figure that keeps appearing in her past, and about the fact that she recognised me as Daniel and not Cassius. Can you help with that?'

'Actually, I can,' Grim stated. 'Take the note out of your inside jacket pocket.'

'Note? What note?' he asked as he fished his hand into the pocket. His whole arm and head disappeared into the enchanted receptacle before he found it. Daniel looked at the note in confusion and read what was written on it. 'Excelsior?' The note instantly vanished. 'What was that all about?' he asked the magical book.

'That was the magic word,' the book replied, 'now you have full access of the spells within. Come and look at this.'

Grim flipped open, and the pages settled down. Daniel read the entry, 'Telepathic Communication.'

'With that,' Grim began to explain. 'You can mentally talk to anyone. As long you can picture them in your mind's eye, you can reach them.'

'Really? That's pretty awesome!' Daniel quickly read the instructions on how to perform the spell and eagerly got to work, giving it a try.

The excitement reminded him just how much he loved magic and casting spells. Thinking about the things that he could potentially do and the things that he would do once he was proficient always made him smile, and now, he felt foolish for letting these Adepts make him even contemplate not going to classes.

Daniel sat quietly and tried to focus on Planetary Essence reservoir. Once he had, he tightened his focus on the arcane element of the cavity. Once he felt the magical energy powering through him, he began the spell casting process. After several attempts and a bit of guidance from Grim, Daniel was finally successful.

'Excellent!' Grim enthused. 'Now, think of Gydion, picture him in your mind and will your thoughts to him.'

'Gydion, can you hear me?'

'You could not have chosen a more Ill-timed moment to contact me, Daniel.'

'I'm sorry. Where are you?'

'That is not your concern at this time. What do you want?'

To say Daniel was a little disheartened by Gydion's reaction would have been an understatement. He was hoping for a little praise at least. 'Well, I'm sorry for disturbing you,' he thought frostily, 'it's just that I thought you might have liked to know that I dreamt about Trinity again, and that same hooded character was there again.'

'That is interesting. At the end of term, I want you to come back to the sanctum; I will have returned by then. Oh, and Daniel, you have done well. Make sure you've read all of my spells and the other books I sent you. Now I must go. Study hard, Daniel.'

With that, Gydion ended the communication.

Daniel sat, grinning and pleased with himself. Gydion had been happy with him after all, and he even gave him his permission to digest everything within his spell-book. 'I can't believe he's given me his grimoire!'

'Excuse me, but I think you are mistaken. Gydion hasn't given you anything. This is just a loan. Once you've finished reading and Gydion is back, I'm out of here!'

'You're joking, right? I need all the help I can get here. I'm failing big time.'

'Don't be silly, Daniel. You're not failing anything. You may not be a Novice and possibly not an Initiate, but you are far above any of these Adepts. I would go so far as to say that you could even become the Adept Altus Vex, if you wanted to.

Daniel laughed until his sides hurt. He hadn't heard anything more absurd in his life. 'Are you out of your mind? Answer me this, have you ever heard of an Altus Vex, the best of their level, the standard bearer, who can't even summon a familiar?'

'No, but I have seen one that made Sayyidah retreat.'

It was true, he had forced her to run, but it was a power he never consciously summoned or controlled. Gydion had said it was a chaos bolt, fuelled by the anger and pain of losing Trinity and that it was something that he couldn't tap into like ordinary magic.

'You have truly done things that not many students at this academy have the ability to do. But if you truly wish to reach the top echelons of this craft, you must stop being so timid; you must have confidence in yourself and your abilities. Once you do, you will find that your magic will flow when unhindered by such negativity.'

Daniel reflected on Grim's words. The magic users who had crossed his path all had a steadfast self-belief in themselves; Gydion, Trinity, Sayyidah, even Philip. Daniel knew what he had to do now, his path and his mind were set.

BOLSTERED BY GRIM'S words of encouragement, Daniel threw on his jacket and slipped the enchanted spell-book into his pocket and rushed off to Professor Milton Fijit's Magic 101 class. When he arrived, class was already in session, the students quietly read pamphlets at their desks.

'I'm sorry I'm late, Professor,' Daniel said between breaths.

'That's quite alright, Mr Welsh,' Professor Fijit replied with a jolly smile. 'I've already been informed about your timekeeping or lack thereof.'

'It was just a little...'

'Yes,' the Professor continued, 'we tutors are always talking, mostly about students. Your name has come up quite a few times, as a matter of fact.'

'I see,' Daniel didn't know what to say to that nugget of information, so he pushed on with his agenda. 'I wanted to ask you about challenging for Altus Vex.'

'Altus Vex? That's taken care of at the beginning of the academic year. Forget about that. No, no, no, my boy, you have more immediate things to worry about, the A.S.Es?'

'The what?'

'The A.S.Es! The Adept Standard Exams. They're taking place today.'

'Oh, vekt!' Daniel exclaimed.

Chapter Ten

The Adept Standard Exam Begins

Daniel found an empty desk and sat down with the pamphlet Professor Fijit had given him. It was a little tattered and discoloured, giving the impression that the exam set up had not changed for quite some time. He opened the booklet and began to read; it was the exam procedures.

'As you can see,' Professor Fijit told the class as all the students but Daniel, who had already finished reading, had their noses in the booklet, 'here at Hartfield Mage Academy, all exams are devised of two parts; the written element and the practical element.' An enchanted marker began to write the professor's following points in a large font so everyone could see. 'The written exam is marked out of one hundred and tests your understanding of the following subjects: Magic History, Magical Theory Knowledge, Runic Alphabet.' Several students groaned at the prospect of trying to remember significant dates of magical history as the marker began to write once more. 'The practical exam will test the eight traits of a Mage: Discipline – to not be distracted and maintain focus. Willpower – to believe you can do anything yet still believe in your humanity, Patience – through meditation. Dexterity – to be quick and accurate in your hand gestures. Creativity and Adaptability – in the use of magic. Sensitivity – to Essence and it's mitigation, swordplay and physical stamina.'

Professor Fijit counted off each trait as he said them, and the marker wrote them in the air. Daniel made a note of them and stared at the sheet as he applied each attribute to himself. He circled willpower and swordplay. The other Mage characteristics he felt he had some ability in; discipline, patience and physical stamina had all been developed back on Earth dealing with his tormentors. While dexterity, creativity and sensitivity had all been touched upon since coming to Ariest. What he lacked was willpower and self-belief, even Grim had said it, and the swordplay trait because the only sword he had ever touched was the Dragon Claymore owned by his dad.

The professor continued with his explanation of the exam format. 'Each level of study, Adept, Initiate and Novice, will be assigned an adjudicator chosen from the faculty. In this role, the professor will be tasked with the running of the exam. They will also pick four of the traits to be tested in the practical exam. Of those traits, two will be randomly set thirty-point maximums and the remaining two, twenty points each, giving a possible total of one hundred. Does everybody understand?

At the end of the exam, the scores for the written and practical elements are averaged, and the total mark obtained. Some of you may be thinking that you should be sitting the Initiate Standard Exams, and although students are permitted to take any standard exams whenever they feel they are ready; they must have passed the preceding level before they are allowed to progress. So, if you have hopes of sitting the next level next term, you need to pass this exam today.'

Daniel immediately let out a despondent sigh. He knew he was in trouble. All around him, he could hear the other students moaning about the written exam. At least you've been to the classes, Daniel thought.

'If you've all finished reading, does anyone have any questions?' Professor Fijit asked and saw Daniel's hand go up. 'Yes, Mr Welsh?'

'I was just wondering, what's the pass mark?'

'Ah, yes. So, for an Adept, you must get 80% or higher to pass; for an Initiate, it's 85%, Novice Grade 1 I'd 90%, and Novice Grade 2 is 95%. As you can imagine, only the best are then picked up by masters to progress their training to become High Mages and ultimately masters themselves. Anymore?'

'Can you tell us who the adjudicator will be?'

'Yes, that honour has gone to Professor Tobias Law. The perfect candidate to put you through your paces,' Fijit said joyfully.

The groans and eye-rolls from the students that met this bit of information told a different story, however. From what Daniel could pick up from the disgruntled muttering, Tobias Law was, as his name suggested, a strict, hard-nosed tutor who taught MPE, Mystic Physical Education.

'Any more questions?' Professor Fijit asked. 'No? Then gather your things, and we'll make our way to the grand hall.' After putting away his marker, the professor waited for the students. Once they were all ready, he led them out of the classroom.

BECAUSE OF HIS PHOTOGRAPHIC memory, Daniel had never worried about failing an exam, since he never had failed an exam. He kept trying to tell himself that it didn't matter if he failed, it was to be expected since he had only just started at Hartfield. But Daniel noticed something that he never really did before; when it came to academia, he had a competitive streak.

Daniel chuckled softly at the idea. It was an absurd thought, but it was the truth nonetheless. As the procession left the main building of the academy, he was beginning to get quite anxious about it. The morning sun beat down on them as they filed past the dormitory manors and into the training fields where the grand hall was located.

It was normally the place where the more destructive and dangerous spell casting lessons took place but, with a little conjuring, it was easy to transform it into the perfect examination hall. Professor Fijit and his students joined the back of the long queue of Adepts nervously waiting in line to enter.

As Daniel approached the front, he could see Sara Yacon with a list checking off the names of the students as they entered. Up close, he could really see how large a structure the grand hall was. Unlike the dormitory manors, it was designed in the same style and colour as the main building of Hartfield. The doors were huge and reminded him of the gates at Almedia, just a slightly smaller version. Engraved on them were, from what Daniel could gather, scenes of magic history. Many of the figures he didn't know, obviously, but he could definitely pick out Gydion battling Sayyidah. There were a few images that made Daniel do a double take and crease his brows, because he couldn't believe it was them; one of a man with a snake in front of him, another of a man holding his fist aloft whilst monstrous creatures bowed before him, and finally a man and woman holding what could have been a grimoire and a tree in the distant background.

'Is that...?' Daniel thought out loud.

Sara shushed him. 'You shouldn't be talking, Daniel,' she whispered, 'especially with Professor Law running this exam. He has strict rules, so pay attention.'

'Oh, right, sorry,' Daniel whispered back. 'What are you doing here anyway?'

'As one of the three Initiate Altus Vex, I and the other two, have to help out on exam days. I'd much rather be studying for my ISEs tomorrow, but here I am marking the register. Now get in there, you're holding up the line. And Daniel...'

'Yes?'

Sara smiled. 'Good luck!'

Her genuine expression of friendliness suddenly put Daniel at ease, and he smiled back at Sara before turning and entering the grand hall. It was hard to imagine it as a place of combat training. With all the silk draping around the hall, in the colours of the academy, it could easily have been seen as a place for some sort of political rally, if it didn't have all of the one-seater desks neatly set up in four rows. A gantry ran around the building where several spectators were already gathering, among them Philip Strath-Holm and Sara's sisters Cara and Mara.

A general hubbub circulated the hall as the last of the students taking their A.S.Es sat down. Sara, with her registration duties over, handed in the sheets and made her way up to the gantry to begin her next duty. From up there, she and the other Altus Vex were expected to watch the exam and make sure no one cheated.

'Silence!' Everyone jumped and immediately obeyed the command. The burly Professor Law walked powerfully down the centre aisle, holding the register above his head. 'On these sheets are the names of all the Hartfield students currently at the Adept level, and now they are all in this hall.

You've got big dreams. You want to be a shining light in the world of magic. You want fame. Well, fame costs, and this is where you start paying, in sweat and tears.' Professor Law paused so the words could be digested by each and every student seated there. 'Those of you that remember I said those same words to you at the beginning of the term. Now is the time to see exactly how much you've sweated throughout the year; now it's time for the tears.

As the adjudicator for these A.S.Es I have decided to give you all an added incentive to perform at your best. The pass mark is 80%, but I have added a failure mark. A result below 70% means you are out. Out!'

'You can't do that!'

'You don't know what you're doing!'

'That's not fair!'

'Silence! Your protests tell me a lot. Each of you, look around. Look at your neighbours because today could well be the last day you see them here at Hartfield Mage Academy.

Now, for this written exam, you have two hours to answer one hundred questions on the subjects of Magic History, Magical Theory Knowledge and Runic Alphabet. After the written exam, there will be a two-hour recess for you to prepare for the practical exam.

For the practical, you will be tested on the following traits: your dexterity, wisdom, swordplay and creativity. I will explain the details of each test further once the written exam is over. Today is going to be a long day, so I hope you are all prepared for it. One last thing, be sure to read all the questions before you begin. Your time starts now!'

Chapter Eleven
The Morning Session

There was a loud sound of rustled paper as all the students turned their exam booklets over and prepared their answer sheets. It was a procedure Daniel had performed plenty of times before. The pages seemed no different to ones he'd taken in the past; exams were no different whatever realm you were on. The only difference he could see were the decorative runes around the edge. The style on Earth was to keep them plain and simple, with no distractions.

He looked down and read the first question: *Put these Mages in order (a)Ptolemy (b)Paracelsus (c)Solomon (d)Agrippa (e)Merlin.*

Solomon a Mage? So, he had been right! That was him on the doors of the grand hall. Daniel wondered if the other images were who he suspected them to be also. He was astonished. 'Unbelievable,' he said under his breath. He went back to the exam question, and something struck him; what did it mean "in order"? Order of what? Birth? Death? Height? He took a guess at it being birth.

The next question he read was just as unbelievable. Unfortunately for Daniel, it was unbelievably hard: When the elf maiden, Kepcaldera defeated the giant, Callaroch, what was the name of the son of the fifth refugee she passed on the way? He had no idea and made another guess.

Daniel was starting to wonder what kind of exam paper this was. Of the twenty questions he had attempted so far, they all seemed to be an incredibly obtuse or hard. And he had yet to come across a single question about the runic alphabet. Since Daniel had been reading them for a while now, he felt he could answer questions about them, and at this rate, he was going to need all the points he could get.

He glanced around and saw students scribbling away. Lots of them seemed to be having no trouble at all, whilst others were sweating more than he was. Panic was starting to set in. Maybe the questions weren't hard. Perhaps he only thought they were because he hadn't been to all the classes. But that still didn't answer the fact that there was nothing asking about runes.

Daniel read the next ten questions, and then the next ten after that and still nothing. Time was getting away from him. He quickly flipped through the rest of the exam booklet and finally found a question about the runic alphabet. It was the last one, the 100th, but it was more of a directive than a question.

100. *Translate the runes.*

He hurriedly flipped back to the first double-page and realised for the first time that the pattern of runes around the edges of the papers were different. Daniel didn't have much time left. He just hoped that it was enough to decipher the message.

Time ticked by unbidden. Pieces of paper could still be heard being rustled, crumpled and scribbled on by students, Daniel among them. He read the completed translation: ***You must only need to answer this question. Write nothing else. What was the first spell you were taught? Using the runic alphabet, write the somatic.***

Daniel looked down at the sheet, dumbfounded. That's all there is to it? He was reminded of a test from his childhood where the teacher told them to read all the questions first. But nobody ever did. Everybody would just work their way through the test, only to get to the last question, which would say, "don't answer any questions. Write your name in the top right corner and put your pen down." If this was indeed the real test, then so be it.

He cast his mind back to when Trinity first showed him magic in the library of his old school and how to see house elves. But they had used a gem, not a spell. His mind raced through the early adventures and encounters he'd had since arriving in the fae world and came to the conclusion that, although he had learnt spells from reading the Book of Azul, the first person to actually teach him a spell was Aradia when they were in the Shade's pocket dimension. She had been the one to show Daniel how to combine the three aspects of spell use: arcane words, hand gestures and Essence control.

Daniel smiled as he wrote down all the necessary information about the Frost Bolt spell and when he'd finished, sat back and relaxed. He had barely let out a sigh of satisfaction when the big arm of Professor Law reached over him and snatched up the page.

'Frost Bolt, huh? Who taught you that?'

'A woman called Aradia.'

'Of Tolgarr? Isn't she a shaman? This doesn't look much like a shaman spell.'

'I had read the spell before, but she taught me how to cast it.'

'I see.' Professor Law turned over the sheet and read the name on the front. 'So, you're Daniel Welsh. I knew your dad.'

'Everybody seems to.'

'Well, Mr Welsh, you have a lot to live up to; the standard of your father and the words of Gydion. Today we get to see exactly how exceptional you truly are.' With that, the professor walked to the front of the hall, turned and cast his piercing gaze slowly over the students. A few moments later, he made an announcement. 'Pens down! This exam is now over!'

There was a collective sigh of relief at having completed what many of them believed was the more difficult portion of the exam. Many of the students were desperate to talk to their friends or neighbours, eager to compare answers, but everybody waited until they were formally dismissed; nobody wanted to feel the wrath of Law.

'Before we move on,' the professor began, 'I would like all of those that answered more than sixty questions to raise your hands.' A smattering of hands went up. 'Congratulations! You've just failed your A.S.Es. You may go to your dorm rooms and collect your things.'

There was a sharp intake of breath from the students as they saw their dreams vanish before them. Some of them broke down in tears, and others needed to be further convinced that this was real and not a hoax. Once the handful had left, Professor Law continued.

'And there you have the tears. Listen up, people. This isn't some jolly wizarding school; this is Hartfield Mage Academy. If you graduate from here, you will be among the best in any dimension. That written exam was simply devised to test your discipline and your patience, two traits of a Mage. You needed to show discipline in going against your natural inclination by following my instructions. And you needed to show patience to continue to read the exam questions, although time was against you. It was an easy test to get a perfect score in, but I can tell you now, that not a single one of you got 100%. Not one! All of you have your work cut out for you in the afternoon session.

'When you come back from recess, we will get straight on with the practical exam. For the dexterity test, you will have a set time to complete the somatic for as many spells as possible. For the wisdom test, you will be tested against yourself. After that, each of you will draw a number to determine who you will face in one-on-one combat for the remaining tests in the creativity and swordplay. Now, enjoy your break and be back here, fully prepared, in two hours. Use that time wisely.

'YOU DON'T KNOW HOW lucky you were to get Law as your adjudicator,' Sara said to Daniel as they ate in the busy lunch hall.'

'He seems kind of harsh,' replied Daniel. 'Look at those kids he sent home.'

'Yeah, he's harsh and tough and works you hard in his class, but he also believes that the practical exam elements are far more important than the written. I've heard him say that "Magical History is only good if you intend to be a librarian." Seriously, Daniel, if you had a different professor, you would have been vekted.'

He knew she was right. At the beginning of the exam, he himself had half expected to be among the students going home. Yet he was still here, surprisingly. He stared thoughtfully at his bowl of rum 'n' raisin ice cream as it slowly melted. 'So, you think Professor Law puts more emphasis on the practical?'

'No doubt about it,' Sara replied as she nonchalantly played with her long single braid. 'If you can excel this afternoon, you'll have a good chance of passing, which would be a good achievement, all things being considered. Anyway, I'll see you at the grand hall. I'm going to go and squeeze in a bit of revision for my exams tomorrow, and I think you should do the same, Daniel.' He said that he would, and the friends said their goodbyes and headed off in opposite directions.

Daniel had barely left the dining hall when he was accosted by Philip, almost as if he had been waiting for him, which could well have been the case, Daniel speculated when he saw Philip's companions; Cara and Mara.

'So, this is where you've been hiding,' the bespectacled student stated. 'I thought you would have been off practising somewhere.'

'Well, as a matter of fact, I was just about—'

'Were you? Really?' Philip interrupted and put his arm around Daniel's shoulder. He pulled him closer in a conspiratorial manner before he continued. 'Or did you have other plans? A little EV session, perhaps?' Daniel shot him a worried look. 'Calm down, calm down, you're among friends here.' The sisters came closer to reinforce the statement. 'You know, I had a little look at your paper, and you only scraped through the morning exam. You're going to need tops marks this afternoon, and you know that there's only one sure-fire way to guarantee that.'

'Let's EV together,' Cara suggested.

'We know a place,' added Mara. 'Nice and quiet.'

It was a tempting offer. Very tempting. The effect of EV was a strong pull for Daniel. He could admit that much. That was easy. The feelings, the confidence, the energy. It was undeniable that he loved the rush that he felt whilst doing Essevate. He knew that if he just did it for a short time, he would be in more than a good enough place to excel in the upcoming exam. He looked at Cara and Mara, from their smiles to their proffered hands and reached out his own hand.

'Hey, Daniel!' Sara said as she suddenly returned. 'You know what? Why don't I just train with — what's going on here?' She saw the suspicious scene and demanded answers.

'Nothing at all is going on, little sister,' Cara replied.

'We're just wishing your friend good luck,' Mara chimed in.

'You're not scared you're going to lose another friend, are you? If you do, you'll only have yourself to blame, Sara, you're just too vekting boring,' laughed Philip.

'Come on, Daniel, let's go,' Sara all but dragged Daniel away, leaving the sniggering trio behind them.

Chapter Twelve

The Afternoon Session

There was a palpable tension in the air as Daniel and Sara trained in silence, a hush that was only broken when she would give him directions on countering certain spells. He had seen the animosity between herself and her sisters, Philip too, and wanted to ask about it, but Daniel also wanted to respect her privacy.

When it was time to finish up and head to the practical exam, Daniel felt quietly confident. He didn't expect to do much in the swordplay element of the exam, but he felt more than prepared for the others. 'Thanks for this, Sara. You've helped me a lot.'

'It was good for me too,' she admitted. 'I was able to try out a few things that I've been desperate to.'

'Like what? That hair thing?' Daniel had been surprised at one point during their sparring when he thought he had her beat by magically binding her hands. Only to see her white hair come alive, grow at least ten feet in length and wrap around his body, squeezing him until he freed her.

'My family are witches,' Sara explained. 'Hair manipulation is something that we can all do, even my sisters.' She hesitated for a moment as Daniel sat expectantly beside her.

'What is it with you and them?' He hadn't meant to blurt out and softened his approach. 'I mean, I always thought triplets are supposed to be close, especially identical ones.'

'I know you've been dying to ask me, but now isn't the time, Daniel. I will tell you at some point. I think you need to know what kind of friends you are making, but right now, the only thing you should be thinking about is your practical.'

'You're right,' he nodded in agreement. 'I'm actually feeling pretty good about it.'

'That's great! Because the format for the practical is different.'

'In what way?'

'There'll be spectators.'

'What?'

'Yeah, it's a way for the academy to make extra gold. It's a weeklong event, and it does quite well. Of course, Mages are invited to see the upcoming crop of talent, in case there are any potential candidates they'd be interested in mentoring and taking on in the future. All other attendees pay a fee. Dignitaries and nobles come from all around to watch. For many, it's their best chance to see Mages doing their thing without the dangers of war or questing.'

'I see. But surely there's not that much interest in watching Adepts. I mean, they're only just starting out as Mages. They must be here for the more experienced students.'

'Yes and no. Master Mages usually only attend the higher exams; the two Novice grades and Initiate grade two, perhaps. The other spectators love the Adept exams for the exact reason you mentioned; they're just starting out. Not many have the nuances of minute control of their spell's outcome, so there are lots of overpowered displays, which the crowds love to see. I've heard that this was a very popular ticket to purchase.'

'Let me guess, they're here to see me.'

'Of course! Daniel, you need to realise how big a deal this is. Your dad did great things leading the Athenathoi and as part of the Fellowhood with Gydion, Thunderbeard and Tavisum. So, when someone like that disappears without a word, and then his son appears, there's bound to be a buzz. No child wants to be forever in the shadow of their parents, and I'm not going to pretend that I know what it's like, but you are always going to be his son; it's up to you if you want your name to come before or after his.'

He had to admit that she made a valid point. 'This is the place to start making my mark, isn't it?'

'Well, you've already started that. You destroyed a Shade, remember? '

'Not single-handedly.'

'And you repelled Sayyidah.'

'Again, not single-handedly.'

'And each time you played the key role, but if you want to look at it that way, no one will be out in the arena with you this afternoon. Make your mark and it'll be all you.'

The queue at the grand hall was already beginning to file in when they arrived. Sara, on seeing this, wished Daniel a hasty good luck and ran off to resume her duties as an Altus Vex. He could see that there was indeed a lot more spectators on the gantry than there had been this morning; even Proctor Goodfellow was there, but somehow not as many as he thought, given the way Sara had talked it up. Two elves stood out, though. Dressed in matching red and silver uniform, Daniel got somewhat of a military vibe from them by the way they stood and scanned the hall. The layout within the hall had also been changed. No longer were the seats in columns, but arranged into more of an auditorium with what Daniel originally thought was a large silver-framed movie screen at the far end. It wasn't long before he would find out that he was right, in a way.

'Settle down, settle down,' Professor Law demanded as he stood before the students, hands clasped behind his back. 'Now that we have weeded out those that lacked the focus and discipline to be truly accomplished Mages, we move on to the practical exams. I hope you all used your recess time wisely.

'In a moment, we will begin the dexterity element. I will call the first five names. You will go behind the screen here,' the professor held out his left arm, 'and you will exit here,' he held out his right arm. 'As each student comes out, I will call the next one to go behind the screen. We will continue in this manner until all students have been tested and then move directly on to the wisdom element which I will explain more of at the time. There will be a short recess after that to prepare yourselves for the combat elements, sword play and creativity. Is that all and understood?' A reply of affirmation came from the students in unison. 'In that case, we will begin.'

A roll of parchment appeared in front of Professor Law, and he read out the first names listed. Alicia Adamson, Tariq Akeem, Renata Alieki, Joshua Allen and Alinadam Anvilcore all stood up and walked behind the screen.

A minute later, they strolled out and were replaced by Gary Appleton, Silver Archus, Canter Avist, Sadio Azuma and Ba'ar.

A little over ten minutes had passed when Professor Law called Trixie Waller, Chris Webster, Daniel Welsh, Tabitha Weston and Andrew Wilson – the one he regarded to be the leader of his dorm room tormentors.

Daniel and the other students rounded the screen, where they found, seated behind small desks, five exact duplicates of Professor Law. The students were instructed by the nearest professor to take up a position in front of a desk. 'For this test, we will hold up one of these.' The duplicate professor pointed to a stack of cards on his desk, which were also on the other desks too. 'On each card is written the name of a spell. You will need to correctly perform the hand gestures to as many of them as possible within one minute. A new card will not be picked up until the current one is demonstrated in the right manner. If that is all understood, then we will begin.'

Sixty seconds isn't long at the best of times, but in these situations, when you need every second of that minute to accomplish something, time seems to accelerate. However, Daniel felt that he had managed his time well. He had gone through a fair amount of the cards, without having any do-overs, so he was feeling pretty good about himself as he retook his seat.

With the last few students having finished the dexterity test and the duplicate professors returned to Professor Law, he wasted no time in proceeding to explain the simple mechanics of the next element of the Adept Standard Exams: the test of wisdom.

'Now,' began the professor, 'there are many ways to test wisdom; some professors would have had you answering questions on a sheet again. I, however, have enchanted this screen to place you in scenarios where your wisdom through humility will be judged. The screen will display the name of the Adept to be tested.'

There was a murmur of confusion among the students as they tried to figure how the test would go. This quickly turned to gasps as Daniel's name appeared on the screen. The professor was a little taken aback also, and glanced at the proctor. He called the young Mage to up to the front before explaining to everyone that the names would be picked at random.

'Stand here,' Professor Law said to Daniel. 'Now, close your eyes and relax. Let the screen do its thing.'

THE WARMTH ON HIS SKIN and the cawing of birds prompted Daniel to slowly open his eyes. He was outside, somehow. In a jungle, by the look of things, he surmised, but he had no idea where. 'I don't even think this is Ariest,' Daniel thought aloud as he glanced around and noticed the single sun above him.

Hearing what he thought sounded like running water, he pushed through the brush, breathing in the fragrant scent of the evergreen foliage. Daniel had been right; it was a river. And where there was water, there would invariably be a settlement of some kind.

Daniel's mind started to wonder; what kind of test was this? What was he supposed to demonstrate in a jungle? Survival skills? But what did that have to do with humility? He scoffed and continued on his way.

A deafening scream broke the silence.

He rushed forward without a second thought, and when he burst out into a clearing, he wished he hadn't been so rash. A two-legged amphibian creature was half out of the river. Its long tongue protruded from its elongated maw and had snared a young girl, presumably washing clothes but now found herself in a life and death tussle to escape the serrated teeth in the animal's mouth.

Thinking that he was safe in the animal's blind spot, Daniel began to formulate a plan and figure out what he could do to save the girl. Unfortunately, he hadn't realised that its eyes were extendable and could be moved 180°, independent of each other.

The girl was used as a weapon by the creature as it swung its head and sent her crashing into Daniel. They landed in a heap, but she was as slight as he was, and he quickly regained his footing to stand beside the semiconscious girl. Their assailant bore down on them, dragging its brightly-coloured armoured body along by its two powerful front legs.

Whatever species of animal it was, to Daniel, it had some resemblance to a crocodile with its hard-scaled back, he just hoped that it had the same weakness as he fired off several ice bolts to drive it back.

Having created the space he needed; Daniel easily recalled the spell he desired from his memory of the Book of Azul. He had to admit, in the little time he had spent at Hartfield, the teaching and training he was getting was paying off. It was the multitasking aspect of spellcasting that Daniel always found daunting, he likened it to plate-spinners, but with the practice, he had been getting, accessing and mitigating the water element of his Planetary Essence, whilst performing the hand movements and somatic, was becoming easier.

With his hands surrounded by blue magical energy, Daniel slammed his palms on the ground and a row of ice spikes raced towards its target, growing in size with each moment until the deadly razor-sharp spikes erupted beneath the creature, impaling its soft underbelly. The animal hissed as it died.

After seeing what Daniel had done and the power he possessed, the girl fell to her knees, speaking rapidly in a tongue he didn't understand before she began to prostrate herself before him, just as he heard someone clapping behind him.

He turned around and felt his blood run colder than the ice attacks he had just unleashed. Before him stood the same hooded figure in the grinning demonic mask that he had seen in Trinity's past lives.

'She thinks you are some sort of deity,' the muffled male voice said from behind his mask.

Daniel stared, too shocked to say anything.

'You look like you've seen a spectre, Daniel.'

'Who are you?'

'I'm you, Daniel. Or the better you really.'

'You're nothing to do with me.'

'If only that were true.'

'Why are you here? How are you here?'

'I can be wherever I want to be, whenever I want to be. And that includes the past of your little girlfriend.'

'Trinity. What do you want with her?'

'Nothing.'

'But I saw you. You were in her previous lives.'

'Only because I was in your mind. It's you I'm after.'

'Me?'

'I'm here to make you an offer.'

Before he could continue, men from the girl's village arrived, responding to her cries. Brandishing rudimentary weapons, they took aim at both of the strangers. The girl, however, intervened, frantically waving them off. Daniel remembered seeing a linguistics spell among Gydion's books and quickly performed the simple spell.

'...has great power,' the girl said to the other villagers. 'He touched the ground and killed the Scalaa with ease. He must be from the skies.'

'I am not a deity. I am just a man.' Daniel was just as surprised as they were to hear him speak in their tongue. Although he still thought in English, what came out of his mouth was anything but.

'And yet you speak our language.'

'It's just magic.'

'Only the gods can do the things Vina said you did.'

'See, Daniel? They say we are gods, so why shouldn't we be?' The masked man held out his hand. 'Take it. Join me, and we will be gods. Together we could rule not just Ariest, but all the realms. We could usher in a new era. Think of the recognition and acclaim you would garner. The respect you desire. The respect that you deserve. More than Eric ever could.'

Daniel stared at the masked man's hand. Could it be as simple as that? Take his hand, and I'll no longer just be Eric Mondragon's son, forever in the shadow of my father. I'll become much more. I'll finally have the respect to be my own man and not have everything I do compared to dad. He hesitantly reached out his hand.

'Don't do it, Daniel!' The disembodied voice of Trinity suddenly rang out. 'He's lying to you. This isn't the way.'

'Trinity? Where are you?'

'I don't know. It's dark. I can't see anything. Just blackness. You have to find me, Daniel. Save me.'

'Shut up!' The masked man waved his hand, and the voice of Trinity was gone. 'It seems I've been too lenient on her.'

'Don't you touch her! You said that you didn't want her, so, where is she?'

'I don't want her. I didn't lie, she's just my bargaining chip, so I'm keeping her safe. For now.'

Daniel clenched his fists so hard they shook.

'Calm down, Daniel. I've been in your mind, remember. I've seen the magic you've learnt, and I could find no sign of that vaulted chaos bolt, which suggests to me that it's not something you know how to call upon whenever you desire. You had an advantage once, but no longer. Besides, you're inherently good, Daniel, you wouldn't attack first.'

'People change.' That one word, "once", suddenly lit a bulb in Daniel. 'You say that you haven't lied, and yet here you are, wearing a mask, lying about your identity.'

'True, but that is easily fixed.'

'Take it off then. Show me who you are.' Daniel looked on with bated breath as the man threw back his hood. His words had suggested to Daniel that their paths had crossed, and as the mask was removed, he found out that not only was it true, but they also shared a deeper tie. 'Tristan?' He stared at the scales that covered half of his brother's face. 'What happened to you?'

'I've been given my true calling, brother dearest. Dragon blood now courses through my veins. It burns,' he whimpered before regaining himself, 'but the pain is matched by immense power and magic! As I said, I am better than you now.'

'Tell me where to find Trinity, Tristan.'

'I don't think so. I've done you a favour taking her away from you. I'm protecting you. It's the brotherly thing to do, right? One brother to another. It's funny that she should say that I am a liar, when in truth, of your friends, I am the only one that has ever been truthful.'

'You still call yourself a friend?' Daniel scoffed.

'You seem unconvinced. Well, I'll tell you. Gydion, Finn and even your beloved Trinity have all lied to you. I've seen the life records. With the right meditation, you can see them for yourself if you don't believe me.'

'I *don't* believe you. That dragon blood must have affected your mind.'

'It has! I have more clarity of thought than ever before. You want specifics? So be it. Where should I begin?' He paced in a circle as he deliberated. Soon he was struck by a eureka moment. 'Finn! Not only did she cheat to win the Beltane Games, but she also lured the Shade to our father...'

'What?' Finn somehow cheating at the games was one thing; he half expected it of her if he were honest, but her bringing the Shade to his dad was another thing completely.

'...but she didn't know about that last bit, so I wouldn't hold it against her. Trinity, too, I guess. She doesn't know either.'

'Doesn't know what?' He didn't believe what his brother was saying, yet he still wanted to hear more.

'What Gydion did to her. She doesn't love you, Daniel, but she has no choice but to.'

'Now I know you're talking rubbish.' He had seen the affection in her eyes.

'When Gydion resurrected her, he added something to the spell. Something to aid her in finding you. Something to make her attracted to the person with the highest levels of Essence. She was enchanted to love you.'

'That's bull!' Daniel yelled and charged at Tristan. He was no match physically for his brother, a seasoned fighter, and was easily tossed aside.

'It never crossed your mind, Daniel, as to why someone like her would be interested in someone like you? Is it your charisma? Your charming personality? Maybe you thought it was out of pity.'

The truth was Daniel had thought about it. Many times. But something like this had never crossed his mind. As he got back to his feet, he remembered what Tristan had said about being inside his mind. 'If you truly have been in my head, you'd know what to say to hurt me. What you're saying isn't the truth.'

'I'm not doing this to hurt you, Daniel. I'm doing it to inform you. To show you that I am the only one you can truly trust. What better way to have you subservient to Gydion than to have his "daughter" seduce you? All because of an iffy prophecy.'

'The prophecy? He thinks it's about me?'

'"The progeny of the champion shall bring death and destruction. The ghost of the dragon shall change Ariest forever. The Mortokai has come." Of course, he thinks it's you, everybody does, and that's why he wants to control you.' Tristan put out his hand again. 'Come on, Daniel, take my hand and together, as brothers, no one could stand against us.

'Daniel shook his head. 'I want to hear it from them. I'll give them the chance to explain themselves. I won't take your word for anything.'

Tristan yelled in frustration and unleashed a stream of intense dragon fire at the unsuspecting villagers. Daniel was forced back by the ferocious heat.

The roar of the flames was terrifying, but the cries of the innocent were deafening as his crazed half-brother reducing them to ashes.

'No!' Daniel was horrified by what he just witnessed. The sound and smell in the air was something that he would never forget. They had revered magic users as gods, and that same magic had wiped them out. Perhaps if they had magic themselves, they might have been able to protect themselves and wouldn't have been blinded by a belief that left them at the mercy of someone like Tristan. 'You're not my brother, you're a monster.'

'And you're obviously the younger, stupider sibling.'

'Those people were innocents!'

'Bad things happen to good people, Daniel. Look at Trinity; she died saving your life. She's dead, and I'm going to keep her like that. But then again, she isn't quite "good" is she? Did she ever tell you that we kissed?'

'Liar!'

Daniel unleashed a barrage of ice bolts at Tristan, who, having gained pleasure from seeing the anguish his comment made, conjured a shield to protect himself. Tristan spat a fireball at his brother. Since that day in Abjuration class, when he was caught off guard by Philip's attack, Daniel had practised diligently until raising his defences had become a quick, fluid action.

'Sayyidah said I should kill you and be done with it, but I wanted to give you the chance to join us. Baelthorn is coming, and this world will be reduced to nothing.'

'Baelthorn? The dragon lord? You truly have gone mad, Tristan.'

'Mad? I'll show you mad!'

At that point, Daniel felt a constant attack against his armour as Tristan cast the same spell that he had used to decimate the villagers at him. His protection was beginning to give out, and he was desperately thinking of a counter-attack he could use when he started to feel his own skin burning. Daniel screamed as pain shot through his nerve endings. He couldn't calm his mind to even begin to cast a spell. His concentration was gone, and soon, so would his armour.

Daniel suddenly vanished.

Chapter Thirteen
The End of The A.S.Es

'Professor Law knew something was wrong straightaway,' Sara explained to Daniel as he propped himself up in the infirmary bed. 'He said that he had barely begun the incantation when your exam started suddenly. The location was wrong too.'

'You could see it?'

'We all could. Everything was projected onto the screen.'

'So, where did I go?'

'Well, you didn't go anywhere,' Sara said. She knew that she'd have to explain further when she saw Daniel's blank expression. 'What you experienced was an Image Generation spell. It creates an illusion directly into your mind. It's not something that you see and think is real and has no tactile substance, like ordinary illusions, but something that your mind tells you is real; you feel, hear and smell everything. It's real to you but no one else. That's why you suffered from shock and collapsed, and that's why you don't have any burns.'

Daniel confirmed that by inspecting his undamaged hands. 'It felt so real... the smell when he...'

'Is that really your brother?'

'Half-brother, yeah.'

'You certainly win the crabby sibling award, hands down. You should have seen the professors when they heard him talk about Sayyidah and Baelthorn; they were frantically trying to break the enchantment.'

'So, what happens now? I guess I failed that, huh?'

'No, they're giving everybody a pass. They don't know how your brother did what he did or if he did anything else, so they decided not to take the chance. We're moving onto swordplay then creative combat.'

AS DANIEL AND SARA walked across the neatly landscaped field towards the outdoor arena, where the last two elements of the Adept Standard Exam would take place, she watched a flock of birds fly overhead, squinting her eyes as they passed the suns of Ariest, which were already to past their zenith.

Thinking about what had transpired between Daniel and Tristan, Sara was reminded of her own situation with Cara and Mara. She sighed deeply, longing for the old days. 'We were close, once,' she said all of a sudden, catching Daniel off guard. 'Really close. We did everything together. Sure, they teased me, called me baby, technically I was, since I was born a few minutes after them, but it was all done with affection. We were always there for each other, said that nothing would come between us. It was a great time; the spells we would cast together were amazing. But something did, or should I say someone did, come between us.

Things didn't really start to change until we got to Hartfield. When I first saw Philip, I liked him straight away. It was a crush. We were twelve, I was excited to be away from Ostia and our parents' constant gaze, and I started spending more time with him without my sisters. I broke the pact.

They started to resent me, reminded me of the promise we had made, but we were growing up. By the time we were fourteen and in the first grade of Initiates, I was convinced I was in love, even though it was the first time I had had these feelings. It felt so good. I was happy. But before I could tell Philip about how I felt, it was over.'

'What do you mean? What happened?'

'My sisters set me up, that's what! They pretended that everything was forgiven, saying that blood was thicker than water and that kind of stuff. They wanted us to get together after their Necromancy class. So, I went there to meet them, but they weren't there. Philip was, though...he was there, kissing Alicia Silversage.

Cara and Mara feigned shock and pretended to be supportive. I crossed paths with Alicia the next day and confronted her about it. She said she had no recollection of it ever happening, saying she was in her dorm all day. The last thing she did remember was my sisters going to see her. I didn't believe a word of it, until later that night when I saw them removing the charm they had cast on her.'

'Wow. So, they did it out of spite? To teach you a lesson?'

'That's the character of the friends you're making.'

'What about Philip?'

'I never did find out his role in the whole matter, and to avoid having to see them even more than I do now, I kept myself back, so we're not living in the same house. I should be sitting the N.S.E level two and not the I.S.E level two, but at least they'll be taking their level two exams, and they'll be out of Hartfield Academy.'

'Looking forward to that day?'

'I'm thinking of having a celebration.'

When Sara explained to Daniel that the final elements of his exam would take place at the arena, this wasn't exactly what he had in mind. He thought it would be nothing more than a part of the field with a ring rope on the ground as a boundary, or possibly the hall again, with a rearranged interior. However, the arena was none of these.

The pair arrived at the site, a large circular magical amphitheatre complete with tiered seating. This was where Mages trained before Hartfield was Hartfield. Mage training had once taken place out in the open, wherever they could find space. But that had its complications. These were Mages learning the craft, after all, so it wasn't unheard of to have spells go awry; fields being pockmarked by Arcane Explosions and smouldering bouldermen running amok in nearby villages was commonplace. The newly formed Mage Assembly, created to be the authority in magical matters, decided that, along with their own headquarters, the arena should be built near the city of the elves and would protect those within and without.

As public interest grew in Mage battles, and Hartfield saw a chance to add to their coffers, more and more tiers were magical added. In fact, the whole structure could be materialised and dematerialised as and when needed.

'It sounds like there's a lot of people in there,' Daniel commented as they made their way to join the other students.

'I did tell you. Don't worry about it. Your brother has far more power and ability than anyone you'll be facing here.'

'You're probably right,' but the problem was that Daniel knew that he was his own worst enemy.

The students sat in their own private box, with the thousands of people in attendance straining their necks to get a glimpse of them, excitedly talking amongst themselves about what they had heard about this crop of Adepts. Several Altus Vex were also in the box, with a mandate to supervise the students and make sure none of them tried to exchange the lot they had each drawn upon entry. Philip and his ever-present entourage, two of the Yacon triplets were amongst them. The bespectacled Novice Mage gave Daniel a pat on the back for encouragement.

He didn't know how to deal with Philip now Sara had told him the details of how their friendship had ended. He liked both of them and didn't really want to be in the middle of any potential issues about loyalty. But as she had suggested, Philip would most likely pass his N.S.Es and be out of Hartfield.

Professor Law walked out into the centre of the arena, and the crowd fell silent. It was a power he had over not only the students he taught. 'I hope you're ready. We're about to get things started,' he said to the examinees, which was greeted with applause from the audience. 'You have all drawn your numbers. The person with the corresponding number will be your opponent for this next exam, swordplay, and the final exam, creativity. So, can the two students that both number one come down to the arena floor, please.'

Variel Faunara, a willowy female elf with an austere face and short strawberry blonde hair, stood up. She looked around to see who her opponent was and saw the black-haired halfling named Anaea Rilka making her way down the aisle.

Daniel watched the match intently, hoping to learn one or two things that he himself could utilise since his own sword skills were rudimentary at best. However, although the contest was best-out-of-three it was over as swiftly as the height difference of the combatants might have suggested, not going long beyond the initial salute of weapons.

Next up was a gnome named Neji Vasconquelme facing off against Robert Masterson, who judging by the smirk on his face, was expecting the contest to go the same way as the first height mismatched battle. How wrong he was. Neji was fast, and he used his stature as an advantage, not a hindrance. It was a clean sweep, 2-0, much to Robert's chagrin.

The time Daniel had been dreading was upon him. He looked down at the number three looking up at him, heard Professor Law call for the next students and slowly stood up. And then, so did Andrew Wilson.

As they stood before the professor, Daniel could feel the electricity of excitement coming from the crowd and, in turn, the growing pressure of expectation weighing on his shoulders. He was the son of a legend whose sword had a name; people assumed he would be a talent too. Little did they know that until recently, he had never picked up a sword, and when he did, that sword had been the fabled Dragon Claymore.

They each picked up a training sword at the professor's behest. It was evident that there was a vast gulf in skill by the way each handled their weapon. And as Professor Law said, 'Begin!' it was plain for everyone to see.

Daniel raised the sword to his face to mirror his opponents salute, then they assumed the ready position. Before he knew it, Daniel had his sword swiftly flicked to one side, leaving him wide open for the lightning-quick lunge which followed. With those two moves, it was 1-0 to Andrew. He smirked up at his friends, Robert and Edward, who both applauded rapturously, whilst Daniel was sprawled on the ground. The crowd were stunned, and then the mumblings began.

'It seems the apple does fall far from the tree after all,' mocked Andrew.

Daniel slowly got to his feet and dusted himself off. When he was struck, it felt like he'd been hit by a forcebolt. He had seen it happen in the other two bouts, now he was feeling it for himself, and it hurt. Not as much as his pride, however.

He stared at the ground avoiding eye contact with the gloating Andrew. For once, Daniel was actually glad to have albinism; it hid the otherwise visible flush he had. He only wished that it could block out the whispers questioning his ability and the deafening laughter of his opponent.

After a moment to recompose themselves, the professor started the next round. After witnessing what had happened in the previous round, people might have been expecting more of the same, but the scores were equalised when Andrew lost the second round by disqualification when he conjured up several swords which all attacked Daniel.

'You know that you are not allowed to use magic for this part of the exam. Mr Wilson,' berated the professor.

Andrew knew perfectly well, but savvy young Mages also knew that the public part of the exam was a chance to put their self in the shop window. Not only to boost their popularity and get their name known among the people for future quest endeavours but also to showcase their talents in the hope of attracting a Master Mage to mentor them.

Winning the second round by disqualification didn't change the outcome, however. Even though Daniel put up more of a resistance in the final round, making several critical blocks and parries, his likely defeat was never in doubt.

Daniel was despondent as he watched the rest of the contests. Even Sara offered encouragement, telling him that Andrew's father was in the military and that he probably learned to wield a sword as a young child, still couldn't raise his spirits.

AT THE END OF THE SWORDPLAY exam, the students were given a thirty-minute recess to prepare for the final A.S.Es element, creativity. Students saw it as a bit of a marquee event of the whole exam process. They were effectively given free rein to, not only flaunt their magical abilities but to do so in combat.

'There you are,' Philip said to Daniel. 'We've been searching all over for you.'

'I wanted to be alone for a while.'

'This isn't the time to be alone. We want to help you, if you're still interested in getting that respect you talked about.'

'Look, it was always going to be a long shot passing the exam with the few numbers of classes I've attended. It's fine. I've resigned myself to not passing.'

'What kind of defeatist talk is that? Then again, you're probably right, especially after what that Wilson kid did to you. You know, you probably didn't notice, because the boy was toying with you, but we had to stand there and watch the crowd's reactions to your performance. And his little disqualification only gave the audience what they really came here for, displays of magic. Why do you think the crowd cheered him so enthusiastically? Let me tell you, it wasn't because he won, but more about the way he won.'

'By showing off to the crowd? I don't see how that has anything to do with passing an exam.'

'Very little, but it has a lot to do with getting you the respect you deserve, not only in Hartfield but outside its walls too,' Cara said.

'All you have to do is put on a show for these people, and everyone will know your name in Imperial City,' added Mara.

Daniel listened to everything they had to say. He may have told them that he didn't mind failing the exam, but in truth, he did. He never had failed one before, and his anxiety about that possibility was growing with each passing minute. The fact that a twelve-year-old could be the one to make him fail rankled somewhat; he still had some pride. If nothing else, that was worth giving his best shot. He didn't want to let his new friends down either.

'Well, Daniel?' Philip asked, seeing a change in Daniel's demeanour. 'What are you going to do?'

'I'm going to win! And do it in style.'

'That's excellent!' Philip then put his arm on Daniel's shoulder and whispered conspiratorially, just in case there were any eavesdroppers. 'You know, if we did a bit of EV it would get your mind right. You've felt how focussed you become after doing it; how alert? It feels good, doesn't it? Like you can do anything. Come on, Daniel. Let's do it quickly, then you'll go and wipe the floor with him and show them what happens when you mess with Eric Mondragon's son, Daniel Welsh.'

'Surely you mean, Daniel Mondragon,' Cara started.

'Son of Eric,' finished Mara.

'Ok, let's do it,' replied Daniel. He began to focus on replenishing his Essence, just as he had been taught by Trinity. He almost immediately reached the essevate zone since his reservoirs were already full. He held it there as his purple essence erupted and sheathed his body, a feeling of euphoria washing over him. It was a feeling that he was beginning to like.

Cara and Mara, standing on either side of Daniel, each took a hand and interlocked his fingers with their own. His Essence field slowly engulfed them also, and as they shivered with pleasure from the EV experience, they held out their free hand to Philip, who took them, completing the circle, so he too could be a part of it.

VARIEL FAUNARA AND Anaea Rilka faced off against each other once more, this time in the exam that always garnered the most interest; Creative Use of Magic. The slender elf had a look of absolute confidence as the capacity crowd looked on. She was no doubt expecting things to go the same way as the swordplay exam.

Unfortunately, for her, she couldn't have been more wrong.

While Variel had been preparing her spells during the recess, Anaea, using a Chameleon spell, had watched every second of it. As soon as Professor Law started the bout, the halfling immediately conjured a stone wall in front of the elf. Variel was proficient in enchantment spells and the ones she had intended to use, Dominate, Confusion and Daze, all needed a line of sight to the target. With Anaea's wall blocking her view, her plans went up in smoke. Every time she tried to get around the wall, Anaea would add another piece to the wall until she had created a stone maze, which was actually the name of the spell she had used, with Variel trapped within it.

The elf maiden tried to blast through the walls and every one that she destroyed was quickly replaced by Anaea, who could easily have waited for her opponent to exhaust all of her Essence and win the contest by default, but where was the creativity in that?

While Variel desperately tried to find a way out of the stone maze, its creator cast another conjuration spell and oily black tentacles rose up out of the ground beneath the maze. They wriggled around in search of prey, and it wasn't long before they grabbed and bludgeoned her into submission.

The gnome, Neji Vasconquelme and Robert Masterson, had a much less imaginative battle literally consisting of running around trying to avoid each other's attacks; Neji's Acid Spit and Robert's Chain Lightning. The gnome's disadvantage and what ultimately cost him the match was that he had to stop and stand still to spit the acid; unfortunately for him, lightning travels faster than spit.

When Robert returned to the student's box, his two friends congratulated him. Sara could see Andrew gesturing to Daniel and laughing with his cronies. She approached Daniel, intending to make sure he was prepared, but she was taken aback by his fidgeting and wide-eyed stare. 'Are you ok?' she asked.

'I'm great! Better than ever, actually. I'm just itching to get down there.' Just then, the call was made for the next two students to come down. 'Awesome! It's showtime!' Daniel almost jumped out of his seats and rushed past Andrew, Robert and Edward, who shouted after him. Philip, Cara and Mara made their way to the front. They were expecting to see something special, and they didn't want to miss a thing; all the while, Sara eyed them suspiciously.

On the arena floor, the professor stepped back and shouted for the two students to begin, but they didn't.

'I'm going finish what I started in swordplay and humiliate you right out of Hartfield,' sneered .

'You sound so sure of yourself.' Daniel smiled. 'But then, so am I. So much so that I'm going to give you the first attack.'

The smile on Daniel's face visibly unnerved Andrew, but how could he refuse such an offer. 'You're crazy, but then again, I understand why you'd want to take the easy way out, so that people don't have to see what a big fraud you really are.'

'Are you actually going to do something, or is your plan to talk me into submission?'

Andrew fumed. He didn't know what to make of Daniel's actions but he was not about to be made a fool of. Andrew fired off a volley of Arcane Missiles, the first offensive spell young Mages learn, only to see their flight deflected by Daniel's Mage Armour. He let loose several more volleys, and Daniel's protection withstood them all. Andrew was flabbergasted, but as he looked up at the crowd, he knew what he had to do to end it, and end it in style.

'Is this still your first attack?'

'Shut up, you crazy kook! I'm going to teach you a lesson! I found this Volcanic Storm spell snooping around Professor Tremaine's office when I was on detention. I've been saving it for this day.'

Daniel felt an unparalleled sense of calm and confidence flowing through his body under the effects of EV. Even when the ground began to shake and crack open, he still seemed unperturbed. Clumps of hot ash and superheated boulders erupted from the fissure Andrew created, much to the joy of the onlooking crowd, aimed toward their target, Daniel.

He evaded the projectiles and rapidly cast his own spell, Ice Vortex, over the fissure, which turned it into a mountain of snow, which drew more applause from the audience. 'Nice spell,' Daniel nodded, still smiling. 'But I think I can do it better.'

From seeing Andrew perform the spell only once, Daniel could replicate it perfectly, but with his more powerful Essence, the effects were much more devastating. The crowd loved it. The professors, on the other hand, were alarmed. They had never seen another Mage do what Daniel had just done, and he was just beginning. A chaos storm was brewing, and he was at its epicentre.

The fissure Andrew's spell had created grew and spewed a column of lava high up into the air and spreading wildfire. A dark cloud rapidly grew localised above the arena floor, lightning flashed from the cloud striking the ground repeatedly, acid rain showered down, the ground shook with a magnitude earthquake, powerful blasts of freezing winds whipped around, a twister swept around the area. It was a weather event of cataclysmic proportions. It was fearsome and terrifying, and it was growing in intensity.

The people in attendance, who were once cheering at the spectacle Daniel created, now realised that they might actually be in danger, and some began to panic. The Mage students looked on in amazement, tempered by fear as all forces of nature were being unleashed simultaneously within the arena. Only Philip, Cara and Mara smiled at the proceedings.

While some professors put up shields to protect the crowd the best they could from the ensuing chaos, Professor Law tried to reach Daniel to get him to cease casting his spell, but to no avail; the wind the chaos storm produced was too strong for the professor to penetrate. He was at a loss as to how he might stop the young Mage.

Suddenly, a portal opened, and Gydion walked out into the arena. The Archmage quickly assessed the situation and flew into action. 'Tobias, get that child out of here!'

Professor Law did as he was told, grabbed the cowering Andrew and headed for the student box. As he ran to safety carrying the boy, dodging lightning strikes, huge hailstones, and smouldering rocks, everything suddenly stopped. Daniel and Gydion had both vanished.

There was a still eerie calm in the air, a silence after the cacophony of the chaos storm. Then the audience broke out into rapturous applause

Chapter Fourteen

A Wolff In Sheep's Clothing

F inn didn't like biting her tongue. She had no qualms about speaking her mind, but usually, there was a time and place for doing it. Riding behind Eamon Wolff's carriage whilst he sat in comfort with Teresa and Jarl, of all people, was not such a time.

'"You'll have an influential position in the crime syndicate," she said, doing a perfect impersonation of the guildmaster. 'I should have known! He's the biggest bandit of us all! He's probably in there drinking mead with the newbies. The newbies! Oh, this is some position, alright! Getting dust and crap kicked up into my face, how did I ever get this far in life without having such a privilege before. And what's with all these cases? How long is he expecting to stay in Imperial City anyway?' Finn looked over at her silent companion expectantly. 'Are you going to say anything, Anju?'

'Angel,' she corrected.

'Exactly. Angel. Well? Are you?'

Once Anjunel had been made aware of their destination, Illandor, the city where the elven queen of Ariest resided, she knew that she couldn't go there in her true form. With dark skin, green eyes and short black hair, the former Shadowdancer had taken on the guise of a young girl from the southern port town of Calandru. 'I've pondered over what you've said about your guildmaster and what he told you of his future plans.'

'Forget that, I'm talking about how he's treated me! Leaving me out here to get saddle sore after I've given him a chance at virgin territory? He would never have access to what I'm giving him, and yet here I am, out here, while he's in there with his new buddies.'

'Since you know him so well...'

'Better than he knows himself, the treacherous dog.'

'...perhaps you can tell me something. This crime syndicate idea of Eamon's, how far do you think he would be willing to go to achieve his goal?'

'How far? As far as he would need to go to get it done, to be honest. Short of killing them all, of course,' Finn replied offhand, but then the penny dropped. 'Actually, he would kill them all. Vekt! Vekt! Vekt! How can he plan something like this and not fill me in on the details?' Finn huffed and shook her head as she gave her sidearms and rifle a once over. 'Another slap in the face.'

'I disagree. He's showing you great respect. He trusts your ability to follow his lead in the event that things get messy. It's evident that he trusts your loyalty too. He knows you as well as you know him; Wolff knows you are capable.'

Finn thought for a moment, let everything she was hearing sink in, and then broke out into a broad grin. 'You know, I never doubted the big guy for a second! He knows he can't pull off this kind of caper without me around!'

They rode through a small hamlet, named Molton, with numerous farms, surrounded by fields of wheat, and all manner of vegetables and fruits. It was obvious that this was a major food source for the city. Anything that wasn't grown here would be procured through trade with other nearby villages. The group followed the paved road towards Molton Wood, getting ever closer to their journey's end.

They could all hear music and laughter, whoops of surprise and cheers of celebration. The reverie got louder and louder as they progressed until they came out into a clearing and discovered its origin; a carnival.

There were fire breathers, animal trainers, acrobats, clowns, jugglers, illusionists and strongmen; it was a very impressive troupe. Finn recognised one or two of the performers from other smaller carnivals. When Wolff's carriage came to a halt, she saw someone else she recognised approaching them, and she leapt down from her horse and rushed towards them.

'Virginia Mason, as I live and breathe!' Finn gave her friend a tight hug. 'What are you doing here?'

'It's so good to see you, Finn! It's been too long.'

'Tell me about it. I think the last time was the Baroness Hildepresseig heist.'

'The one where your escape route didn't exist, and we ended up escaping through the poop shoot?'

'Any job you can crawl away from, with the goods in pocket, is a success, as far as I'm concerned, Vee,' laughed Finn.

'We were covered head to toe! I think a little bit might have got in my mouth,' Virginia recollected with disgust as images of the two thieves' daring escape flashed through her mind. 'And you don't want to know how many times I had to wash my hair to get that stench out.'

'Ah, good times! You always did treasure that silky, black hair.'

'Yeah, good times,' Virginia agreed.

'So, Ringmaster, huh?'

'That's me,' she replied, straightening her top hat and tails. 'The Wolff pulled some strings for me here and there. Started off with a few disgruntled acts from other carnivals and kept growing to what it is now.' It was hard for Virginia not to notice Finn's disbelieving raised eyebrows. 'Yes, they came legitimately, all of their own accord.'

'It's just that you have been quite the mesmerist.'

'I still am, thank you very much! Honestly, once I told them that they'll be part of something big, I couldn't beat them off with a stick.'

'You know about Eamon's plans?'

'Sure, the troupe are involved in it. We'll be part of the spy network since we'll be travelling far and wide. Our animal trainer will be sending reports by bird, back to Wolff. That's if everything comes together, of course.'

'This guy's been playing his cards close to his chest for a long time. This isn't a plan that you hatch overnight.'

'That's for sure. Anyway, I'd better check in with him, let him know that the other guild-masters have already arrived.'

Virginia went off to speak with Eamon Wolff while Finn slowly made her way back to Anju and her horse deep in thought.

'You look troubled, Finn,' Anju said once her young companion had climbed onto her saddle.

'It's just dawning on me that this is actually happening; it's not a pipe dream of Eamon's. He's already set things in motion. But what if the other guild heads don't want to give up what they have? Things could go south really quick. What if I don't get to see my dad again?'

'Don't focus on what might happen, Finn. Think about the things you can do to make sure that they don't and we'll get through this.'

'You're right! I always wanted adventure. To break out on my own and see the world. The world has dangers, simple as that, you just have to face them.'

Just then, Virginia Mason returned. 'Who's your friend?'

'Oh, this is Angel,' Finn replied.

'Well, I guess you must be in the business if you're hanging around with this scoundrel,' Virginia joked.

'Hey!' Finn exclaimed.

'Just don't let her get you into any trouble. Anyway, I suppose I should be getting back to the troupe, but I'll be seeing you around, Finn, especially since we'll both be in this new world of Wolff's. If you ever need a new endeavour, I could always do with a sharpshooter act,' she said, squeezing Finn's knee as Eamon Wolff's carriage began to pull away. Virginia Mason waved them off as they left the throng of the carnival.

Above the tips of the fir trees, in the distance, the party from Almedia could see the majestic city of Illandor, suspended, unmoving above Imperial City. It loomed large in the sky like a gleaming beacon of aesthetic perfection. The grounded city was no less impressive and was distinctly influenced by its elven twin, so that their architecture complemented each other.

As the group continued towards their destination, Finn tried desperately to remain nonplussed by what she was seeing, and failed miserably. She wanted to stay cool and edgy, but her eyes were wide like someone who was seeing precious stones for the first time. And in a way, she was.

Finn had always considered Almedia to be a large town, and it was, with its almost five thousand residents. Imperial City, however, was at least five times bigger with a population to match. People that she knew that had been here, Quinn, Eamon, traders and adventurers, all described the vastness of it, but she had never been able to picture it.

In a strange way, it reminded her of Daniel's world; the hustle and bustle of it, the cacophony of sound and the diversity of its people. She was seeing people of varying backgrounds from the far reaches of Ariest, some for the first time, traders, adventurers, tourists, all congregating in that magnificent city.

Trade flourished here, it was Imperial City's lifeblood. The Central Government made its money from taxing citizens and more importantly the Merchant Guild on the products coming in and out of the city walls. Merchants distributed their goods to others in specific markets scattered throughout the city but the biggest and oldest market was the roofed Illandor Market at Port Illandor. And as the convoy from Almedia trotted pass the building, Finn craned her head, intrigued by traders peddling their wares.

They passed several temples devoted to different deities, a testament to the multi-faith nature of the capital. The red and white robes of Imodae, goddess of honour, justice and valour; the black and white of Nethys, the god of duality of destruction and preservation; the black and yellow of Calistria the hedonistic goddess of lust, revenge and trickery and the black and brown of Norgorber, the god with four aspects; greed, murder, poison and secrets. All garments of the clerics, priests and paladins Finn saw, she could identify. All except one that she couldn't place whose priests and paladins wore black and white with a red crescent overlaid with black wings on their chest.

But it wasn't the strikingly, beautiful, brightly-coloured buildings or the lively atmosphere of the city that held her gaze, but all the potential marks she saw. She couldn't help it. For every person Finn saw, an idea of how she would alleviate them of the burden of carrying such heavy money purses, popped into her mind.

They finally arrived at their destination, an exclusive venue called Landon's, named after its owner, Landon Skipton, the thieves guildmaster of the capital city. Situated near Illandor Lake, it was the place to be seen for the wealthy elite of Imperial City. Finn could imagine that this was the kind of place Mavis wanted The Dirty Dog to be, but she had a long way to go to accomplish that. Dedicated games room, restaurant, music hall and three floors of exquisite rooms and suites, put it a cut above any other such establishment, something that didn't go unnoticed by Eamon Wolff or Finn.

'Well, that's one hell of a statement,' she said as Eamon stepped out of his carriage and stood at the bottom of the stairs beside her. The pair looked up at red-carpeted marble steps that led to the palace-like building.

'Isn't it just,' he replied, lighting a fresh cigaro. 'I had heard rumours about the grandeur of this place; it seems like they weren't lies.' The Wolff blew several smoke rings into the air. 'Doesn't change a thing, though.'

'Are you vekting me?' Finn was beginning to think that Eamon wasn't taking this whole situation as seriously as he should, especially since it was all of his own making. He had been the one to call this meeting of the heads, and Landon had insisted that it took place here, on his home turf. 'Maybe you should reconsider this whole thing. We knew Landon was making gold, but this much? There's no way he'll give up all this money and power easily. And by insisting that all the heads come here and not somewhere neutral makes me think that he's up to something himself.'

'That's why I like you, Finn,' he smiled and lay his heavy arm around her shoulder. 'You always think the worse of everybody. That suspicious nature will serve you well.'

'I learnt from the best, didn't I?'

'That you did, young Finn, that you did.'

'You're determined to do this, aren't you?'

'Yup.' Eamon took a long drag of his cigaro. 'Let me tell you something, I never dreamt of getting Landon to go along with this idea of mine. My goal has always been to get the other heads onboard. If I can get enough of them to support it, then Landon won't have a leg to stand on. And coming here, having our host flaunt his opulence in front of all of us is bound to have one or two of them turning green with envy.'

'And the contingency plan? You do have a contingency plan, right?'

'What are you trying to say? Just because I have you numbskulls doing my dirty work for me doesn't mean that I've forgotten how to do field work. For your information, I've got contingency after contingency after contingency. I just hope you and your little companion are ready, if need be.'

'Don't worry about her; she's got plenty of surprises, and you know I'm always ready.'

'Why do you think you're here, Finn?'

'For my charming personality?'

'Bah! You don't have one! Now let's go introduce ourselves.'

Chapter Fifteen

A Trip to the Realm Where the Wise King Dwells

The feeling that you get immediately after having an EV session, was completely opposite to how you felt during it. Gone was the elation, confidence and the sense of empowerment, only to be replaced by apathy, doubt and temporary debility before the person's normal state was returned.

Daniel was beginning to hate the after effects. He wished he could be on EV all the time. He would have no worries in life, no disappointments, no stresses. Life would be perfect.

He was tempted to give in to the lure and find somewhere to Essevate again, but looking around, he didn't know where he was; fragrant, lush green grass was all around and Daniel could feel the spray on his skin from the raging waterfall nearby. As his mind cleared, the last thing he remembered was being in the arena taking part in the A.S.Es, but how did he get from there to here.

'What the hell do you think you were doing, Daniel?' Gydion seemed to appear from nowhere and grabbed his arm tightly. 'You could have killed that boy and a lot more besides! Magic is serious. You can't be irresponsible with it. The chaos storm is a dangerous spell to be playing with. Where did you learn it?'

'Andrew Wilson. He cast it, I copied it,' he said petulantly, the words of his brother's revelation still ringing in his ears. At his announcement, Daniel felt Gydion's stare boring into him, and his painful grip loosen. He shrugged himself free and rubbed the circulation back into his arm. 'What's the big deal? Everybody can probably do that, right?'

'No, Daniel, they can't. Not without having learnt the spell from a grimoire or scroll.'

'I guess you should have trained me after all, huh? You could have kept a close eye on me. It wouldn't have been a stretch from what you've already done.'

Gydion raised a quizzical eyebrow. 'What is that supposed to mean?'

'It means I know what you did to Trinity and what you really think about me.'

'Perhaps you would like to enlighten me, in that case.'

'As if you don't know!' Gydion's seemingly indifferent attitude was beginning to grate on Daniel. 'Let me enlighten you then, shall I? Trinity doesn't love me; she never has! It wasn't her own free will! She loved me because she had no choice. Because you made her love me!'

'And where exactly did you hear this?'

'Tristan told me. He said that he read records and saw you do it.'

'But of course, Tristan, that trustworthy, fount of wisdom. This is the same Tristan that has vowed to kill your father, am I right? I don't recall him using magic before.'

'He said that he has dragon blood inside him now. That it gave him power, but he seemed to be in pain.' Gydion said nothing, just stood looking at Daniel with his hands clasped behind his back. 'Aren't you going to say anything?'

'What would you like me to say?'

'I want you to admit what you did!'

'Yes, I did it.'

'No! I want the truth, not you saying it because I told you to!'

'That is the truth, from a certain point of view.'

'What?'

'There are a multitude of timelines, Daniel. Every decision you have made in this one, in another timeline, you made a different choice. In one, you could be the bully, in another, you may not have gone to the library with Trinity, and in yet another, Eric may not have gone to Earth, and you may not exist as you are.'

'What's this got to do with anything?'

'Everything. I did consider putting a spell on her, but it would have made her seek out youngsters with exceptionally high levels of Essence. Obviously, in the timeline, Tristan saw *that* Gydion went ahead and did it.'

'How do I know you're not lying to me?'

'Are both the Mondragon boys so incredibly dense? I've never lied to you. At times I may have only told you what I deem you need to know, Daniel, but I have never lied. Trinity gave her life to save yours. It was a selfless act, born out of true love, something magic cannot create.'

It was Daniel's turn to be silent as his mind tried to make sense of it all. He went over everything Tristan had said, then Gydion and finally all those moments with Trinity that he cherished. 'And what about the prophecy? You think it's about me. You think I'm the destroyer?'

'I do think it is about you, but not in the way you think. It's not you that is the destroyer... it is your child.' Gydion turned around and began to walk across the neatly landscaped gardens of the Manor House that had not been there a moment ago and away from Daniel.

'Hey! You can't drop a bombshell like that and just leave,' the perplexed youth said, chasing after the Archmage. As he did so, he looked at the world around them, which was changing with each moment. 'And what *is* place?'

'This is my little internal realm. I come here when I need to talk and get advice.'

'From who?'

Gydion gestured with his hand. 'From them.' Numerous people all of a sudden materialised out of nothingness. 'They are past Archmagi, or rather their Essence echoes. Most are from Ariest, but I open it to all realms.'

'I knew I'd be seeing you again, Mr Welsh,' a familiar voice called. 'Archmage Penwyll!'

'Well, it's Grandmagister, actually. There is only ever one Archmage per realm. Those that have passed on are given this new title. So, why are you here, young man? Haven't died already, have you? I had such high hopes for you.'

'Firstly,' Gydion stated, 'he's not dead. And secondly, if you haven't noticed, I'm still Archmage.'

'And we both know that's something that can't last forever. How long do you have left?'

'I don't know. I stopped using the watch.'

'What? Why?'

'I decided that I didn't need to know when my time was up.'

Whilst Penwyll expounded the virtues of knowing when your time was up to Gydion, Daniel watched something peculiar going on behind them. A disembodied hand with a striking ring, appeared and two peaches suddenly began to roll out of the fruit bowl they were nestled in, and down the banquet table toward it. The hand grabbed them, and they all vanished.

Daniel was so distracted that he hadn't heard Penwyll's question the first time.

'I asked how are you, lad?'

'Oh, sorry. Well, I had another dream about Trinity.'

'You did? What was her name?'

'Lady Bianca, and I was Cassius Stewart.'

'That's it then!' Penwyll said excitedly.

Daniel was perplexed. 'That's what?'

'The last of her three key incarnations; Alosia, Bianca and Trinity. So, what did you observe?'

'What? Nothing.'

'There must be something. Some commonality between those three lives that you saw.'

'I can't think of anything.'

'Nothing?'

'You were there Penwyll, what did *you* see?'

'I wasn't there for all of the entirety of it, neither was I there in France or her most recent life. Like it or not, Daniel, this all comes down to you. You are the one she chose. You must figure it out because you are the only one that can help her manifest into her final form.'

Daniel felt the weight of expectation on his shoulders, holding him down, but when the realisation of Penwyll's words sunk in, he felt invigorated. The grandmaster was right, Trinity had chosen him because she believed in him, and he wouldn't let her down. 'Don't worry, I'll figure it out. I'll get it done, and I'll bring Trinity back.'

'I never doubted you for a second, my boy.'

Daniel had been itching to ask Gydion or Penwyll about the regularity of disappearing fruit in this realm but, before he could, the Archmage informed him that they were going.

'Going where?' Daniel asked.

'You wanted answers, Daniel, the truth. Well, we are going to see someone that is a damn sight more reliable and trustworthy than your twisted older brother.'

'You're taking him to Solly, aren't you? Are you sure he's ready for this?'

'*He* is standing right here, and yes, I am ready.'

'Really? Because unlearning knowledge is a lot harder than learning it in the first place.'

'And impossible for someone with a photographic memory,' added Gydion.

Daniel looked from one to the other, and as the phrase "curiosity killed the cat" passed through his mind, he nodded. 'I'm ready.'

IT IS SAID THAT "A journey of a thousand miles begins with a single step." It soon became apparent to Daniel that it literally was the case in Gydion's internal limbo world. Daniel, Gydion and Penwyll all began to take a step, and the scenery around them rushed past. When their feet touched the ground again, they found themselves standing in front of a golden hall with huge pillars. Daniel didn't have the chance to see what was etched on all the gold, as much as he would have liked to do, because Gydion and Penwyll were moving at a determined pace.

'What's the hurry?' Daniel asked.

'You cannot shirk your studies, Daniel. You have to get back to school.'

'And,' Penwyll added with a smile, 'old Solly likes to give advice to Gydion about how he should be running things.'

'And who is this "Old Solly" anyway?'

'Solomon,' Gydion replied with a grimace etched on his face.

'Solomon who?'

'Well, I don't mean Solomon Grundy. King Solomon? Son of David? Ever heard of him?'

'*The* Solomon? You're kidding, right?'

'Oh, how I wish I were.'

'But why is he here?'

'How do you suppose he convinced those demons to build his temple? Ask them nicely? He was a Mage, of course. Now get in there, ask him what you need to know and don't tell him I'm here. Great! Now run along.' Gydion pushed Daniel towards the palace entrance. As he was just about to open the door, he called after him. 'By the way, he has a thing about riddles. Make sure to be a good lad and answer it. Who knows what kind of forfeit he has these days?'

'Forfeit?' Daniel responded, suddenly having second thoughts. It was a moot point, however, as the palace door slowly swung open. 'Perhaps next time you should lead with that titbit of information, just some friendly advice.'

INSIDE, IT WAS DARK, moody with a single light source, with no apparent point of origin, shining down on a throne which was occupied by a man in a yellow three-piece suit, with a matching tie and a black shirt.

'Well, this wasn't what I expected,' Daniel mused.

'And what were you expecting? Gold? Robes? A crown? A bit outdated, don't you think? But I'm sure you're not here to admire my stunning fashion sense. So, why are you here?'

'I'm not actually sure, to be honest. I was talking to Gydion—'

'Is he here?' Solomon sat up excitedly on hearing the Archmage's name.

'Uhm, no. No, he just pointed me in the right direction and sent me on my way.'

Solomon slouched into the throne with a bored expression at the news. 'That's a shame. I have quite a few ideas for him about the Mage Assembly. Anyway, continue.'

'So, I was talking to Gydion about a prophecy that some people believe is about me...'

'And who, exactly are you?'

'Daniel Welsh.'

Solomon sat up; his interest piqued again. 'Daniel Welsh? Really?' He scrutinised Daniel more thoroughly. 'Yes. Yes, of course you are. Well, well, well, what an honour this is.'

'It is?'

'Oh, for sure! I have so much to tell you. But first, you must answer my riddle.'

'Gydion mentioned as much. So, what's the—'

'What do I have in my hand?'

'Hey! I was about to ask you what the forfeit is. How can I decide if I'm going to play unless I know what the stake is?'

'Unfortunately, you have no choice now,' Solomon admitted. 'Once the question has been asked, it must be answered.'

'That's not exactly fair.'

'My palace, my rules.'

'I'll just leave then.'

'If you do that, you automatically forfeit.'

Daniel stared at Solomon. He was beginning to understand why Gydion had an obvious dislike for the man. 'Fine, I'll play. What was the question again?'

'What do I have in my hand?' Solomon replied triumphantly. 'And the forfeit? It's not much; we just swap bodies for a while, a few hours, then we swap back.'

'Swap bodies?'

'Just for a few hours.'

'Just a few? I suppose I could do that,' Daniel replied reluctantly. 'Which hand is it anyway?'

'Your choice,' the playful king answered and pointed behind Daniel.

Rows of arms protruded from the ground; some chubby, some skinny, different colours but all with clenched fists.

'What the...? Each hand has something in it? How am I supposed to know what's in it any of them?'

'You can pick any hand and I suppose I could give you a clue.' He thought for a moment, stroking his bearded chin. 'What is in my hand is something you have seen before.'

'I see. That doesn't really help in any way.'

Solomon smiled at him. 'Just let your intuition guide you.'

What a joke! Daniel thought. He walked amongst the little forest of arms, hoping that one of them would jump out at him. And one did. He saw the ringed hand he had seen earlier.

Daniel smiled, but identifying the hand was only half of the conundrum.

'So, it was your hand I saw taking the peaches. But where are they now? If we assume that you've eaten them, that would leave only one conclusion. You have two peach stones in your hand,' declared Daniel.

Solomon applauded and conceded defeat. 'Very good, Daniel, very good, indeed. It was worth a try on my part. So, what do you wish to ask?'

He was so elated about guessing the riddle correctly that Daniel had completely forgotten about the reward that came with that success, and he uhmed and ahhed, trying to think up a suitable question.

'Why don't we start with what Gydion told you. He speaks the truth. You are the bringer of destruction. That destruction shall be wrought by your child.'

'I still don't believe it! That's not possible. How could I have a child that would cause devastation? I would bring it up with the same values that I was given by my parents.'

'Do you dispute that you are the Mortokai?'

'I can't. I spoke to the magic entity.'

'That entity is called Methys. By its very nature, it must be truly neutral; good and evil, chaos and order, it encompasses them all to keep the balance. A cosmic balance has to be maintained. Just as Methys is neutral, so must its agent be.'

'I don't understand,' admitted Daniel. 'Methys is neither good nor evil, and as such, so are you, Daniel. The Mortokai must be both chaos and order. But you are not in sync. You have only accepted one half of your true self. Have you noticed when you unleash certain spells they are powered by negative, destructive emotions?'

As Daniel thought back, he realised that Solomon was right. When he fired the chaos bolt at Sayyidah, he was full of anger and rage. When he had let loose the chaos storm against Andrew Wilson, it had been bravado that had fuelled it. Even against the Shade, he had felt disdain for them.

'You may not think it, Daniel, but your chaotic side is in ascendancy. And although you must live in duality, both sides must be in balance. You must awaken your other half, the light to the dark, the order to the chaos. You must become the Spell Sage.'

It all became too much for Daniel to process; he was on the verge of wishing that he had never listened to Trinity that day in the library. 'Spell Sage? What is that?'

'The Mortokai has two aspects; the chaotic Harbinger, whose magic is powered by negative emotion and the orderly Spell Sage who is powered by positive emotion. The Harbinger has immense power and can cast spells without somatic, just a thought. On the other hand, the Spell Sage can learn and cast spells of all classes of magic users, druid, cleric, shaman just to name a few. You must be both aspects equally, but you have been leaning towards the former.'

'Not by choice. Things happened that guided me towards it. When I was facing the Shade at the Beltane Festival, I became this Harbinger out of desperation. When I faced the Shades on Earth, I died and accepted the gifts of Methys out of self-preservation. When Sayyidah killed Trinity, a voice told me to feed off the hatred. If I had known any of this back then I would have made different choices.'

'You still do not understand, Daniel. You have no choice. To truly become the Mortokai, you must be both the Harbinger and the Spell Sage. Just as the universe must be balanced, so must you. That is why your familiar does not answer your call.'

'So, I'm not a useless Mage after all.'

'Far from it. You will do great things, from both points of view.'

Daniel looked at Solomon with concern on his face as the realisation of what he was being told struck him. '"Great things, from both points of view"? This cosmic balance you mentioned, you mean good and evil, don't you?' He suddenly felt lightheaded as Solomon nodded. Daniel was a good person; he knew he was. He didn't have an evil bone in his body, but now he was being told that he had to develop one. 'What if I don't? What if I only choose to be on the side of order?'

'Then you'll die, along with many of the realms you are supposed to maintain.'

'How am I supposed to do something bad? It's not how I was brought up.'

'Don't think of it like that. This is bigger than your upbringing. You are the enforcer of a natural balance. Those who worship the perfect balance of nature, particularly druids have a similar path, only on a smaller scale. Those who seek a cantered existence, with moderation in all things, who take no side and instead seek spiritual perfection of the self are an example of being neutral. Do you think them to be evil?'

'What must I do to awaken the Spell Sage within me? Raise my Essence levels again?'

'No. Your aspect of order doesn't depend on raw power as the Harbinger does. It relies more on getting your mind into a state of calmness.'

'Meditation?'

'Correct, only a deeper kind. There is a race of people called the Tolgarr who use ritual magic and have special connections with the deities and can teach you how to get into a deep meditative state so that you may become the Spell Sage.'

'I guess I have a busy summer then,' mumbled Daniel and then remembered that there was something he had meant to ask. 'I don't suppose you know who the mother will be?'

'Unfortunately, no. The Mortokai draws suitable mates towards it, and there are a few.' Solomon grinned.

'Great. I suppose I'll just have to swear off women and stay celibate then.'

'You can't escape your destiny, Daniel. Your child will destroy, and it will be down to you to rebuild.'

SOLOMON WATCHED DANIEL leave. It wasn't until the youngster was out of sight that he rose up from his throne and slowly walked towards the protruding arms as they disappeared, one by one, until only the ringed fist was left.

Its fingers slowly opened.

Within its palm, however, was not the two peach stones Daniel had guessed and what Solomon had said was in it. The king took the folded silver object out of the hand, opened it flat and smiled. It was the FTN ticket Daniel had used when he first arrived in Ariest.

Chapter Sixteen
Revelations

Several days had passed since the incident at the A.S.E's and Daniel's impromptu visit to Gydion's personal limbo realm. All the exams had been completed, and now it was a waiting game for the results to be published. In the meantime, students and teachers of Hartfield Mage Academy were winding down to their summer holidays. With the curriculum having been completed, lessons had become incredibly relaxed, students were given free rein to practice with their spells, under supervision, or use their free time to do extra study in the library.

Daniel sat at a desk; a few opened books were strewn across it. They covered many subjects, but he barely glanced at them, because Solomon's words still troubled his mind. Daniel didn't know if Philip or Sara knew about the prophecy and didn't particularly wish to divulge it, especially now that he finally discovered that it was about him, indirectly. Hence the reason why he had been hiding from them as much as he could.

The thing that tormented him was what he should do now. Every parent only wants the best for their child, but if they knew that child would commit heinous atrocities, would they still have it? If the parents of Adolf Hitler or Pol Pot were told in advance that their baby would cause death and destruction, would they still give birth to them?

Daniel pondered over his dilemma and was so deep in thought that he forgot to change his location until it was too late.

'There you are!' Philip said triumphantly. 'I've been looking all over Hartfield for you. Anyone would think that you were avoiding me, but that couldn't be the case, especially after all I've done for you. Have you seen the way others look at you now? That's respect! None of them will be mocking you and making fun at your expense anymore. Vekt no!'

He had to admit that things had changed. Daniel noticed it the day after he got back from Gydion's realm; his dorm mates made sure they were out before he woke up and would return when he was asleep. 'What do you want, Philip?'

'I came to get you because the Adept results are out, dummy.'

Daniel looked up at Philip, not knowing how to react. Staying in Hartfield could be the reason his child turns bad but then again, not mastering his magical abilities could also be that reason.

They left the library and made their way to the magnificent academy's entrance hall where the A.S.E results were displayed. Students they passed stood and stared as the two most well-known attendees of Hartfield walked down the corridors. Daniel hid his smile as he noticed them looking at him in awe. He was finally getting the respect he had always wanted.

'Move aside!' Philip yelled at the Adepts that crowded around a silver table. It wasn't until the junior Mages turned and saw Daniel that the sea of blue uniforms parted. There was a large scroll gently bobbing in the air above the ornate table. On the enchanted paper were the names of the Adept students of Hartfield along with their pass mark. 'This is the announcement scroll,' Philip explained. 'All news about Hartfield and the magic world, in general, is displayed here. Your imminent arrival at the academy was on it; that's how we all knew. To see your results, all you have to do is stand before it and say your name.'

Daniel did as Philip instructed, took a deep breath for courage and said, 'Daniel Welsh.' The Hartfield Mage Academy lettering on his school badge changed to display his name. Once identification was confirmed, the names listed rapidly changed until it came to rest on his. His were not the only eyes interested in seeing the results.

Philip read it out aloud. 'Daniel Welsh, written exam 90%. Impressive!'

Sara had been right about the benefit of having someone that had so little regard for historical knowledge in charge of this exam.

'For the practical, you got 72%! Look, you got top marks in creativity, 30 out of 30! I told you going all out and not holding back would do it.'

Daniel read over the grades now he could see what the marks available were. For wisdom, like everybody else, he had been given full marks out of 20. For dexterity, he got 17 out of 20, being the perfectionist, he was, he tried to figure out what he had got wrong. For swordplay, he had understandably been awarded a low mark, 5 out of 30. But it was a moot point. With the written and practical exam scores together, Daniel had an overall result of 81%.

When school resumed after the holidays, he would be an Adept Grade II.

Philip took his arm and held it aloft for all the other students to see. 'How many of you could have done what my friend has? How many of you could have started at Hartfield with only a few weeks left of term and passed it first time? I know that I couldn't, but then again, I'm not the Shade Slayer!'

A Shade Slayer chant suddenly rang out, and although it initially embarrassed Daniel, he soon began to revel in it.

From a doorway, Sara turned away as she saw him slowly start to show signs of being taken in by the trappings of fame.

SARA WAS DISAPPOINTED in Daniel and headed towards the campus gardens. She never thought that he would be so superficial and so easily fall under Philip's spell. She suddenly heard someone calling her name.

'Miss Yacon! Miss Yacon!'

It was a young boy, an Adept, with two girls. As an Altus Vex, anyone junior to her had to address Sara respectfully. She would have had to have done the same to Philip and her sisters, but avoiding that scenario gave her added motivation to pass the test.

'Yes, what is it, Adept, and why are these girls not in uniform?'

'They are not students. They're here to see someone.'

'You know that is not allowed during term time,' Sara said to the nervous boy before addressing the two young women. 'I'm sorry, but I'm going to have to escort you out.'

'They're here,' the boy swallowed, 'they're here to see Daniel Welsh.'

Sara Yacon looked from the student to the two girls. 'I see. You may go; I'll take care of this.' Sara watched the boy almost skip away, happy that he didn't have to be in the presence of the Shade Slayer. 'My name is Sara Yacon. You're friends of Daniel's?'

'Yeah, very close friends, actually. I'm Finn, and this is Angel.'

'Your timing couldn't have been any better.'

'Why, what's wrong?'

'Daniels been getting in with the wrong crowd. He's being influenced by them. Maybe you might be able to get him to open his eyes before he's sucked in too much.'

Finn scoffed. 'Are we talking about the same guy here? Daniel? In with a bad crowd? I find that hard to believe. That guy's got a bad case of Saviour Syndrome, a hero complex, probably from having a dad like his.'

'Did you see the way that boy reacted?'

'Well, now that you mention it, he was a bit jittery when we said we were looking for Daniel.'

'Trust me, he's not the only one. During his exam, he almost killed his opponent. Now a lot of the other students are scared of him.'

'You're kidding, right?' When Sara shook her head, Finn finally realised her friend really was in some kind of trouble. These things were so out of character for him. After all, this was the guy that set up himself as bait to lure out a Shade. 'Who is this *wrong crowd* you talked about?'

'Philip Strath-Holm and my sisters, Cara and Mara. He's the most popular student here.'

'Your sisters? This isn't some sibling rivalry vekt, is it?'

'What? No! Daniel's a good guy, and the way they're building his reputation is wrong. If he doesn't distance himself from them, it may never recover.' Sara paused a moment, stared intently at Daniel's friends. 'There's something else. I think he's on EV. I know they are; I've seen my sisters do it.'

'What the vekt is that?'

'It is a Mage drug,' Angel suddenly spoke up. 'Just like most drugs, it gives the taker a sense of euphoria but takes away their sense of morality.'

Finn looked at her companion cockeyed. 'How do *you* know so much about it?'

'In the slums of most cities, you will find Mages that have overindulged in EV and succumbed to its effects. They become addicted to it, but the more they do it, the more their abilities diminish, then they become desperate, and they do things to get that next fix. In those areas there are slum Mages that feed their addiction, for a price of course. And sometimes they cross the wrong person that has deep pockets.'

Finn knew what Anjunel implied, but to keep her true identity hidden, she didn't see the need to vocalise it. 'Well, if he is doing this Mage drug stuff, it would explain that exam incident.'

'My thoughts exactly,' Sara replied.

'Ok, it seems I get to save him for a change. I've got some pull, so I'll put him straight. We've shared a lot; I was his first kiss after all,' she said with a grin. 'Lead the way!' Then she headed back towards Hartfield's main building.

The swell of Adept students had grown as more and more came to see their results and to make sure they hadn't wasted their first year in the prestigious Mage academy.

'I don't know where my sisters are, but that student with the slicked-back hair and glasses, next to Daniel, is Philip.'

'If we could somehow catch Daniel's eye and bring him over here, I could talk to him away from this guy.'

'I'll take care of that,' Angel announced before turning to Sara. 'Give me your blazer.' Sara did as she was told. She and Finn watched her button it up, and as she slipped out the door, the skillful assassin said, 'I'll be right back,' and disappeared into the crowd.

Anjunel liked what she did. Although she was no longer a Shadow Dancer, the skills she had honed to perfection were hers and hers alone. Unlike her status among the Krez, they could never be taken from her.

The assassin moved unhindered and unseen through the mass of students, in no time she had snuck up behind Daniel and tapped his shoulder. 'Excuse me, I have a friend that would like to meet you, but she's too shy to come over herself.'

'Sure,' Daniel said, enjoying his sudden popularity. 'Let me just tell my friend.'

'That won't be necessary,' she replied before she struck his pressure points with lightning-quick blows, and he immediately felt his body go limp into her arms. She half dragged, half carried him away back to the others with Philip none the wiser.

'Vekt, Anju! What did you do to him? How am I supposed to talk to him now?'

The Krez assassin released Daniel's pressure points, and the stunning effects began to lift.

'What the... Finn?'

'Surprise! How you doing, consort?'

'What's going on?' Daniel looked at the three women in confusion.

'This is an intervention. I've heard some worrying things about you, so we needed to get you on your own away from your new friend so we could talk.'

'Who? Philip?' Daniel scoffed. 'I've heard some things about you too, actually. Tristan told me that you cheated at the Beltane Games.'

'And?' Finn replied unapologetically. 'You said so yourself; I'm a scoundrel. Me cheating is not that big of a stretch. I don't cheat at gambling, though, no matter what you've heard! I like you, Daniel, you know that, but at the time I couldn't bring myself to tell you. Which is so unlike me,' she shook her head still in disbelief. 'So, I got a little help from Hyasda, big deal!'

'You bringing the Shade after my dad is a big deal!'

'What are you talking about? How exactly could I have done that? You know the Shade were already in your world.'

'But it wasn't until you got there that their attacks began to lead towards my home!'

'Vekt, Daniel! You want to know something? After what you and Trinity did, I wasn't even going to go with you! It was Hyasda that persuaded me! And as payment for helping me win the games, she wanted me to look at Eric! That's all! She was pretty insistent about it, actually.' Her voice trailed off as things suddenly became clear. 'It was Hyasda.'

'What was?'

'Everything! Vekt! She asked me about you. I thought she was just being interested, but it all makes sense. Isn't it possible that she could have put some kind of spell on me so the Shade would follow me?'

'I don't know much about the Shade,' Sara admitted, 'but there are spells, charms, even potions that could do that.'

'During the Battle of Almedia,' Finn continued, 'Tristan told me he saw her surrounded by Shade duplicates but that she turned them away before they could attack her! What if they didn't attack her because she was controlling them?'

Daniel looked at her sceptically. 'That's a pretty big what if.'

'Is it really?'

'Ok, so what does she have against my dad? Why would she want to send them after him? And how exactly did she get them to Earth?'

Finn thought for a moment. 'For Tristan, of course. He blames your dad for dishonouring him, and she brought him up as her godson. Why wouldn't she help him?'

'The portal corridor,' Daniel said as a light switched on in his head. 'Gydion told my dad that Fungal accused an old woman of putting it there. It could have been her that did it and how they got to Earth.'

'See? Now you're thinking like me.'

'It all fits. But If Hyasda knows where to find my dad...'

'We have to assume that Tristan does too,' Finn said, completing Daniel's spoken thought.

'We have to warn him!'

'But you can't leave, Daniel. It's against academy rules. End of term is in a week, though.'

'Don't worry, Anju and I will go. I'm sure Fungal has an FTN stop around here. She'll need your ticket, though.'

'And you'll need some money. Thank you, both of you. In the meantime, we'll tell Gydion what we suspect. Maybe he'll want to look into Hyasda himself. Daniel paused in reflection. 'I can't believe that I let myself be drawn in by him. That I listened to him and believed everything he told me.'

'Don't be so hard on yourself, Daniel. I've known Tristan a lot longer than you. The guy has charisma and a silver tongue, not bad looking either. He's like an evil version of your dad. Convincing people of things is pretty easy for him. But he's not the only one you shouldn't be listening to, in my opinion.'

All of a sudden, a door opened, and Philip stood in the doorway survey-ing the scene. 'What's going on here?'

'These are friends of mine from Almedia,' Daniel replied. 'We'd made arrangements to meet up and go to my dad's place.'

'That's ok,' Philip said, putting his arm on Daniel's shoulder. 'I'm sure you didn't know that visits aren't allowed during term, but Sara certainly did. I think Headmaster Zislaa should be made aware that you are not fulfilling your duties as Altus Vex.'

'Come on, Philip, you don't have to do that. They were leaving. I just need to give them some things.'

'I suppose Sara could wait with them at the entrance, then afterwards we can go find Cara and Mara. Just don't slip up again, Sara, or I will have to go to the headmaster.'

She sneered at him as he and Daniel left.

'He's a bit of a vekt, isn't he?'

'You don't know the half of it,' answered Sara.

Chapter Seventeen

Familiar Surroundings, Faced by An Unfamiliar Foe

The world around Trinity was still spinning as she slowly opened her eyes. As her vision cleared, she raised her head. She found herself bent over a table; her head had laid on her arms; there were red from where it had been, as if she had been dozing, but Trinity knew that was far from the case.

She had once been in a dark, formless place. For how long, she didn't know. She could sense nothing; neither physically nor mentally. It was as if she were in a place of no existence. A Lumin spell revealed nothing. She had changed into various beasts with senses keener than her own, and still nothing.

Then the place her captor held her had wavered; for just a moment. She had heard him trying to convince Daniel, her beloved, to join him. Using that fleeting weakness to her advantage and with all her strength, she had reached out mentally to contact him.

He had heard her! But she had paid for it and suffered an angry backlash from the man that imprisoned her.

It was a small price to pay now that she knew Daniel was alive. It made her smile. She had given her life to save his, and they had triumphed over Sayyidah.

Trinity blinked her eyes into focus and looked around. She immediately recognised the place; she was in The Dirty Dog! Mavis and Eveline, their backs towards her, busied themselves at the bar, unaware that she had woken. Upon seeing familiar people, Trinity, almost leapt out of her chair and rushed towards them. 'You don't how good it is to see friendly faces!' Neither of the women responded to the young druid's enthusiastic calls. 'Mavis? Eveline? Are you ok? It's me, Trinity.' She touched each of them on their shoulders and they turned to face her. She gasped when she saw that their eyes and mouths were sealed shut

'It's so much quieter this way, don't you think?' It was the muffled voice of the man in the demon mask. He sat at the table she had just vacated. With a wave of his hand, the faceless Eveline brought over two mugs of honey mead. 'Come. Sit down. We should talk.'

She was reluctant to do as he bid, but at the same time, Trinity knew that he was the only one who could give her the answers she desired and sat down. 'What is this place? Why am I here?'

'This?' He gestured to the surroundings. 'This is a gift to you. The previous place was a bit harsh. I see that now. So, I thought this would be much more comfortable for you, and I'd have no more trouble from you. After all, you're going to be here for a long, long time.'

Trinity scoffed. 'We'll see.'

'You still believe Daniel will come to your rescue?'

'Of course! I have the utmost faith in him. He loves me as much as I love him; that's why the universe chose him.'

'To be the one to bring you back? I hope so; I'm banking on it. When he sees you imprisoned and powerless to save you, he will finally realise that accepting my offer is the only way to guarantee your safety. I had originally planned to steal his powers of chaos, but then I saw an opportunity, and I took it.'

'I don't know what you're talking about.'

'You, my dear, you. When your subconscious brought Daniel into your past, I was in his mind, at the time, as he slept, and I was taken along for the ride. What an interesting life you have led, or should I say lives. Who exactly are you? What will your next life be?'

'I am who I am, that's all.'

'We both know that is not true; you are something more. Maybe I should let Daniel rescue you, just so that I can find out.'

'Maybe you should, to save yourself.'

He chuckled. 'You are unaware of the things that have happened since your apparent death, Trinity. The world didn't stop, as it did for you. The magical hierarchy is about to be shifted. Sayyidah will topple Gydion, and if Daniel does not accept my offer, then I will expose him to be nothing but the useless fraud he really is.'

'Sayyidah? You're a student of hers? Well, that explains it.'

'Explains what?'

'Why you're so crazy, unhinged and power-hungry.'

'And what of Gydion? The arrogant, self-important betrayer. Besides, you can thank my father for my state of mind!' A momentary ripple suddenly went around the tavern. 'Sayyidah just gave me direction and purpose.'

'Who are you?'

'I think our discussion is at an end; I have already said too much,' and he rose up from his seat. 'Besides, I would much rather get to know you better.' He stroked her cheek but Trinity slapped it away, so he forcefully grabbed her face, the claws of his hand slightly indenting the soft flesh of her cheeks. 'Still the feisty one? In time you will succumb. You and I make a much more believable couple. You'll come to learn that I can give you so much more than Daniel.'

'Not love.'

'Love? Soon you will see exactly how weak and inconsequential love truly is.'

'You obviously have never loved.'

The masked man was about to respond, but he stopped himself, glanced at the bar before turning around and leaving without another word.

'Well, that was enlightening,' Countess Bianca Daumier said with her French lilt as she appeared beside Trinity.

'Aye, but I wish you'd have let me unleash my druid's wrath on him,' Aloisia added as she joined the others.

'You will get your chance at the appropriate time.'

'So, what was so enlightening, Bianca?' Trinity asked.

'There are a few of things, mes amis,' replied the astute French aristocrat. 'Firstly, it would appear that our esteemed captor has a liking for you.' The observation caused a look of indignation to cross Trinity's face. 'Secondly, he does not seem to be as all-powerful as he claims to be, else he would have sense Aloisia and myself. Thirdly, his emotions are a weakness; when he was angry, his control slipped, and when you talked of love, he retreated. And finally, this setting; he claimed it was for you, but I dare say that it holds more significance for himself, especially one or both of these women, why else have them here at all. C'est ma conclusion.'

Bianca's reasoning resonated with Trinity. 'I know who he is! Or at least I think I do. I don't know how, but it all fits, well most of it does.' Bianca and Aloisia both looked at her expectantly. 'I think it might be Tristan, Daniel's half-brother.'

'Le plus intriguant!'

'Magic runs through their bloodline?'

'No, he was a swordsman, a warrior.'

'He did say that you were unaware of things that have happened since your death.'

'He also said that he was a student of Sayyidah's, but he fought, by our side, against her the day I died.'

'I still think you should tell us everything you know about him.'

'It could take a while.'

'Do you have somewhere else to be, cheri?'

Chapter Eighteen
End of Year

The door of Daniel's dormitory suddenly burst open. 'I can't vekting believe it!' Sara yelled as her hair bristled with anger.

'Hey! Sara, calm down. What's wrong?' He stopped packing and offered his friend a seat on the edge of his bed, which she took and sat down in a huff. 'So, what's happened?'

'I passed my exams, that's what's happened.'

He looked at her, perplexed. 'Isn't that supposed to be good news?'

'It's excellent news,' she said, still downcast. 'I passed with the highest marks.'

'That's amazing! Congratulations! So that means you're a Novice now?'

Sara nodded.

'Then why aren't you happy about it?'

'Because the one thing we thought wouldn't happen, happened. Philip, Cara and Mara all failed their exams. So, we'll all be sharing the same building like a dysfunctional family. It's bad enough that I have to go back home for the summer and play happy sisters there, but now I have to be around them here too.'

'Why don't you come with me then? I'm going to see Gydion, then he's taking me to stay at my dad's estate at the edge of town. I'm sure it'll need work done. Finn and Anju are coming too.'

'Is Finn here already?' she probed.

'No, but I'm expecting them at any minute. I hope nothing happened to them back home. Trouble has a knack of finding her.'

'She seems very capable, though. I really would love to hang out with you all over the summer, but it'll be Lammas. It's customary in my village for one family to host the proceedings, and this year it's mine, so my parents want all hands on deck, which means I get the pleasure of travelling with my sisters for four days. What joy. At least I'll have Fisama with me.'

Hearing his name, the curious sprite, who had been searching, whilst invisible, through Daniel's trunk, suddenly materialised. 'As always, Sara,' he said in a high-pitched voice.

'Oi, get out of there!' Daniel shooed the diminutive creature away and finished off packing. When he had finished, the two friends made their way downstairs, safe in the knowledge that their heavy trunks would be taken care of and delivered by the magic of Hartfield when their transports had arrived.

Fisama flew back to Sara, with his wispy, moth-like wings, and landed on her shoulder. 'Sorry about that,' she said. 'Sprites have a healthy curiosity for all things magical in nature, be it people, objects or buildings. It's a trait that often gets them into trouble,' she added for the benefit of her familiar. 'I've been thinking, if you have time, perhaps you'd like to come to Ostia.'

'That'd be great! The festival doesn't have any kind of contest attached to it, does it? I'm not going to end up with a wife or anything am I?' Daniel's experience at the Beltane Games flashed through his mind as he observed the mayhem of students leaving the Mage academy by a procession of carriages, oblivious to the fact that most of the students still made a point to steer clear of him.

'No, it's nothing like that,' she chuckled. 'It's a celebration of the harvest and the god Lug, who is the god of craftsmanship, so it's all about good food and people sharing their skills and creativity.'

'Sounds amazing! If I can make it, I'll let you know.'

'Excellent! Just send me an astral message, and of course, Finn and Anju are invited too.' Just then, Sara saw Cara and Mara approaching with Philip. She quickly hugged Daniel and hastily entered her carriage. 'And so, it begins,' she said with a deep sigh. 'Please, Daniel, I'm begging you, come to Ostia and save my summer!'

Daniel laughed. 'I'll do my best!'

'I hope our little sister isn't harassing you, Daniel,' Cara said.

'No, she was just inviting me to your village for Lammas.'

'That's actually a good idea, especially for her,' Mara added. 'I think you should come. We'd have so much fun.'

'If I can make it, I'll be there.'

'Good!' The sisters said in unison, before blowing air kisses to Daniel and Philip and heading off to the carriage their pit upon sister waited in.

'Oh, and sorry about your exams results,' Daniel called out.

'Don't be!'

'We're not!'

The carriage pulled away, and as it swung around, Daniel saw Sara pretending to hang herself before starting to laughing and waving goodbye. Although their first meeting might have been a bit frosty, things had changed quickly after they had gotten past the initial preconceptions, and Daniel now believed that he could count her among his good friends. A list that was growing.

'Those condolences go to you too, Philip. I was so sure that you'd pass.'

'Don't worry about it. It wasn't meant to be. We can't all be as exceptional as you Daniel,' he said, patting his friend on the shoulder.

'Come on.'

'No, seriously.' Philip flicked his hand in the general direction of the last remaining students. 'You think any of these jokers could have done what you did? You've been here for a few weeks, and you passed your exams. They've been here all year and some, not only didn't pass, but they got kicked out of Hartfield altogether.

It was a true fact, but Daniel still couldn't bring himself to blow his own trumpet. 'I couldn't have done it without your help, Philip.'

'We all need a bit of guidance from time to time, Daniel.'

The last students were picked up, leaving the two friends alone in the courtyard. 'At least it's not only my ride that's late,' Daniel said as he gazed up at Hartfield, taking in its magnificence. He knew from living in London that it's usually a good idea to look up at old buildings to admire the intricate and often impressive stone work. Daniel wasn't expecting to see a shadowy figure looking down at them, from one of the windows.

Phillip interrupted his thoughts. 'I said that nobody is coming to pick me up. My parents won't be back until next month, so I'll be staying at one of the inns.'

Daniel looked back up to the window, but the figure had gone. 'Look, if that's the case, why don't you come and hang out?' Just then, he heard his name being called by a familiar voice and turned to see Finn and Anjunel running into the courtyard of the school.

'Sorry we're late. There were a few things that I had to take care of.'

'Is everything ok? How are my parents?'

'They're fine, Daniel, don't worry. I'll tell you more about it later. So, when are we getting out of here?'

'I wish I knew. Gydion was supposed to pick us up.'

'And he will,' Proctor Goodfellow said as she exited the academy with some of the other tutors. 'He just contacted me and said your carriage is on the way.'

'Excellent! Will you be staying here over the summer?'

'No, all staff and students leave the academy during the holidays to allow the—oh, here they are!' They all turned to see a procession of goblins wearing overalls with the Ganygu logo on them, marching into the courtyard and up the steps to Hartfield. 'These contractors will be staying here cleaning and maintaining the academy while it's empty, so it's spick and span when we all return.'

'So, it's empty?' Daniel asked, looking up at the window again.

'Of course. I've had a last look around with the headmaster. Ah, here he comes now.'

Headmaster Radek Zislaa strode out of Hartfield Mage Academy and began to converse with the lead goblin, who then put its clawed fingers to its lips and whistled. Four goblins immediately carried in two large crates past the confused looks of Proctor Goodfellow and the others.

'What are they bringing in?' she asked.

'Nothing much, Morgana,' Radek replied. 'Just some equipment I'll be needing in the new year.' He strode off without another word.

Just then, a screeching could be heard overhead, and a shadow fell across them as they gazed up into the bright morning sunshine. It was a carriage being drawn by two griffins, one in front of the other. They circled a couple

times as they descended to the ground and drew up to a halt in front of
Daniel once they'd landed.

'That Gydion; always the extravagant one,' the proctor said with a shake
of her head. 'That just leaves you, Philip. We've already sent your trunk to the
inn you said that you would be staying at. They're expecting you anytime.'

'Well, actually, I'll be going with Daniel.'

'What?' Finn had climbed into the enchanted carriage and taken a seat
on the plush cushions when she heard that nugget of information.

'It seems like your friends aren't overly thrilled with the idea. I guess they
don't like me very much.'

Finn nodded behind his back.

'That's only because they don't know you.'

This time Finn shook her head.

'What better time to get to know you than now? With us all at my
home.'

Finn rolled her eyes as Daniel waved Philip aboard the carriage before
getting in himself. As he did, he noticed the shadow in the window again. He
called the proctor's attention to it, but she waved it off, claiming that it was
probably one of the goblins. He was about to tell her that he had seen the
same figure before the workers had even arrived, when the griffins began to
move off, and he was thrown back into his seat.

'Don't worry, Philip!' Morgana Goodfellow called out. 'I'll have your belongings redirected to Gydion!'

As the carriage with the students left the academy grounds, a chill ran
down the proctor's spine, and she spun around to look up at Hartfield. If she
didn't know any better, she could have sworn she was being watched. Not
seeing anything there, the proctor picked up her belongings and headed out
to begin her summer break.

THE GRIFFINS COVERED ground at a rapid pace as they charged down
the streets of Imperial City. Onlookers stood and stared when the creatures
thundered past with the carriage in tow. Daniel held his head out of the win-

dow, squinting his eyes to stop them from being dried out by the onrushing wind.

As they approached traffic ahead, the griffins extended their wings, flapped them a couple times and soared into the air. The unexpected manoeuvre jolted the other passages, Finn was even thrown into Philip, which brought a smirk to his face, and she made sure to cause him as much "unintentional" pain and discomfort as possible in her attempts to regain her seat.

Of the four, Daniel was the only one that had seen the amazing city from this vantage point before and they all marvelled at its size and architecture. Anjunel's gaze was drawn to the elven city, Illandor, floating above, lauding over the heads of its subjects. She wondered if any other Krez had ever been so close to the ones that had banished her people.

From here, Finn could see Landon's, although she suspected that now that Eamon's plan to consolidate the guilds into a crime syndicate had come to fruition, he would no doubt rebrand it. She just hoped that it would be something a bit more imaginative than Eamon's.

'Is that Gydion's sanctum?' Philip said, pointing at a brilliant white tower.

'Yeah, it is.'

'The way the sun catches it really does make it stand out. I'm surprised I didn't notice it before.'

'He said he made some changes to it when he got back from Salamida. But I don't remember it being this close to Hartfield when I stayed here, though.'

The griffins began to spiral down until they came to land in front of Gydion's tower. They all disembarked, and as soon as they did, the griffins along with the carriage, shimmered and vanished before their eyes, which brought gasps of surprise and nods of approval from them.

'Wait a minute,' Finn said with a quizzical look after turning back to face the tower and noticing for the first time that there were no doors or windows. 'So how exactly did you get in and out of this place?'

'Well, you announce yourself of course,' replied Daniel matter of factly and cleared his throat. 'Hello, Anna. It's Daniel Welsh to see Gydion.'

Finn had heard it all now. 'Anna? His home has a name?'

'Trust me, it's no ordinary home.' As Daniel said that, part of the masonry in front of them rearranged to resemble Gydion's face.

'Ah, greetings, Daniel. I wasn't expecting such an entourage in tow,' the Gydion facsimile said as his eyes flitted over the four of them.

'Oh, yeah. They're coming with me to Mondragon Keep.'

'I see. Very well, take them to the drawing-room, then come and see me in my study.' The stone face rearranged once more to form an opening, allowing Daniel and his friends entrance into Gydion's tower.

Daniel looked at their faces and saw the same look of astonishment that he himself must have had when he first arrived here. The interior of the tower was a stark contrast to its exterior. Impossibly so. It wasn't circular, as the shape of the tower would suggest, and with its large foyer, it was more in keeping with what you would expect to find in a country mansion than an austere tower.

As Daniel was about to leave the library to find Gydion, Finn hooked her arm in his and walked with him outside. 'We need to talk, Daniel.'

'Is something wrong?' He could see that she wasn't her usual happy-go-lucky self.

'I need you to do me a favour. Well, actually, it's not for me; it's for Anjunel. And it's not really you, it's Gydion.'

'Ok, you're not making much sense, Finn, so spit it out.'

'She's going to die if we don't help her.'

He didn't know elf assassin half as well as Finn did, but she had known the consequences of helping to fight the other Shadowdancers, and yet she did it. With her abilities, it would have been easy for her to escape the first chance she got, but she fought beside them against Sayyidah and Ch'tan. Daniel owed her his life now, he was being given the chance to save hers. 'Ok, we'll both go to Gydion, and you can tell him everything.'

THE PAIR ARRIVED AT the Archmage's study, where Finn explained the whole situation to the Gydion; from her arrival at the Krez capital to Anjunel's eventual banishment. He listened intently, asking questions about the

Shadowdancers reaction to the news of Sayyidah's return. When Finn had finished recounting the events and made her plea, Gydion sat back in his chair, and let it all sink in. He lit his pipe and as the puffs of sweet-smelling smoke drifted to the rafters, he thought for a moment.

'This is quite a quandary. The Quelling is such a tightly kept secret that, although I have been to The Hollow and spoken to Loscivia and Pharinox, it would be difficult to replicate it. It's not so much a spell,' he explained, 'but a ritual. Each Shadowdancer is a part of its casting.'

'So, you're saying you can't save her then?'

'No, I can't. It's not just the somatic and verbal components of the ritual that I'd need, but also the ingredients within the brazier, plus the same amount of willing sacrifices. As you can see, it is quite an impossibility.'

'Then she is dead.'

'I wouldn't say that. We know what The Quelling does, essentially anyway.'

'Yeah. The tattoos her people have are almost like imprints of the people's souls they've assassinated. Without The Quelling, those souls rise up and attack their minds, driving them crazy and ultimately killing them.'

'Exactly, it's a curse. We just need to stop that from happening.'

'You can do that?' Finn asked, leaning forward in her chair.

'No, but I know someone that may be able to brew up some sort of concoction that Anjunel could inhale to suppress those spirits. It may not be work as well as the real thing and she will probably have to use it more often, if it even works, but it's worth a shot.'

'Who is this person? Where can we find them?'

'In Daniel's pocket.'

'Aradia?' whispered Daniel. Still held in the green peridot gem in his pocket, the same he had used to save the elderly Tolgarr shaman, now it turned out that she was Anjunel's hope of survival.

Chapter Nineteen

A Mondragon Returns to Home

The matriarch of the Tolgarr people had been the one to give Daniel the final critical instruction of spellcasting that had made the snippets of knowledge he had obtained from Trinity and the spells he had read in the Book of Azul come together successfully. Without her, he knew there would be no Shade Slayer because there would be no Daniel. That's why he was intent on fulfilling the promise he had made to her.

'That kind of makes sense, actually,' admitted Finn. 'The Tolgarr travel all over Ariest; no one knows as much about its flora and fauna as they do, not even Hyasda.'

'You mean Sayyidah,' Daniel retorted.

'You mean maybe Sayyidah,' corrected Finn.

Gydion looked quizzically at both of them. 'What are you two talking about?'

'Well,' began Daniel as he prepared to deliver his explanation. 'It's more of a hypothesis more than anything, but we believe that Hyasda is either Sayyidah or she is a close ally of hers.'

'And what makes you say that?' Gydion asked as he got out of his chair and stood by the window. He relit his pipe with fresh herbs and puffed at the long stem thoughtfully as he listened to what he was being told.

'Ok, during my exam, Tristan said that you had all lied to me; you, Finn, Trinity.

'He tried to put a wedge between you and people you know. Cut you adrift from your support system and make you more inclined to accept whatever he was offering. It is a rudimentary tactic, but still quite effective at sowing the seeds of discontent. Continue.'

Finn took up the narrative. 'He told Daniel that I had brought the Shade to Earth. But I only went with him because I owed Hyasda for rigging the Beltane Games so that I'd win. She pushed me into going there.' Finn saw the perplexed look on Gydion's face as he glared at her over his shoulder and knew that she needed to add a bit more exposition. 'You see, it all began when I first saw Daniel. He looked so—'

'No no no,' Gydion cut in, slightly exasperated. 'That will not be necessary. I am still waiting to hear why you think Sayyidah and Hyasda are one and the same or in league with each other. Her telling you to follow the one you are smitten with is hardly a crime, even if Shade did turn up. That could be nothing more than coincidence.'

'And what if she was seen talking to Shade, several of them, during the battle of Almedia?'

'What?' Gydion shot a glance at Finn. 'You saw this?'

'No. Tristan told me before he switched sides.'

'Well, what do you think?' Daniel asked impatiently.

'It is hard to say. The thing is, Hyasda has been a proprietor of that shop in Almedia for a long time before the third war even started. It is not as though she just appeared overnight. But I do think it warrants further investigation, all the same.'

'Let's go there now then. We have to stop her.'

'No, Daniel. She is no doubt long gone from there if Sayyidah is in fact Hyasda.'

'But we can't just sit here twiddling our thumbs waiting for her next attack.'

'And we have not been. You have been studying, and I have been checking on my wife's former allies. News of her return has spread quickly amongst them, and there have definitely been some stirrings among their ranks'

'Stirrings?'

'Yes. Secret meetings among the Warchiefs of different Orc clans. Disguised messages being sent to Gnoll and Hobgoblin encampments.'

'So, they are violating the treaty they signed at the end of the war? 'Admittedly, not all, but the majority, yes.'

'Does the queen know?'

'She does, but she won't act on secret meetings and rumours. There is unrest in some of the remote northern settlements. Rumours that I have yet to prove or disprove, either way.'

'What are they?' Finn scoffed. 'What could be more unsettling than an Orc uprising?'

'There have been sightings. Parties of ogre's heading north, beyond the Goddess Spine Mountains. Apparently, they are in search of frost giants.'

She burst out laughing. 'Giants! You must be joking! There haven't been any giants here for millennia. And they think they're going to conveniently find a living giant now?'

'Who said anything about a "living" giant?'

Finn was silent for a moment until the implications of what Gydion was alluding to manifested in her mind. 'Vekt!'

'Wait a minute! Zombie frost giants?' It was Daniel's turn to be incredulous. 'You've got to be kidding.'

'I wish I were. No matter how improbable it may sound, there is still a hint of the probable. The orcs, for instance, are no slouches when it comes to necromancy, and the ogres, being distant cousins of giants may know a legend or something else we don't know, that may hint at a graveyard of the giants or some other such thing. I have asked Milos Yacon to spare a couple of his best scouts to do a bit of reconnaissance for me.'

'Yacon?' Daniel repeated, hearing the familiar surname. 'As in Cara, Mara and Sara?'

'Yes, the triplets! Milos, their father, is the mayor of Ostia. Three extremely talented girls individually, as I recall, but when their minds are linked, they can perform a gestalt spell which is simply marvellous!'

Knowing the level of dislike between Sara and her sisters, Daniel had the feeling that it was something that he would never get to witness for himself. 'They actually invited me to Ostia for a Lammas feast.'

'Is that so? Did you accept?'

'I told Sara I'd let her know if I could make it or not.'

'It would help me greatly if you could, Daniel.' Gydion sighed. 'You would be able to obtain a status report from Milos for me.'

It was the first time Daniel noticed how tired the Archmage looked and he felt like such a fool. All this time, he was thinking that he was being abandoned by Gydion when in actual fact, he was doing the right thing; he would be nothing more than a hindrance on such dangerous missions, especially with his current level of ability. Going to Ostia was the least he could do to help the cause.

'But Sayyidah is not the only thing we need to be concerned about,' Gydion added. 'There is also the imminent return of Baelthorn, the dragon lord. Given the way she was so desperate for the Book of Azul, I surmised that it must be of more importance than I was led to believe.'

'When she was asking me for the book, she said that she would have them all and that not even I could stop her. How can I stop her? Her abilities are incredible!'

'But even she had to run from that thing you fired at her,' Finn reminded him.

Daniel nodded, but he knew that casting the chaos bolt then had been pure luck, a spontaneous reaction to the killing of Trinity, and he was reluctant to revisit those feelings again anytime soon.

'The Book of Azul is but one of four books; the Books of Roj, Clar and Ma'on being the others. I would assume that they are of no lesser importance. But why, I have no answer. I even spoke with the scholars of Par Atreia, and even they could provide little help. As far as they know, they are just four ordinary spellbooks that specialise in the elements.'

'So, where are they? We should go and get them, before she does, right?'

'One is in the north with the Mulanaari in Falias. One is in the south in the capital of the Salamanders, Finias. The final one is in the east in the Sylph city, Gorias. I have already messaged them and warned them. Once you leave to find the Tolgarr, I will go in person and discuss matters with all of them face to face. The only race I would expect trouble from are the Salamanders since they were allies of Sayyidah's during the war.'

'Aren't you worried that she's gotten a head start on us?'

'In all honesty, Sayyidah has a fifty-year head start on us. We have been involved in a game with her, and we did not even know we were playing. Whatever her ultimate goal is, we can assume that it will need all four books to succeed. If we keep our book safe, then we foil her plans. Now, let us make haste to Mondragon Keep, for I fear that moments of cheer will be few and far between in the foreseeable future.'

WHEN DANIEL AND FINN returned to the library, they found Anjunel glaring at Philip. As they looked from one to the other, it was plain to see that her intent stare made him uncomfortable. 'What's going on?' Daniel asked hesitantly.

'Finn asked me to watch your friend,' Anju replied. 'He has quite the curiosity. Who knows where he would have gone?'

'How could I *not*? It's not every day you find yourself in the home of the Archmage.'

'Indeed,' Gydion said as he joined the others after a change of clothes. 'But this sanctum is no playground, young man. There are protection wards here that would reduce you to dust.' He paused a moment to let them fully comprehend his words before he continued. 'Now then, if we are all ready, let's be off.'

A look of fascination was etched on Daniel's face as he watched Gydion begin to cast a spell. The speed with which Essence flowed down his arms to his hands in order to empower the somatic he traced in the air, was truly impressive, and Daniel could appreciate the process more now that he had spent time at Hartfield Mage Academy. Reciting the runic sigils in his head, Daniel tried to identify the spell by its somatic alone since he couldn't hear Gydion's hushed tones. He guessed it was the teleportation spell he had read in Grim, and confirmation of that came swiftly as the air before them began to shimmer, and a small hole opened in space and rapidly widened until the portal was big enough for the party of five to walk through.

The journey was instantaneous, and as they stepped out, they found themselves standing before a set of large double doors. None of them, however, were expecting to be confronted by what was before them. Mondragon Keep was almost derelict. One of the doors hung precariously on its single remaining hinge, while the once red paint that coated both was flaking off.

Parts of the defensive walls were crumbling, other parts seemed to have been taken, and most of what was left had graffiti painted on them.

'Is this really the place?' Daniel asked, his eyes wide in astonishment.

'Yeah, maybe you took a wrong turn somewhere,' Finn smirked at Gydion, who returned a less than impressed look. 'Not too late to go back to yours, is it?'

Before the Archmage had any time to respond, Daniel had decided that they weren't going anywhere as he tentatively opened the door and entered his ancestral home.

The dilapidation which had greeted them outside continued within as they passed through the entryway. Despite this, the further they moved into the complex, it was plain to see that, once upon a time, it would have been an impressive sight to behold.

The outer wall was a perfect square and rose some four metres high. In each corner stood a tower, but they were in an even worse state than the rest of the keep due to their elevated position placing them more at the mercy of the elements, and it had taken its toll.

Ahead of them was an arched bridge, one of three, wide enough for two carriages to pass side by side. It crossed a meandering stream which had an almost horseshoe shape; it flowed down one side from the north of the complex, across in front of the southern main gate, where they stood, and back up towards the north. The sounds of bubbling brooks and splashes from fishes gave it all an air of serene tranquillity, which made Daniel smile.

However, it quickly vanished as they traversed the bridge, with its elaborate bas-relief carvings along either side and came to a building that appeared to have been gutted out by fire.

'This was the home of Joseph and Madeleine Archer,' Gydion related sombrely. 'He tended the grounds and gardens to the back whilst she was the head housekeeper. Good folk. I hope they are alright. There was other staff too. Guards were once stationed at the entrances, there were stable hands, cooks, there was life here, and although it was a keep, Eric made sure that the militaristic was balanced with the tranquil.'

As they all turned, about to continue on towards the main building of the keep, there was suddenly the sound of movement coming from within the burnt-out home.

Chapter Twenty
Friends Reunited?

'**A**stray animal?' Daniel ventured. But Gydion was not taking any chances. He put a finger to his lips and took a position in the front of the party. He gestured for the others to remain behind him and readied himself.

However, Anjunel, used to giving the orders and not taking them, had already moved into action. She swiftly and silently positioned herself to flank the door of the seemingly derelict house. Having quickly scanned the ground and found what she was looking for, she stooped down and came back up with a small stone.

They watched as she threw the piece of gravel at the window, causing a distraction for whatever was inside before she kicked in the door. The groans which accompanied the sounds of punches landing that could be heard by Daniel and the others outside were definitely humanoid. And when a person holding a sword was tossed out and landed in front of them, they saw that it was indeed a middle-aged man.

'Look, I told you before! There's nothing left to loot!'

'And why would that be, Joseph?' Gydion said to the man at his feet.

The voice was familiar to the man. He squinted and shielded his eyes from the sun so he could see more clearly, make sure he wasn't imagining things. 'Gydion? Is that really you?'

'It is indeed,' replied the Archmage with a smile as he helped Joseph to his feet. 'Sorry about my companion's heavy handiness. Let me introduce you. This, my friends, is Joseph Archer, custodian of the estate.'

'No, not at all,' Joseph said, dusting himself down and picking up his sword. 'People that come by these days don't tend to do so with a smile and a handshake, hence the sword.'

Gydion gave voice to the burning question. 'What happened to the keep? What happened to your home? And where are all the staff? Your wife?'

'Thunderbeard happened. Madeline and I are the only ones left now; the rest were either dismissed or left of their own accord. Come on,' Joseph said excitedly. 'She'll be happy to see you.'

The custodian led the way to the main house. He took the time to explain how tough it had been to maintain the estate between himself and his wife. They did as much of the work as they could, but every time they made progress, they would suffer a setback at the hands of Thunderbeard. 'He's not the same person you knew, Gydion. He drinks like crazy.'

'He's a dwarf! They all do.'

'Maybe, but he's taken it to another level. In a day, he spends more time drunk than he is sober. It was him that set our home alight. In one of his stupors, he claimed that the dwarfen god of blacksmithing had told him that he needed a new blast furnace and that it was to be my home.'

Gydion stared in disbelief. Grimgaard Thunderbeard was a capable and ferocious warrior, and why he was second only to Eric Mondragon. He had a berserker rage within him, and the strength of a giant, but he also prided on being honourable and against harming the innocent.

The Archmage was about to make a comment about the virtues of his dwarf friend but, as they approached the estate's principal abode, they heard a commotion coming from within.

'Oh vekt. I was hoping that he'd still be in a drunken sleep somewhere.'

'Where is it!' The voice was deep, gruff but slurred. 'I know you've taken it!'

'I already told you, I don't know what you're talking about!' Joseph's wife was just as ferocious and gave just as good as she got.

'You're lying! The thunder ale! Where's the thunder ale? I know Eric has a secret stash, you hag!'

'You've drunk it all, you useless dung muncher!'

Sounds of glass smashing then rang out as the custodian opened the door and lead the way inside. They all ducked as a vase, thrown at Madeline, crashed against the wall beside them, and as they looked around, it was obvious that it wasn't an isolated incident. Furniture that had not been smashed, was strewn everywhere. Random weapons were embedded in walls and doors. If Daniel didn't know any better, he would have said the place had been ransacked. It was like a storm had gone through, but the storm was still there, and it had a name.

'Grimgaard Thunderbeard!' Gydion yelled angrily. 'What is the meaning of this?'

Madeline's eyes lit up when she peered over the shield she hid behind and saw her husband with the Archmage of Ariest. Perhaps this nightmare would finally end, and a bit of normality could return.

The unkempt dwarf, another object in his hand ready to be thrown, paused upon hearing the voice he had not heard for so long. 'You!' Thunderbeard snarled. 'Of course, it was you. You stole my grog!'

'We have not seen each other for many years, not since that night Queen Rhiannon woke from her dream sleep and shared her prophesy with us, and the first thing you do is accuse me of a petty crime when it is plain to see who the real culprit is.'

'Because you have a forked tongue. You are the master of lies and the king of half-truths,' he spat with venom as he swayed on unsteady feet.

'We have all chosen the path that we take, unfortunately, I cannot divulge all that I have seen or experienced along mine. The planes of existence are too vast for many to comprehend. The interwoven fabrics of reality, its intricacies, could drive you mad.'

'This is all your fault!'

'This is your doing, my friend.'

'You could have stopped, Eric. Stopped him from leaving, convinced him to stay. Then the Athenatoi would still be here. I would still have something...'

'The Athenatoi are no more?' Gydion asked Joseph, who shook his head in reply. 'If I had known his plans, I would have had just as much chance of convincing Eric to stay as you did of convincing Narla.'

'Don't you speak her name!' Thunderbeard yelled. There was a rapid shift in his mood and a raging fiery tempest in his eyes.

Grimgaard was what the dwarfs called a berserker; during battle, he could tap into an inner fury, a rage that could empower him. When they are young, berserkers have to partake in a ritual to be chosen by an aspect to channel through their rage; some are taken by an animal, some take the rage of a lesser dragon, others have a deep and personal fury inside them that they can tap into. It was no surprise that, with his bright-orange hair, Thunderbeard was chosen by the aspect of the fearsome, militaristic Fire Giants.

His powerful stature became even more so; his veins and muscles throbbed as the dwarf flew into a rage and charged at Gydion. Whilst those around the Mage were shaken by the sudden aggression of Grimgaard, Gydion, who may have seen it all before, forgot how quickly the dwarf could cover ground in his enraged state, and barely erected his Mage armour before he was blasted out through the door by the powerful shoulder barge.

'You sent my Narla away!' Grimgaard roared as he pressed his advantage and leapt at his prone foe.

Gydion rolled out of the way and struggled to regain his feet as the dwarf landed where he had just been. 'I did nothing of the sort. She was not the type to stay at home and do nothing, waiting for you to return from some adventure or other. You know that as well as I.'

The comment did nothing but fuel Grimgaard's berserker rage further.

'Shouldn't we do something?' Daniel said as he looked on with the others. He knew Gydion wasn't in his best condition, he had seen it in the Mage's features when they were in his study. All his secret escapades must be more dangerous than he had let on. Perhaps he hasn't fully recovered from what happened to him on Salamida. Facing a god and being on the brink of death has got to have an effect on you.

'Come on, are you kidding me?' Finn, eyes wide, had a huge grin on her face. She was in no hurry to see this battle end. She couldn't believe her luck. Not only did she get to see Eric Mondragon in action, but now she was getting the chance to see Grimgaard Thunderbeard's fabled berserker rage. 'I'm sure Gydion will be fine.' That sentiment quickly changed as they saw the enraged dwarf pick up the door, which had been ripped off of its hinges in the initial clash, and swing it, swatting the Archmage like a fly. He followed up it up by charging in and getting his hands on the shaken Gydion. 'Ok, on second thought, maybe you should do something.'

'Like what?'

'I don't know. You're the Mage.'

'Noxious cloud,' Philip said.

'No! I don't want to kill him.'

'You control the intensity of the poison.'

'You think I have that kind of control?'

'Yeah, probably not.'

'This rage doesn't last forever,' Madeline revealed. 'There's a time limit. it goes away after that or if he's unconscious.'

'Unconscious?' There was a spark in Daniel's eyes. 'I have an idea, Finn. Remember back in Almedia when I was falling, and Princess Nyriel saved me?'

'Yeah, she caught you in that globe of water.'

'Exactly, and when I was inside, I couldn't breathe.'

'You can do that spell?'

'It was in the Book of Azul, so it's in my head too, so in theory, yeah.'

Daniel stepped out, took a deep breath and began the incantation. His Essence aura briefly flared as the magic energy flowed from its reservoir, expanding through his body and down his arms to empower the sigils he traced in the air. He moved his hands in a fluid motion, coaxing water from the nearby stream to raise into the air, and form into a rippling globe of water around the head of Grimgaard Thunderbeard.

It took a few moments for the berserker dwarf to react to the sudden lack of air. When he saw that it wasn't Gydion but someone else that was weaving the magic, he turned his attention to that person.

Daniel sustained his spell. It was becoming apparent that the dwarf's lungs had a larger capacity than he had anticipated. Thunderbeard continued to bare down on him. He knew a blow was coming from this bulging veined thick set dwarf, knew that it would hurt. What he didn't know, as he tried to keep the distance between them, was if he should drop the water bubble and raise his shield or hope that his attacker used his last bit of air.

'Don't you lay a finger on him, Grimgaard Thunderbeard!' Gydion yelled at his old friend as the dwarf reared back a huge fist. 'He is Eric's son!'

The fire in Grimgaard's eyes diminished as he and the Archers stared at Daniel. Then several volleys of magic missile blasted him in the back, and he dropped to his knees. 'Ow,' he said and fell face down, unconscious.

Chapter Twenty-One
A Tale Told

Joseph and Madeline Archer had dealt with the unconscious warrior dwarf many times before. Usually, after he passed out drunk after one of his outbursts. It was usually a sombre affair, seeing how far the once great commander had fallen. This time, however, they did it with huge smiles on their faces. A Mondragon had returned.

'You don't think Gydion was lying about the boy, do you?' Madeline asked her husband as they lay Grimgaard down.

'Why would he do that.'

'To placate this raging buffoon,' she said, gesturing to Thunderbeard. 'You know as well as I that the Archmage would say or do anything to obtain the desired outcome.'

'Maybe so, but I am sure that he could have dealt with the situation a number of different ways than claim the boy is master Eric's son if it were not true. Besides, I've heard talk in the markets of an extraordinary boy at Hartfield, and our guest fits the description.'

She thought for a moment, mulling over everything, remembered the day Joseph had shared the gossip about the Mage exams. She and her husband had devoted their lives to the Mondragon Keep and were disheartened to see where it now lay. 'I hope it is true,' Madeline smiled. 'Maybe he will bring glory back. We should have a feast,' she said excitedly.

'We should! Do we have enough provisions, though?'

'Definitely not for the things I would plan, but I will make do. Come, let us at least greet the new master properly.'

'That was good work, Daniel. Very fluid casting and no mistakes. Creative too.'

Daniel tried hard to hide his pride. He didn't seek recognition or affirmation for what he did, but when it comes from the Archmage it's hard not to beam.

'Didn't quite stop Thunderbeard, though,' Philip said.

'Didn't exactly see you busting your ass to help,' Finn retorted.

'I could say the same about you.'

'That's because I'm waiting to bust your ass,' she said with a malicious grin. 'I'm just waiting for the right moment.'

'What's with all this hostility?' Gydion asked, but before anything could escalate or be explained, Joseph and Madeline returned.

'Uhm, I take it people are getting a little hungry,' Madeline said, sensing the tension in the air. 'We don't have much in the pantry, but I'm sure I can whip up something palatable.'

'Oh, wait, I have money,' Daniel said taking a handful of coins out of his pouch. 'I guess the upkeep of this place is down to me now, since my dad's not here.'

'Ah, Yes. I have yet to introduce you. Madeline and Joseph Archer, meet Daniel Welsh.'

'Pleased to meet you,' Daniel said, shaking their hand in turn.

'Welsh?'

'It's the name dad took when he first arrived on Earth,' he explained. 'Is that going to be enough money?'

'More than enough. I'll be able to hire someone to help with the repairs, and once the word gets out that a Mondragon is back at the keep, staff will come flocking back too!' Joseph said excitedly.

'We'll have Mondragon Keep back to its former glory in no time!' Madeline was just as enthusiastic as her husband about that prospect. They loved the place as much as Eric had and hated the fact that they couldn't do more to stop it from declining to the condition it was currently on. She gave Joseph a long shopping list of items and told him to hurry before sending him off to the markets.

'Excellent,' Gydion said with a clap. 'I am going to check on our little berserker. Madeline, perhaps you could find rooms for Daniel and the others, maybe show them around as well.'

'It'll be a pleasure.'

DURING MADELINE'S TOUR, Daniel could see that the main house was deceptively larger than the front had him believing. It was an extensive walkabout she had given them, taking in many potentially wonderful rooms, the grand reception hall in particular. However, since Eric's disappearance and dignitaries no longer visiting, the Archers had taken it upon themselves to put as much of the furniture and decorations as they could into storage. Much of what was left had been damaged or totally destroyed by Thunderbeard in one of his frequent tirades.

What the legendary dwarf warrior had become was a far cry from the tales Daniel had been told about him by his dad. Even Finn had waxed lyrical about the exploits of the fearsome berserker. Now he was unkempt, unwashed and barely sober.

'Who's Narla?' Daniel asked Madeline suddenly. He suspected, given the way Grimgaard reacted when Gydion mentioned her name, that whatever happened to him was in part down to this person.

'She was Grimgaard's lover,' answered Finn.

'Actually, Narla was Grimgaard's wife,' corrected Madeline. 'She was his childhood sweetheart, always excited by the adventurer's life he led with the Athenatoi and The Fellowhood. Like all dwarfen women, she could handle herself, but Grimgaard was protective of her, maybe a little too much.

Narla was intrigued by magic, had a talent for it, and desperately wanted Gydion to tutor her, but Grimgaard wouldn't allow it; he feared she would want to join The Fellowhood and the thought of losing her in combat haunted him.'

'You stifle someone, don't allow them to be who they're supposed to be, and you can still lose them,' Finn said wistfully.

'Someone in the group had a similar sentiment.'

'Gydion?' Daniel offered. 'Is that why Grimgaard blamed him?'

As if by design, they arrived in yet another hall. The disturbed dust was clearly visible as particles drifted through the rays of sunlight that streamed through the large windows. Several sconces with unlit torches adorned the walls, for the occasions when moonlight was not enough to illuminate the hall and the meetings that were conducted around the large oak table that dominated the floor, much like the huge painting that dominated the wall.

In it were the core members of The Fellowhood in their younger days before Gydion became Archmage, before Tavisum became archdruid and when the Athenatoi were in their infancy; Eric Mondragon, Grimgaard Thunderbeard, Tavisum, Gydion and next to him stood...

'Sayyidah? But I've read quite a few accounts of the exploits of The Fellowhood, and I didn't see any mention of her, even in the royal library of Murias City.'

'This all happened long before her change of heart and her ultimate assault leading the Shade during the last war. Once that was over, all of her previous good deeds were erased from the history books.'

'By who?'

'Who else? The queen, of course. As they say, history is written by the victor.'

'I see. Gydion couldn't have been happy about that; he must have said something.'

'You'll have to ask him that; he's not really one for sharing his feelings and thoughts willingly. But saying that, you should know that he was supposed to execute Sayyidah and not exile her.'

'And you say she was the one that taught Narla magic?'

'Yes. She advocated people being allowed to reach their full potential to be who they could be. It wasn't a lot, just enough to get her started. The thing is, Narla went searching for more and fell in with a group of adventurers called The Collective.'

'I've heard of them,' Finn said as she dipped into her well of adventurer knowledge again. 'They are all Mages, each of them a specialist in a different school of magic. They're not the most heroic of groups, though. They can get a little heavy-handed and overzealous judging by all accounts.'

'That's putting it mildly. She kept her involvement with the group hidden from Grimgaard for a quite a while. It wasn't until somebody approached The Fellowhood about The Collective that things were revealed. They had accepted a quest to rescue the mayor's daughter but after they did, they changed the terms of the reward, saying that the information received about the strength of the kidnapper stronghold was incorrect. They wanted triple and ransacked the village as a down payment.'

'What? Are you kidding me?'

'See, I told you, Daniel. Not the most heroic of groups.'

'And that's when Grimgaard discovered Narla was in The Collective. It turned out the group needed the girl for their own devices, a ritual. It wasn't about the money at all. When Grimgaard and the others arrived, it was all but complete. There was a skirmish. The girl was saved, Tavisum took her to safety, but whatever creature they had summoned still needed to be appeased, and with no offering, one of the summoners would have to be forfeit. The members of The Collective made their choice of who it would be when they teleported away leaving Narla to her fate.'

'I don't understand,' Daniel said. 'He can't really blame Gydion for any of this.'

'It's not for that,' explained Madeline. 'They fought the demonic creature, but they were vastly outmatched. However, if they didn't stop it there, there was no telling the death and destruction it could have wrought. The only way to send it back to the abyss was to give it what it wanted. Gydion knew this, as did Sayyidah. They told the others, but Grimgaard was obviously reticent of the idea. Narla took the decision out of everybody's hands. She intended to sacrifice herself for the greater good. When Grimgaard tried to stop her, Gydion and Sayyidah cast a sleep spell on him and the others. When they awoke, Narla and the demon were gone.' Silence pervaded as Madeline finished her tale.

Chapter Twenty-Two
Secrets Revealed

Gydion stood with his hands clasped behind his back, scrutinising the golden Athenatoi armour that hung in the corner of Grimgaard's room. Everything else there was in a dishevelled state, but this piece of equipment and the dwarfen war axe, which was propped up against the wall beneath it, were in pristine condition.

He could still sense the enchantments that he and Penwyll had cast on all one thousand two hundred and twelve suits of armour that the Athenatoi wore; special armour for a special unit of soldiers.

The selection process was gruelling. All the provinces of Ariest put warriors forward for this military order, but only the best of the best was selected.

Despite the honour and prestige that came with being in the Athenatoi, some hard choices were made by the twelve hundred and ten. The military order became their life. Their comrades, their family. Their identity was only known to each other – all for a psychological edge over their enemies. If one of their number were to fall in battle, then another would be recruited to take their place, always maintaining their ranks of 1212; they were an immortal army.

Gydion could hear the occupant of the bed stirring behind him. 'I must say, I am impressed with the condition you have kept your armour in,' the Archmage said without turning.

Grimgaard sat on the edge of his bed, rubbing his head. 'What are you on about?' he growled. 'It was you that enchanted the damn thing.'

'Exactly. So, I know it does not protect it from dust nor wax it. Shows that you still cherish it, despite what you say about the demise of the Athenatoi.'

'You sound as though you don't believe me.'

'You must admit that it is hard to. The Athenatoi have been a celebrated unit to the throne. You have won countless battles in her name.'

'And yet Queen Rhiannon still decommissioned us. She summoned me to the throne room and told me that our services were no longer needed since the war was at an end.'

'When did this take place?'

'Barely a week after she awoke from her Dreamweave.'

'She should not have been making decisions like that so soon after such a long slumber.'

'Indeed, but there was no one here to give consul; you and Eric were gone, Tavisum had returned to the Druid Glade to tend to the injured Cernounos, the Sisters of Calatin were too busy sifting through the dreams she had during her sleep and I'm a warrior not an adviser. Besides, I'm not so sure it would have made a damn bit of difference; Rhiannon is not like Alina one bit.'

'That is how it works; you know this as well as I. When the elven queen has her recuperating sleep, she keeps her memories, but everything else about her changes, her look, her personality, even her name.'

'I get that, but you've spent time with her, haven't you seen it?'

'Seen what? What I saw when I returned from Salamida was that the water supply of Illandor had been poisoned. It was causing a miasma to control the city. The people had no inclination to do anything, not even to eat or drink. I purified the system but have yet to find the culprit.'

'And what of Rhiannon? How was she when you helped her and her elven people?'

'She was grateful, of course.'

'As Alina would have been? Smiling and hugging?'

'Well, no, but I already said- '

'Yes, Yes, Yes, different personality, I get that. Do you know what one of the reasons she gave me for dismantling the Athenatoi was? She didn't like the fact that there were other races in its ranks. That the elite army of the ruling royalty of Ariest was not wholly made up of elves.'

'I see.'

'Well, you know me, I didn't take too kindly to that and told her that the Athenatoi is made up of the best of the best, and if it's not overrun by elves, it just means that they're not as good with a sword as they think they are,' laughed Grimgaard.

'And how did that go down?'

'She exiled me from Illandor.'

'This is all very troubling.'

'Not dissimilar to the dark fae of old, I'd say.'

'Let's not get carried away here, Thunderbeard. However, I will admit it does warrant a closer look.' Gydion scrutinised his old comrade closely. 'And what about you?'

'What about me? I'm fine.'

'Are you sure? You did not seem it when you were blasting through that door.'

'Of course. I'm-I'm sorry about earlier. Things have been pretty tough. In the old days when there was peacetime, I had the Fellowhood to fall back on, but I didn't even have that, and adventuring on your own just isn't the same as when you're in a party.'

'So, you needed something else to occupy your time.'

Grimgaard nodded. 'Drinking to forget was easy to do, until I ran out, which didn't take long. Then I started on some of the taverns until the tabs got so high that they wouldn't serve me until I'd paid.'

'And now? Have you come to terms with things? Because peacetime is over. I need you, Grimgaard, Ariest needs you. Sayyidah is back and I will need your help.'

'Dealing with your vekt of a wife wouldn't be my first choice of breaking the lull, but I will be with you, of course. Now, tell me about Daniel, is he really Eric's son?'

'He is, but not the only one.'

WITH THE FOOD THAT remained at the keep, Madeline was able to whip up a well-received meal. Daniel and the other unexpected guests were already filling their stomachs with the delicious food when Joseph returned from the market with some drink.

'Whilst I was out, I was also able to hire some builders to start the repair work, with the money you gave me, Master Daniel,' Joseph said as he poured everybody a drink.

'Just Daniel is fine.'

'You should let Quinn, I mean my stepdad, redesign the keep for you, give it some upgrades.'

'That's not a bad idea,' admitted Daniel, nodding. 'Because I've been considering the idea of making a change. I'm not a warrior like my dad and I don't think the military moniker fits if I'm going to be living here. I feel that Mondragon...Mondragon Estate may be more my style.' It was his legacy, his inheritance from his dad, now he wants to put his mark on the place.

'I think that is a wonderful idea, Master Daniel,' gushed Madeline. 'I often told your father that the name intimidated people. This is a much more welcoming name.'

'I agree. A new name and a new master of the house,' Grimgaard Thunderbeard said as he appeared at the top of the stairs. He stood resplendent in the golden armour of the Athenatoi. His hair and beard were no longer the unkempt mess they had been but were both now neatly trimmed and plaited. This was the image of the dwarf warrior Daniel had pictured in his mind, not the drunkard he had first seen. 'Your mother must be quite the woman to have snagged Eric; he always said that he would never marry.'

'Especially after our failed attempts at it, my friend,' Gydion added.

'And Tavisum being married to the trees, he didn't have particularly good role models for it!' Grimgaard and Gydion both laughed. He offered his hand to Daniel, who shook the weathered and calloused hand gratefully. 'My name is Grimgaard Thunderbeard, and it is a pleasure to meet you, Daniel.'

'I suppose you'll be wanting feeding too?' Madeline smiled at the dwarf, happy to see him back to his old self. She knew that he would never admit it, but it wasn't just the adventure he missed but the being among friends too.

TIME PASSED INTO EARLY evening as Grimgaard regaled his captive audience with tales of adventures with The Fellowhood and skirmishes with the Athenatoi during the war. Finn's knowledge of his deeds, although garnered from bards and tavern tales, hence subject to some creative embellishment, was extremely detailed, non the less. She often prompted him to recount certain episodes. It was clear for all to see that he was thoroughly enjoying himself in this impromptu double act.

As the evening began to wind down, Grimgaard was smiling to himself as he had a contemplative smoke of his pipe outside. He reminisced about the times The Fellowhood had nights just like this, after completing quests, a sort of celebration of life, happy to have survived another adventure. The warrior heard the patched-up door being pushed aside and saw that Finn had brought two flagons of honey mead with her.

'Not interrupting anything, am I?' she asked, handing over one of the drinks.

Grimgaard shook his head. 'Not at all; I'm glad for the company. You're a good kid, Finn.'

'I'm glad you think so, because I've got a proposal for you.'

The dwarf had his drink up to his lips when she spoke, and he slowly took a mouthful. 'I appreciate what you're trying to do, kid, but I don't need charity gigs. I rarely do signings anymore. Besides I'm sure your schoolmates would get a bigger kick out of seeing the Archmage.'

'Yeah, probably not the mates I hang around with,' Finn replied as she flipped her coin in the air.

'Thieves Guild?' Grimgaard asked, seeing the emblem on the golden disc. 'That explains your worldly behaviour. So, I guess this is bigger than some appearances in your hometown then?'

'Much bigger. Think The Fellowhood evolved to the next level big... potentially.'

'I'm listening,' Grimgaard replied as he knocked out his pipe and refilled it with fresh herbs. His interest was certainly piqued.

'Ok, so, Fungal, I'm assuming you know him...'

'Our paths may have crossed.'

'...well, he has a corridor of portals to other realms that he wants to turn into a travel business. The thing is, he needed people to scout them, find out the rules and dangers, to act like ambassadors really. So, he offered Daniel and me the role.'

'Just like that?'

'Well, no. It's so we don't tell Gydion that he still has the corridor. But that's neither here nor there. Anyway, my boss, Eamon Wolfe, had a plan to consolidate the guilds to create a crime syndicate...'

'What? That's a big power-play.'

'...so, I told him about the Fungal gig so he could sweeten the offer with the other guild heads, not knowing that he already had a fool proof plan in effect. The Syndicate is going to be a thing, and he still wants a piece of my action. But his actions got me thinking, what if I set up an organisation myself, a secret society, a society of adventurers, so to speak.'

'And what would this society do?'

'The same kind of things that you and The Fellowhood used to do; rescuing people, finding lost treasures, battling monsters and more.'

'The thing about them is that we were all seasoned professionals.'

'And so are the people I have in mind to kick start this venture.'

'Who might that be?'

'Me, Daniel, Anjunel, who is a Shadow Dancer by the way and the Undany princess, Nyriel. She's into archaeology and historical stuff. And when we expand, and we will, the new recruits will get specialist training from us and you if you come onboard. So, what do you say? Are you in?'

Grimgaard took a deep pull on his pipe and let the smoke slowly escape from his nostrils as he contemplated everything the youngster had explained. He eyed Finn to get the measure of her, to try and see if she had the drive, the ambition to accomplish all she had set out. He found his answer in no time at all. 'What you planning on calling this outfit of yours anyway?'

'That's still kind of up in the air, but I was thinking maybe the Seeker Society or the Wayfarers or the Acquirers. Or even the Adventurers Alliance.'

'If you'd pitched your idea to any of the others, especially Eric or Tavisum, you'd probably have fallen flat, what with your shady background and dodgy partners.'

'I'm not so sure they're as squeaky clean as they used to be, but Gydion wanted the corridor destroyed. And that's why I'm talking to you. I know you can appreciate what's on offer here; a new family, new adventures, new realms and a new purpose.'

Finn had seen aged thieves at the guild before, seeing how they would drink themselves into a stupor when the one thing they were good at was taken away from them. She had seen the same signs in Grimgaard. This was an offer for a desperate man, a chance to relive their youth, and Finn knew that he was far from ready to be put out to pasture. She knew he still had it in him; he was still a force to be reckoned with. Getting the mighty Grimgaard Thunderbeard to join her would be a major bonus to her plans; she just had to dangle a big enough carrot.

And there was only one thing that she could think of, although she didn't particularly like the idea of using it, but needs must.

'You never did get closure with Narla, did you?' Finn said, looking up at the stars as they began to appear in the ever-darkening sky. Out of the corner of her eye, she could see Grimgaard's pipe pause at his lips. 'Yes, the demon took her,' she continued, 'but we don't know where or what happened after that. She might have escaped.'

'And she might be dead.'

'Maybe, anything is possible. But what if one of these portals led to the realm she was taken to. What if you could finally find out what happened once and for all? And if we do find out that she is tragically killed, wouldn't you want the one responsible to feel your wrath? You should do the right thing and come with us, Grimgaard.'

Before the young thief could push him further on the matter, Gydion suddenly came out of the house to join them. 'Not interrupting anything, am I?'

'No, I was just getting some more tales of the Athenatoi, and trying to convince him to come with us to meet the Tolgarr.'

'That's actually what I wanted to see you about.'

'Finding the Tolgarr?' Grimgaard asked.

'Well, yes, but also regarding the Athenatoi. Do you still have contact with any of the Major Generals? Do you know what happened to them? I need to know the depth of the talent pool we will have if Sayyidah does indeed mount an attack.'

'I've seen some of them. Alexander Black is hiring out his spymaster skills to anyone with enough coin to pay his exorbitant fees. Kayvan has all but disappeared. I had a few drinks with him not long after the unit was dissolved, but I haven't seen him since. Cassidy is around somewhere, no doubt partaking in two of his three favourite things, fencing, women and gambling. Which two? Only the gods know. Torbin Asker took up a new mantle, Mage hunter. When you left, some spellcasters became a bit unruly, he took it upon himself to protect those that needed help. He even managed to jury-rig some spells for himself. Darrow returned to his first love, hunting and the forest, and Crystal Webb is now a successful bounty hunter, of course, considering what a formidable trapper she is.'

'Crystal?' Finn's eyes were wide in surprise. 'There were women in the Athenatoi?'

'We were the best of the best. It didn't matter if you were man or woman, human or Orc, if you were good enough you were in, simple.'

'Hmmm, I quite like that edict,' Finn said as she rubbed her chin.

'I assume the elves of the Athenatoi were absorbed into the royal army. No problem, if Sayyidah does attack, even Queen Rhiannon would not turn her back on Ariest.'

Grimgaard looked sceptical, and he didn't share his views on the new queen's separatist attitudes, nor his worries for Imperial City and beyond that, Ariest.

Chapter Twenty-Three
The Party Sets Off

Finn slowly made her way upstairs to bed. The two drinks she had initially brought outside had turned into a few more once Gydion had joined her and Grimgaard. Night had fully fallen by the time they had drunk their fill and decided to turn in.

As she passed Anjunel's room, Finn thought she would first check in on her since the assassin had felt unwell and retired early, before calling it a night herself. She gently eased open the door of the Krez elf's bedroom. Once inside, it was obvious to the young thief that her friend was in the midst of a restless sleep; the bedsheet clung to her body as she tossed and turned, and her pillow seemed damp.

Although she was concerned about the condition Anjunel was in, there was nothing she could do about it right now except find a cloth, wipe her down and straighten the sheets, try to make her as comfortable as possible. Finn was certain that it had something to do with The Quelling, that she was no longer going to be a part of. Were the spirits of those she had slain already assaulting her mind, or was it the prospect of it happening that was troubling the Krez. She mouthed a prayer and hoped that they not only reached the Tolgarr in time but that they would be able to help Anjunel.

She left as quietly as she had entered and stepped away without making a sound. Finn contemplated going to see Daniel, whose room was next to hers, to inform him of Anjunel's condition, but she thought better of it, thinking that he would be deep asleep by now.

Then she heard voices from within and a light from under the door.

She could hear Philip urging Daniel to raise his Essence. Reminding him how good he had felt each time he had used EV. Telling him that everything is better on EV. That he was better on EV. That he could do anything on EV.

Grimgaard is right, Finn mused. I am worldly, far more than Daniel is, at any rate. I know pushers when I see one. I've come across addiction before, alcohol and other substances. Seen people get into a zoned-out state where they couldn't distinguish between fantasy and reality. There's no vekting way I'm letting Daniel go down that route.

Her dislike of Philip grew with each passing moment. She envisioned kicking the door open and beating him silly. She smiled broadly at the idea before she turned on her heel and headed towards Gydion's room.

WITH THE BEAUTIFUL sunrise came an equally fine breakfast, the aroma of which had acted as the best wake-up call Daniel had ever received. As he came downstairs and entered the dining area, he saw Anjunel and Philip already seated, but Daniel almost collapsed when he saw that the chef making the delicious smelling food was none other than Finn.

'What's your problem?' she asked in response to Daniel's open mouth. 'Just because I kick a little butt now and again doesn't mean I don't know how to cook a mean feast. Madeline and Joseph are busy sorting out provisions and stuff for our journey so I said I'd help out.'

'I didn't say a thing,' Daniel said, his hands up defensively. 'You'll make someone very happy one day.'

'Oh, I know that! The thing is I don't think there's anyone out there good enough to deserve me, much less able to handle me,' laughed Finn as she handed Daniel a plate of food, which he thanked her for. 'Besides, I think they should be the one to make me happy.'

'True. Any sign of Gydion and Grimgaard?'

'They've been outside talking for a while. Business not for young ears, no doubt. They need to come in though, before their food starts getting cold.' As Finn was about to make a move to get them, in walked the legendary men. 'Just in time, I was about to come get you guys.'

'Tight breeches Gydion here was just asking me a favour and, when I so kindly accepted, began laying down some rules for me,' Grimgaard said despondently.

'What kind of favour?' Daniel queried.

'Grimgaard has agreed to go with you to find the Tolgarr,' announced Gydion. 'Whilst I continue my investigations, beginning with Almedia and Hyasda.'

'Can't I go with you?'

'It's too early for that, Daniel. I'm not going on a picnic.'

'But I've improved so much, you've seen it yourself.'

'And yet you cannot summon a familiar; child's play in the scheme of magic, and I have also seen you almost kill people through a lack of control.'

Finn still couldn't believe that this was the same Daniel she had been attracted to the moment she first saw him from atop the Almedia city wall. When she had spoken to Gydion last night and told him about what Daniel was doing, the Archmage had expressed his concern about him losing control of a spell he cast during his exam, that people's lives had been put at risk.

'That wasn't my fault! It was...' he stopped himself when he saw Philip glaring at him.

'Really? Is there anything you want to tell me, Daniel?'

The inner turmoil was almost visible on Daniel's face. He didn't like hiding the truth from Gydion, but he also didn't want to betray Philip's trust either. Having someone like him as an enemy would make his life at Hartfield Mage Academy a nightmare, and right now, he was enjoying his status there. 'It was... it was a mistake.'

'I see. Well, Daniel, as a Mage, mistakes can cost lives and much more. Only when you are true to yourself will you be ready to reach your full potential.'

'Come on, Daniel. Have you forgotten that he's sending us to Ostia? Why would you want to go back to Almedia and Hyasda's stinky shop when we can go to a village of witches in the centre of a haunted forest!' Finn beamed with excitement.

'Wait a minute,' Grimgaard suddenly piped in. 'Nobody said anything about going to Ostia.'

'It must have slipped my mind,' Gydion said sheepishly.

'You're not telling me that the big bad berserker dwarf is afraid of ghosts?' Finn mocked. 'Come on, it'll be a blast! We'll be there for Lammas, so just think about all that food and grog that'll be there mmmm, mmmm-mm.'

'For the record, I'm not afraid,' grumbled the dwarf. 'I just know that there's more in that forest than just ghosts, but those witches do make a mighty fine wine!'

'OK, THAT'S IT,' JOSEPH announced as he loaded the last of the provisions into the horse-drawn caravan. 'You're ready to go whenever you want.'

'Thank you, Joseph,' Daniel replied as he shook the hand of the groundsman. Madeline couldn't restrain herself any longer and threw her arms around Daniel and squeezed him tight.

'Make sure you wrap up warm at night and stay close to the fire. It can get a bit chilly out there,' she said motherly as she released him.

'We will,' he replied and handed her a coin bag. 'This should be enough to get this place back into shape and some for the two of you for being so loyal to the estate.'

'When you get to Almedia, don't forget to tell Quinn what I said, Gydion,' Finn said, then remembered something herself and handed the Archmage an envelope. 'And give him this too. It's a few of my own ideas for the renovation.'

'That reminds me,' Daniel said as he fished out a letter from his own pocket and gave it to Grimgaard. 'My dad wanted me to give you this.'

The dwarf looked at it for a moment before hesitantly taking it, without saying a word, and immediately slipping it into his pocket before walking over to the Archers to apologise again for his actions and say goodbye.

Finn leaned against the wagon, her arms crossed, and glared at Philip as he whispered close to Daniel. She spoke in hushed tones as Anjunel joined her. 'He's no doubt praising Daniel for not saying anything to Gydion about what they've been up to. Probably reminding him not to tell anyone as well.'

'If it is not stopped soon, he will develop an addiction that will be hard for us to break; much like we Krez are addicted to The Quelling.'

'This is totally different!' Finn was all for enjoying life but what rankled her was people choosing to take it to excess, to the point they were no longer in control of themselves. 'The Quelling has a purpose, not a great or whole-some one, admittedly, because of the curse, but it has a purpose. It keeps you from going insane, from killing you. Daniel and that vekt are doing it just for pleasure. When I spoke to Gydion, he told me that this EV thing has been known by other names for centuries, probably since people first started using magic. It was rife. He said If you go to any slum that has drug abusers, you will find out that some are Mages that abused their gifts.'

'So why didn't the Archmage do anything?'

'Apparently, there haven't been occurrences like this for a long time. How to do it isn't even written down, so someone must have taught Philip. That's who Gydion wants.'

'And what of Daniel?'

'He told me to keep them two separated as much as possible and try to make him come to his senses before he gets dragged too deep into this vekt. You keep watch of Philip, and I'll handle Daniel.'

'Agreed,' Anjunel replied.

Having completed her clandestine discussion with the elf, Finn turned her attention to the party. 'Well, if we're all packed and ready, we should make a move, people. At this time of year, the Tolgarr should be in the north-ern plains getting ready for their migration south. It's about a six-day ride, so if anybody is too delicate to rough it, or isn't up for it, now would be a good time to change your mind... Philip.' She glared at him as she said his name.

'No, I'm here for Daniel, so I won't be leaving anytime soon,' he said and smiled thinly back at her. The lines of battle had been drawn.

Chapter Twenty-Four
Firelight Admissions

Before Daniel knew it, four days had flown by, such was the fun he was having. Although he was a city boy at heart and had never been camping before, he did still appreciate nature, especially when it was as idyllic as this.

The aroma of the trees, grass and the multitude of flowers they came across was distinct and pleasurable. The streams and bubbling brooks produced relaxing sounds to perfectly accompany the rhythmic clip-clopping of the horses' hooves and provided them with the chance to do some fishing for extra food and a dietary change from their provisions of salt beef.

These scenes of a blissful, carefree life didn't mean that they slept without having turns at watch during the nights. As wonderful as things seemed during the day, Grimgaard warned that night could sometimes bring its own dangers; cutthroats, bandits, wild animals and more.

The warrior suggested they each take an hour stint, with the least experienced pairing with someone else. Finn had insisted that Daniel stayed with her, just as she had told him to sit up front when she was driving the caravan. He didn't mind that, though, because, on occasions, she'd hand him the reins, put her feet up and tell him what to do. Not the most professional of teaching he's ever had.

'I know what you're doing, Finn,' Daniel said as he sat staring into the crackling campfire, the ever-present sounds of Grimgaard's nightly snores invading the clearing they had set up camp.

Finn aimed down the sight of one of her guns before returning to cleaning her precious pistols. 'Really? I don't know what you mean. I like spending time with my consort. Or have you forgotten that I'm the goddess and you're the consort? And surely you couldn't have forgotten that kiss.'

'No... it... it was my first kiss,' he replied shyly, then seeing her pride-filled smile strengthened his resolve. 'But you know that's not what I'm talking about. I'm talking about you separating Philip and me.'

'Why would I do that?'

'Because of that crazy idea you and Sara have about Philip. You think I forgot about your little intervention stunt? You knocked me out.'

'Well, technically, that was Anju so, if you want to, you can wake her up and have it out with her,' she chuckled. 'But I don't like him.'

'Why not? You don't even know him.'

'True, but I know you, and it's plain to see that he is a bad influence on you.'

'He's helping me. He's made me someone at Hartfield; I would never have passed the exams without him.'

'You would never have put people's lives in danger without him. And you wouldn't be getting jacked up on this EV. I don't want you to become an addict, Daniel.'

'What? I'm not an addict!'

'Has he told you the facts about the continued use of EV? That those addicted eventually lose their magical abilities?'

'And who told you that? Sara? You do know that they used to be a couple, right? Not exactly getting an unbiased view about him, are you?'

'In my experience, that just means that she'll know more about him than you ever will.'

'I imagine that's a lot of experience.'

The barbed comment stung. 'I live my life the way I want to live it, Daniel. If you don't like that suddenly, then maybe you should take your friend and go back to your precious Hartfield.' Tension hung heavy in the air as Finn stood up. 'You know what? I'm going to sleep. You can do the watch yourself. And while you're sitting there doing your Mage drug thing, maybe you should try and imagine what Trinity would think of you right now.'

He sat there in silence, for how long, Daniel didn't know, until he heard Finn's rhythmic sounds of sleep. He thought about what he had said to her. And although at the time, he had said it to hurt her, he hadn't meant it. As soon as the words left his mouth, he had been sorry. He had lashed out in retaliation and, in doing so, had hurt Finn.

Wiping his moist eyes, he took a couple of deep breaths to prepare himself. If Finn thought that he was an addict, who was he to disappoint her opinion of him. It would just be for a little while, Daniel convinced himself, to get over the stress of their argument.

As he was just about to begin to raise his Essence, a thought crossed his mind; what if the brightness of his aura woke up his companions. Being caught red-handed doing EV was the last thing he needed.

With the idea of moving away from camp into the surrounding trees prevalent in his mind, Daniel stoked the fire and added another log, so that he would be able to see its glow from afar and easily find his way back.

'I think that would be a bad idea,' Anjunel suddenly said from behind him. Daniel hadn't heard her get up, let alone walk behind him.

'I don't know what you're talking about,' he replied, regaining his composure after the assassin's startling appearance.

'Well, If I were in your shoes, all alone, I would likely take this opportunity to get a fix.'

'What? I wasn't thinking that at all. Whatever Sara told you and Finn, I am not addicted to EV. I don't need it. I can do fine without it.'

'I, myself, am feeling the pull of The Quelling. The voices of those slain by my hand grow louder and stronger with each passing day. They crave vengeance. They haunt my sleep. Forcing me to relive each of their deaths from their point of view. Feeling their pain, their agony, over and over. A time will come when I will no longer be able to tell the difference between these nightmares and reality. If I could have just a bit of The Quelling, I would gladly, but that would negate and invalidate the sacrifice I have already made and the sacrifice made by both my lover and by my mother.'

Daniel was stunned by Anjunel's frank admission. He could see in her eyes that she was more agitated than he ever remembered seeing her. It strengthened him to reveal his own inner demons. 'The reason I do EV is not dissimilar to your own, but the voices I hear are mine, telling me that I'll never achieve anything, that I'll always be in the shadow of others, that I'm not good enough. When I do EV, I have none of those fears.'

'I have fought by your side, Daniel, and I have seen with my own eyes that you have something within you. People follow you without condition. They risked their lives to rescue you. And this was all before you started to use this Mage drug. You have already achieved much. This drug may make you feel great, on top of the world. However, true greatness takes time and a lot of dedication. We all begin our journey with flaws, granted, some more than others, but we must all work hard to conquer and overcome those flaws to achieve the things we desire. When we achieve our dreams, we become a better person for it, a humble person who will remember when they started with nothing, because when we toil and learn the right way, no matter the hardship, those lessons will stay with you forever. You were right when you said that you don't need EV, Daniel, now you have to believe it.'

Anjunel's words rolled around in Daniel's head and hung heavy in his mind. EV made everything easy, but she was right; it didn't make him a Mage, it didn't give him magic; it just made it easy for him to access what was already there. What was the harm in that?

But what if Finn was telling the truth, that I could lose my magic altogether if I continued to abuse it? I can't believe Philip wouldn't tell me that! It wouldn't be worth taking the risk just to experience that euphoria. Or would it?

Daniel pondered hard. Thought about those closes to him and how they always encouraged him, believed in him, especially Trinity and Finn. So why was it so hard for him to believe in himself? How was he supposed to save his love if he couldn't even save himself? If he lost his magic, lost who he was, then she would be lost forever.

That was something that he couldn't let happen.

She had given her life to save his. She had trusted him to resurrect her. Believed that he was capable of succeeding, and he wasn't about to let her down.

Daniel eyed the assassin; the fire of determination blazed in his eyes. 'Anjunel, I need you to teach me how to fight.'

Chapter Twenty-Five

A Trap Sprung

C onsidering that he only had a couple hours of sleep, to say that Daniel was buzzing the following day would have been an understatement. After training with Anjunel, he stayed up and trained with Grimgaard. They were completely different types of teachers, teaching completely different fighting styles, and Daniel loved every second of it, soaking up every bit of their instruction.

Although they differed in combat techniques, Anju preferring to use finesse and precision strikes to overcome her adversaries, while Grimgaard used strength and power to batter opponents. There was one thing they could both agree on. That the best teacher of martial prowess was Master Kay Haiche of The Hidden Path Monastery. The master's school was in the eastern kingdom of Gorias. Although they were headed in that direction, Grimgaard had told him getting there would take them too far off their current course, especially since they were to head north to Ostia after their visit with the Tolgarr.

'Hey, Anju,' Finn called the elf as everything was packed, and the party readied themselves to continue their journey. 'Why don't you ride up front with me?'

'See, I told you,' Daniel whispered to Anjunel. 'Letting her sleep last night didn't make any difference. Finn hasn't forgotten a thing; she still hates me.'

'All you need do, Daniel, is apologise,' the elf replied as she climbed into the back of the carriage. 'And there is no better time to do so, than now.'

Daniel stared worryingly up at Anju as he mentally prepared himself to step into the lion's den. He made his way to the front of the carriage, expelled his doubt and took in a deep breath of courage and climbed up next to Finn.

'About time,' Finn said before she saw that it was Daniel and not Anjunel climbing up to take the seat next to her. 'Oh, it's you.' The coldness of her reply stung Daniel. However, he wasn't expecting this to be an easy conversation but one bumpy as the well-worn trail that they now rode along.

Several minutes passed before that breath of courage began to take effect, and Daniel finally opened his mouth. 'Do you remember the Beltane Games? The feast after the Wheel Run?' Finn made no acknowledgement or response as she continued to ride the horses as if he were not there. 'You had snuck away from your chaperone and had a go at me for calling you a bandit instead of a scoundrel,' scoffed Daniel.

He glanced at his friend with a smile as his recollection of that day became clearer in his mind, which was gently nudged by the morning sun's glint off her engineer's blast goggles and her violet hair with its purple streaks.

'Don't you remember how impressed I was with you; with your life and the way you were... are. You're Finn Jesson, you are what you are, and if people don't like it, then they can shove it.'

'Does that include you?' She spoke without taking her eyes off the road ahead. 'You're right, I don't care what most people say about me. But you're my friend, we've shared moments together. I have a love for you, Daniel, and to know that you think so little of me hurt.'

'You know I didn't mean it.'

'Do I?'

'They were rash words spoken in the heat of the moment.'

'Spiteful words.'

'Granted, but without the weight of meaning. I was angry, I lashed out because you were needling me about the EV, so I retaliated.'

'By implying that I'm a harlot and devoid of morals.'

'I was angry, but not at you. Now I see that I was angry with myself. You could see what I couldn't.'

'You were too close to see what was right in front of you.'

'They say that we hurt the ones that we love, and I do love you, Finn. You are undoubtedly the best friend I have, and I am genuinely sorry for hurting your feelings. It was insensitive and judgemental, and I hope that you can forgive me. I messed up, but I'll be more mindful of what I say.'

'Stop using EV because that's what's fuelling your little outbursts,' pleaded Finn. She turned to face Daniel for the first time and showed the anguish in her eyes. 'Don't let this drug control who you are, Daniel. You don't need it, no matter what other people say. And if you need help, you know I'll always be there for you.'

'Thanks, Finn. So, are we ok?'

'Yeah, as long as you stop acting like an asshole.'

'Excuse me?'

'You heard.'

'Yeah, I did, but where did you...?'

'Come on, Daniel,' chuckled Finn. 'I've been to your world a couple times now. Me and Anju watched that box thing with your dad. It's fascinating!'

'Oh, you mean the tv,' Daniel replied as he tried to imagine these two loose cannons running wild on the streets of London. 'I've been itching to tell you, whilst you were sleeping last night, Anju and Grimgaard have been teaching me how to fight.'

'Really? When I left you, I was worried that you would do your thing.'

'I'm not going to lie; I was tempted. But Anjunel talked me out of it. Talked about her own addiction and the fact that her people have no choice. Addiction to them is life, whilst I wasted mine by choosing to become a slave to EV. I felt ashamed.' Daniel noticed that Finn was only half paying attention as her gaze was fixed firmly down the road ahead. 'What is you, it?'

'There's something up ahead. Looks like a carriage, with three people...no four people with it.'

Daniel squinted as he tried to see what Finn could but to no avail. Her sharpshooter's eyesight was too much for him to contend with.

Finn opened the flap to the carriage and let the others know what was ahead. She told Daniel, who in turn warned Philip, to be on his guard, as some bandits occasionally played possum to lure unsuspecting marks before striking.

The four men and their caravan were stood by a lone tree that seemed to have been split by lightning. As they neared, Finn saw that, judging by the tools on the ground, they must have just finished repairing a wheel on their caravan. One of the men suddenly stepped out and waved down Finn, who reined in the horses and came to a halt.

'Afternoon, there,' the man said in a genial manner. 'Nice day for a ride, huh? Especially a beautiful, young couple such as yourselves.'

'Hi,' replied Finn as she jumped down and stretched her legs. 'yup, just me and my man doing our thing.' Two of the men began packing away their tools whilst the third busied himself with reading.

'My friends and I are merchants on our way to do a spot of trading in Imperial City. Where might you be heading with such fine horses?'

'In the opposite direction. You having some trouble?'

'A little, but we have it in hand,' the man stated and intercepted Finn as she tried nonchalantly get a closer look. 'I won't keep you, I'm sure a young couple, such as yourselves have places to be. I just wanted to warn you that the road ahead is in some dire need of repair, so I'd take care riding over those potholes.'

'Thanks a lot, friend! Maybe I could buy some of your wares as a way of thanking you,' said Finn and began to lift the cover of the cart. It was filled with toys; figures and dolls of all kinds. One fell on the floor, which Finn bent to retrieve, in so doing, gave one of the men time to cover the cart. On the bottoms of the doll's feet was engraved the name "Lily". As she stood up, the young thief found her entrance to the cart blocked by the sinewy tattooed arm of one of the men. 'So, you and your men are toy sellers?'

'Indeed, we are,' the first man replied. 'But unfortunately, these have all been prepurchased, hence the names on the toys, so they know which is to be given to whom.' He took the doll from Finn and gave it to his compatriot, who quickly put it with the others. 'Now, I've taken up enough of your time, so I'm sure you'd like to be on your way, as do we as we are in a bit of a hurry. A diviner we passed said heavy rain was coming.'

Finn looked up at the clear sky. 'I don't think much of their talents,' she scoffed. The trader helped her up into the carriage, and she saw the same tattoo on the inside of his arm as the other man had. This time she got a longer look at it.

She could see that the design was a red crescent, but rather than like a waning moon, its points were facing down. Over it was a pair of black wings with an oblong shape in the centre, where they met. There were symbols on it, that much Finn could see, but she didn't know what they meant, but it looked familiar. She had seen many tattoos in her time running with the guild, but this one drew a blank. Then she remembered that she had seen the same pattern on some clerics and paladins back in Imperial City.

Just as she was about to ask him about it, he noticed her staring at the artwork. 'It's our company logo,' he explained. 'Kind of like our advertising.'

She creased her eyebrows. 'Wouldn't it have been easier just to paint it on your cart?'

'Sure, but everybody does that. This way is much more striking, don't you think?'

'Well, it's certainly made an impression on me,' she said with a congenial smile and started the horses. 'Good journey! And thanks again for the advice!'

As they continued riding down the path, Daniel looked back. 'That's odd,' he said.

'What is?' Finn asked.

'They don't seem to be in any hurry at all. Three of them are talking amongst themselves, and the one that was reading is now standing in the middle of the road watching us.'

Finn didn't give voice to her fears, just geed the horses to a gallop.

TIME PASSED INTO LATE afternoon uneventfully. Even the potholes they were warned about never really materialised. There was indeed wear and tear, which was to be expected on a trade route, but nothing to the extent that the merchants had implied.

The plains were, as Daniel was learning, exactly as their name implied; plain. But he had developed a love for exploration, taking in new things. And the company and conversation were pleasant. He and Finn talked as if their disagreement had never happened, as is the way with true friends. With the hatch to the back open, they could hear Grimgaard Thunderbeard and Anjunel telling tales of their exploits whilst Philip quietly read his book.

Everything was proceeding smoothly until they came to a stop so that Grimgaard might relieve Finn. Daniel and Finn both climbed down and began stretching out their bodies. As she leaned back, letting out a huge yawn, which was mirrored by both Daniel and Grimgaard, the sky above them suddenly darkened, unleashing a sudden deluge upon them.

The rain pelted down, stinging their flesh as it struck them, such was its force. Climbing back onboard, they drove the carriage headlong into the downpour in desperate need of some sort of shelter. The trees dotted here, and there were few and far between, not enough to give any sort of protection.

When it looked like huddling up in the carriage for the night was beginning to look like a distinct possibility, Finn, through squinted eyes, sighted a structure in the distance. They closed in on it rapidly, soon discovering that it was a seemingly abandoned rustic wooden shack with a covered well. They were glad to see it all the same and spared little time disembarking and piling into the building to escape the downpour.

They were all glad to be out of the rain, even if their impromptu accommodation was very sparse to say the least, a hearth, table, a couple chairs and not much else. Each of them looked around the small space, their backgrounds and interests drawing their attention to different things. Daniel noticed all the graffiti and hastily scribbled words scrawled on the walls: "run, lost, trust". And one that seemed unfinished, "don't take the-". Whilst the combatants picked up small tell-tale signs of some sort of skirmish that happened on the site, scorch marks, small nicks in the wood from a sharp edge, some of them possibly having specks of blood in them, the party's thief however, struck gold.

'Well, well, well,' Finn said to herself in hushed tones. 'What have we here?' She bent down and picked up the small ornate gold ring. Giving it the once over, she blew the dust off of it. 'Finders keepers.' She smiled and slipped the ring on the ring finger of her right hand. At which point they all collapsed to the ground.

Chapter Twenty-Six

A Ghost's Story

Daniel groaned as he slowly opened his eyes. He blinked them several times, not because he couldn't see. On the contrary, he could see perfectly. Everything was crisp and sharp, in ultra-vivid colour.

'Finally, he stirs,' a familiar Celtic voice said. 'How are you, husband?'

Glancing to his left, Daniel saw the beautiful and brave Dobunni princess, Aloisia.

'Ah, mon amour, it has been too long since we parted,' on his right, the astute and self-assured Countess Bianca Daumier peered down at him.

'What is going on,' asked Daniel, thoroughly confused.

'I don't really know to be honest. We've been combining our efforts to try and get through to you for... I don't actually know. I have no idea how long we've been here but it feels like forever.

'Instantly recognising the voice, Daniel sat up. 'Trinity!' He jumped to his feet and rushed to hug her. 'It really was you I heard during my exam.'

Trinity nodded, and they kissed. 'We have been trying to contact you again ever since.' The shivers that ran up and down the spine of Trinity was also felt by both Aloisia and Bianca, as if they were also being held in the embrace.

It was the happiest Daniel had been for some time, and a smile crept onto his face as the couple stared into each other's eyes. 'Where are we? How is this even possible?' He didn't know how, but by the look of things, he could have sworn they were in The Dirty Dog tavern.

'I don't know,' Trinity admitted.

'Come, come now, cheri,' interjected Bianca. 'As we are one and the same, what I know, you know. Or perhaps because we are all standing here, independent of one another, you no longer have my piercing intellect. No matter, I will do my best to explain. To answer your second question first, you and Trinity have a connection, a bond, a mind-link, if you will. It was no doubt established at the time of her death. Don't look so troubled, Daniel. It was a subconscious act to connect to the person that she trusted most and had the belief and capability to be the one to resurrect her.'

'Gydion was there too. Surely he would have been a better candidate.'

'Perhaps, but it is you we love, Daniel. Throughout our many lives, we have always found that one person that we love above all others. I had my bien-aime, Cassius. Aloisia had Donal. And now in this life, Trinity has you.'

Daniel instinctively squeezed her hand.

'Now, as for where we are, that I cannot say, but, for sure, it is some sort of construct of Tristan's.'

'Yes,' Trinity replied in response to Daniel's surprised expression. 'We know he is the masked man and behind my prolonged imprisonment, but not how.'

'Dragon's blood. He has it coursing through his veins now.'

'You have to be careful, Daniel. He's insane. I'm just the bait to lure you to him. It's you he wants.'

'And I won't disappoint him, because I will rescue you. I need you, Trinity.'

'Then don't lose yourself, Daniel. Don't lose the man that I love.'

Hearing her words, he reflected on his actions of late. How he'd spoken to Finn and Gydion. He suspected that she knew more than what she was letting on, then Finn's words about letting Trinity down and what she would think suddenly reverberated through his mind.

'Something is not right,' Aloisia suddenly said. If Trinity was the compassion, the keen mind of Bianca was the intellect, then the Dobunni princess was undoubtedly the source of power for this triptych. They were three aspects of one being. 'I can feel that Daniel is asleep, but I can also sense that is anything but natural.'

'We're in a cabin, sheltering from the rain. But we hadn't gone to bed yet.'

'If I can just extend my awareness outwards... through you... I might be able to... sense... more.' Aloisia fell silent as she concentrated. 'You are not alone!' She finally panted. 'There are men, searching, you and your friends. You must wake up. Dispel the magic and wake up, now!'

'You must go, Daniel,' Trinity said as they kissed and hugged tightly. 'Be safe, my love, and take care.'

Bianca said her goodbyes next, and as they embraced, she whispered to him. 'Do not tarry, Daniel. You have seen what you need to know from our pasts, even with Tristan's interference. He has designs on Trinity, despite what he says. Figure out what the theme is and bring her back, Daniel.

'Strengthen your willpower and mental defences,' said Aloisia as she hugged him. 'Tristan has been in your mind as you slept, trying to steal your chaos magic. Protect yourself at all times. Now go.' She pushed Daniel hard in the chest and sent him tumbling through different planes of reality until he was back in his body with a start and opened his eyes.

As Daniel lay there, pretending to be asleep, he watched them, deciding what his course of action should be.

'This is going to be our best haul yet!'

'Will you be quiet!' The man Finn had spoken to, seemingly the leader, reprimanded his colleague in an agitated whisper. His speech was less refined than it had been, which was put on to play the part of the amiable trader. 'Do you think Kastor will be happy with only three recruits for the cult? I don't think so.' There were mumblings of agreement. 'Exactly. So that means that we're going to have to do this again and hopefully get a family or something.'

'I didn't know these three were in the back, though.' It was the one that had been reading the whole time.

'Neither did I, and judging by their gear, they're fighters. Luckily, your spell affected them all. If we had just jumped them, things could have gone south pretty damn quick.'

'Vekt!' The fourth man had been searching Grimgaard, looking for the clasps to remove his armour.

'What is it?'

'I thought this was a fake Athenatoi armour, a pretty good fake, but a fake none the less.'

'So?'

'This is the genuine article. It's enchanted; I can't undo it. And there's on-ly one dwarf in Athenatoi armour that I know of.'

'Thunderbeard, but nobody's seen him for ages.'

'I heard he was a drunken bum.'

'What are we going to do, Ken?'

He thought for a moment, weighed everything up and came to his con-clusion. 'This doesn't change anything. We stick to the plan. Kill the elf and the dwarf. Stuff the armour. They can bury him in it for all I care. We take the youngsters to the cult, and we sell the gear. Simple.'

Upon hearing their footsteps getting closer, Daniel knew that the time to act was now. 'I can't allow you to do that,' he said, getting to his feet. Daniel tried to project his voice, give it more gravitas, like his fathers. If it worked, he didn't know. They seemed more concerned about something else.

'What happened?' Ken was angry. Things were beginning to go wrong. 'Why didn't the spell work?'

'It did work! Look at the others; they're still fast asleep.'

'This one might be more valuable than we thought.'

'Yeah! Look how they reacted when you gave them Lily.'

'Grab him, boys!' Ordered Ken.

Daniel looked down at the others and realised that maybe he should have formulated his plan a little bit more. He was outnumbered, alone against four. He needed time to cast Dispel Charm. Somehow, he had to delay their course of action. 'Let me get this straight,' he said, holding up his hands to stop their advance. 'So, you're bandits, right? You select potential targets on the roadside. Use some sort of sleep spell on them.'

'A Scroll of Fatigue.'

'A Scroll of Fatigue, yes. And then they come here to rest...but we could have stayed in our caravan, except for the rain...'

'Another scroll.'

'Another scroll, of course, forcing your victims to shelter here in this cab-in. But why this cabin? And we didn't feel tired in any way, it happened all of a sudden.'

'That's because that little ring on your girlfriends' finger is the trigger. Once someone puts it on, it activates the curse.'

'Ah, I see. So, they all fall asleep, and then when you rob and kill them. Is that how it works?'

'Not bad, but only partially right,' Ken admitted. 'We're not bandits; we're slavers for the Black Wing Cult,' he showed off his tattoo proudly. 'We bring youngsters, like yourself and younger, to the leaders to be indoctrinated. The older ones are killed, but we don't do the killing.'

Suddenly, there was a wailing from outside, which grew louder until it reached a point where Daniel felt pain and had to cover his ears to try and shut it out. Running to the window, he looked outside. The rain lashed the cabin in sheets making it difficult to see anything at all. Then, as lightning repeatedly struck the ground around the well, a glowing ethereal form, half-human, half-snake, slowly rose from within it. 'Where is my ring? Where is my ring?' The creature said the phrase over and over as she slowly slithered toward the cabin and through its door.

Daniel's blood ran cold as he watched the creature approach. He backpeddled, aghast at the scene before him and shot a glance at his four captors. Each one of them had wicked smiles on their face, and Daniel noticed that not only did their tattoos have a strange glow but also something that was around their necks, tucked under their shirts.

'She's not here for you,' Ken shouted over the lightning strikes. 'But that can easily be changed.'

He saw that the apparition was almost upon Anjunel. His mind raced as he decided his next course of action. His spell to counteract the sleep charm his friends were under was ready to be cast, but he had to protect them from the immediate danger first.

Despite his initial fears at seeing the ghostly figure, and the desire to cower away from it, Daniel knew in his heart that wasn't really an option, not with his friends in imminent peril. Now was not the time to hesitate.

He tightened his hands into fists, took a deep breath and squared his shoulders, making himself as tall as possible. His heart rate increased as a surge of adrenaline fired through his body, quickly followed by his Essence.

That's when he heard the voice again. The same beguiling voice he had heard when he had faced Sayyidah. Its words were so compelling, so appealing, so attractive, so tempting.

Use the power of chaos, he could hear in his head. *Chaos is true freedom, my friend. It is so easy to grasp, yet few can master it. I can teach you. Show you the way. Chaos is not restrained by laws of order, neither is it limited to the ideas of good and evil.*

Who are you?

I know your pain, Daniel. I know your dilemma. You fear having to be the balance between good and evil, between order and chaos. I am the one that can teach you to be all you can be. I have waited a long time for your arrival, Daniel. Your brothers and sisters have waited. Seek me out, Daniel, and together we will do great things. Now, finish them. Finish them all.

Daniel was confused by that final remark. Finish who? Suddenly, he seemed to wake from a trance and realised that mystic energy, similar to that which he had struck Sayyidah, was reaching out from his hands. Not only was it wrapped around the chest and neck of the four slavers, but it also held the human snake apparition in a field of chaotic energy, which, judging by her wails, caused her great pain.

Finish them. Finish them all. The voice reverberated and faded away the more Daniel came to his senses until it was completely gone. With the chaos spell no longer being sustained, it immediately vanished. Even though Daniel had no knowledge of what had just happened, the four men did know, and they had no desire to be caught off guard again. They had underestimated him once, now they intended to cut their losses and be rid of him; the other boy and girl would have to do for the cult.

Daniel heard the sound of blades being unsheathed and turned to see the four men advancing towards him, their faces twisted in anger as a couple of them rubbed their throats after their brush with death. The ghostly figure was still slowed after its imprisonment, and Daniel seized the opportunity to cast his spell.

A wave of sparkling purple radiated from Daniel in an ever-increasing circle. It passed over his friends, Anjunel, Grimgaard, Philip and finally Finn, then one by one, they began to stir.

'Kill them!' Ken yelled in desperation. The plan they had executed numerous times before was unravelling. This group was turning out to be more trouble than they were worth. As he pushed his comrades to engage, Ken quietly slipped away., leaving them to their fate.

Even in their groggy state, Grimgaard and Anjunel were more than a match for the remaining slavers, leaving the apparition to the three teens to take care of.

'She's a spectral banshee,' the dwarf shouted as he head-butted one of the slavers and kicked another. 'A naga, by the looks of it. She must be given what she seeks; that's all she wants.'

'The ring,' Daniel said, remembering what she was screaming for when she had first appeared. 'Give her the ring, Finn!'

'What? No! Finders keepers. That's the law in any realm... I'm sure.'

'The ring, Finn!' Daniel became more agitated as the spectre made a bee-line for him. She knew that he had been the one to cause her harm.

Seeing her friend about to be attacked convinced her to do as he asked, although it pained her... greatly. She slipped the ring off of her finger and, against every fibre of her being, and against everything she had learnt from Eamon Wolff and the Thieves Guild, tossed the ring towards the spectral banshee.

It passed right through it.

'And still, she persists. Vekt, Daniel! You best hope I find it again!'

Daniel had no worries about that, especially since the naga was baring down on him, desperately clawing at him with sharpened nails, at least three inches long. He managed to narrowly evade each swipe she made. Philip sent a volley of magic missiles at the creature, which struck true. In response, she unleashed a haunting wail which brought them to their knees.

With Grimgaard and Anjunel unable to defend themselves, the remaining slavers ensured that every one of their unanswered blows counted. The spectral naga turned her attention back to Daniel. She rapidly slithered towards him, claws raised again, and that's when he saw it.

'It's not the ring she wants,' Daniel screamed over the ringing in his ears. 'It's her ring -finger. But how are we supposed to find that? Where would we begin to search?' As the slavers continued their beat down of the warrior and the assassin, one of the men bent down to retrieve their blade, so they could put an end to the proceedings. As he did, his necklace slipped out from beneath the shirt and hung down. On the cord, still surrounded by the strange glow, looked like what seemed to be a piece of bone. 'Finn! Their necklaces! Get their necklaces!'

The three slavers were unperturbed by what they perceived to be just a young woman, struggling to her feet, hands covering her ears. Unfortunately for them, Finn was no mere young woman, as she proceeded to give them a beating with nothing more than her feet, knees, elbows and head.

The moment she had the chance, Finn ripped off each of their necklaces. The spectral banshee instantly stopped her attack on Daniel and focussed her attention on the four men. They tried desperately to escape, but there was none to be had. She killed each one of them by passing her hand through into their body and crushing their hearts.

As the last slaver died, the bloodlust of the naga apparition was still evident. Before it began to make any further moves towards her friends, Finn threw the bone necklaces to her. She reached out and grabbed them, and with a flash, her wild, spectral banshee appearance vanished, to be replaced by a demure, kind-faced woman. 'Thank you all for releasing me. My name is Dana,' she said it a gentle voice. 'I have longed for this day to be free.'

'What happened to you?' Daniel asked. 'Were you one of their victims?'

She nodded. 'One of their first. Ken was my husband, and these three,' she gestured to the slain bodies, 'were his brothers.'

'Your own husband murdered you?'

'Yes. I am a naga, but I chose to live my existence as a human. I loved him very much, but I never told him my origin. Life was wonderful. Well, until he became mixed up with the Black Wing Cult.'

'I heard him mention it. Can you tell us any more about it?'

'Not much. I know their leader is a high priest named Kastor and is said to be an ancient holy man from another realm and that he speaks of a god returning to give salvation and redemption. Many have listened to him, and many have been swayed by his doctrine. But he also swells the numbers of his congregation by convincing members to do as my husband did.'

'You mean kidnap children?'

She nodded. 'The young are particularly valued so as to begin their indoctrination. No doubt, in time, those will become his staunchest supporters. Although I took no part in my husband's activities, my knowledge of them and inaction made me just as guilty,' sobbed Dana. 'It wasn't until the day he wanted to take our daughter there that things changed. I refused; tried to make a stand.'

'Your daughter?' Daniel said. He and Finn looked at each other, remembering the doll in the back of the men's cart.

'Yes, my daughter, Lily. Where is she?'

'And you didn't fancy joining the club?' Finn asked.

'Only humans are accepted,' replied Dana. 'After I refused to allow him to take our daughter, he brought one of the ministers to our cabin, a man named Milton, hoping that he would be able to persuade me of the good wholesome life my daughter would have amongst the other kids in the cult. But it didn't quite go like that. Somehow the minister could see through my transformation and revealed my true form.

Ken and his brothers derided me, called me abusive names, but it wasn't until Minister Milton got involved that I met my end. He told them that I had forever tainted their family name and that they would no longer be welcome within the Black Wing community, unless they proved their worth.

The brothers brutally attacked me, beat me half to death. Ken tried to take my wedding ring back, but couldn't, so he drew his knife and cut it off,' she instinctively clutched her hand and took a moment to compose herself, recalling the events of that night distressed her deeply. When she could, she continued. 'He stabbed me and they threw me in the well. Somehow, I became trapped on this realm, a tortured spirit, the ring, cursed. The fragments of my finger that they wore offered them protection from me, but now I have had my vengeance.'

Hearing that it was cursed, Finn surreptitiously slipped the gold ring off of her finger and placed it on the nearby table.

'We're sorry for what happened to you,' Daniel commiserated.

Dana nodded and accepted his kind words with a smile. 'Thanks to all of you, I am now able to cross over. I can already feel it happening. I ask one thing of you, find my daughter.'

A light suddenly emanated from her chest, getting brighter and brighter until they had to shield their eyes against it. When they looked back, all that was left was her ornate golden wedding ring.

'I guess where she's gone, she won't be needing this,' smiled Finn as she retrieved the ring once more. Her desire for riches had finally dominated her fear of curses.

Chapter Twenty-Seven
A Promise Fulfilled

Grimgaard unfastened the remaining horse from the slavers cart. When they had ventured outside of the cabin, it immediately became apparent to them that Ken had taken the other horse to make good his escape.

'I don't like this idea,' Daniel said.

'We came to the same conclusion, Dan,' Grimgaard replied.

'All those whose opinions actually count,' corrected Finn loudly to make sure Philip heard the remark.

'We all wanted to find the kid, and right now the only person that knows where she is, unfortunately, is that Ken fellow. We can't let him get away, and you're on a time sensitive quest, so we have to split up. There's no other way.'

'I found his trail,' Anjunel reported, returning from her excursion. 'He is headed north-west, not hiding his tracks either, so you should have no problem following them.'

'Good.' Grimgaard nodded, thankful for the information and mounted the horse. 'If all goes to plan, I'll meet you in Ostia. Watch over each other and we'll be reunited soon.' With that, he was off.

They watched him ride off in the direction Anjunel had instructed before they themselves finished packing the carriage to continue their journey east. Finn had taken it upon herself to empty the slavers cart of the children's toys. She collected them in a sack, hoping to somehow, one day, reunite them with their owners. She kept Lily's doll aside and vowed to make it the first one.

With both Finn and Anjunel otherwise occupied, Philip seized the opportunity to talk to Daniel away from his shadows. 'I think this was a bad idea me coming,' he admitted to Daniel once they were out of earshot. 'Your friends are never going to warm to me. It's obvious that they think that I'm a bad influence on you.'

'Don't worry about them, I know the truth,' replied Daniel. 'All you have to do is ingratiate yourself with them, and everything will be fine. Actually—,' it was Daniel's turn to look around and make sure they were alone. 'I wanted to talk to you about something.'

'Sure! It'll give me a chance to feel useful!'

'Ok, so last night, before you guys woke up, I heard a voice trying to convince me to use chaos magic against the banshee.'

'A voice? What kind of voice?'

'I don't know...just a voice.'

'Male? Female?'

'Male.'

'Was it accented?'

'Well...yeah, now that you mention it. And it was soothing, calm, never urgent.'

'Is it the first time you've heard this voice?'

'No. I heard it when I fought the Shade and again when I fought Sayyidah. Each time it has sounded stronger. Yesterday I was even using chaos magic without even knowing it.'

'Hmm, this is all very interesting. I know someone that might be able to help.'

'You do?'

'Yeah! No one knows more about chaos magic than them. I'll introduce you when we get back to Hartfield.'

'Who is it? A tutor?'

'Finn says that if we leave now, we should reach the Tolgarr encampment by early evening,' Anjunel suddenly said from out of nowhere. Neither Daniel nor Philip heard her approach. She really was the best of her race.

THE REST OF THE JOURNEY passed by uneventfully. The Spine of the Goddess mountain range ever visible on the distant northern horizon, its many peaks hidden by cloud cover, Daniel and Finn happily chatted up front, whilst in the back it was deathly silent.

Finn saw this leg of their journey as the ideal opportunity to let Daniel in on her plans regarding Eamon Wolff, Fungal and the corridor of portals. Even though she had given Grimgaard the impression that Daniel knew everything about her idea and was fully on board, this was, in fact, the first time the young Mage had heard anything about it, and his initial reaction wasn't anything like what she had envisioned.

'Are you mad or just crazy?'

'What are you talking about? I thought you'd be impressed.'

'Oh yeah, it's a wonderful idea,' Daniel applauded sarcastically. 'except for the part where you double-cross a boggart that can hold a hell of a grudge and someone else who is the head of the Thieves Guild, just for good measure. And not only that, you want me to train magic users!'

'Technically, it's the Syndicate now,' Finn nonchalantly stated, which drew a stern look from him. 'Don't look at me like that, Daniel! I don't take any vekt from them, and I'm not about to take it from you either! This was my job offer, and I'll be damned if I give Eamon a bigger slice than I think he deserves! And for your information, I'm not double-crossing anybody. They both get what they want; Fungal gets his information about local customs, and places to go for his clients, and Eamon gets some loot, minus my 90% finder's fee.' Daniel raised his eyebrows at that. 'What? He should be thankful it's not 99%. Besides, what he doesn't know won't hurt him.'

'And what if he does find out? Didn't you say that he's sending a couple newbies with you? What if they're spies?'

'I'd be disappointed if they weren't, but I know what drives thieves.'

'And what's that?'

'A desire for a greater slice of the pie, a big score,' smiled Finn.

'A bribe?'

'Let's not label these things. Let's just say that they'll be making more for telling Eamon what I want him to know than what they'll be getting for telling him what they actually see.

Daniel shook his head. It was obvious that she had given her idea a lot of thought, that she had covered every eventuality. He didn't know how long she had been planning it all, but he had to admit, he was genuinely impressed. 'So, what drives you? The 90%?'

'Nah, it's something intangible. I've always been told that I'd amount to nothing. That I wasn't ladylike. Or I wasn't this. Or I was that. But I'm the best thief the guild has ever had. I got their respect; now I want everyone else's. And with The Fellowhood, I can get that. And it'll be something I built up from scratch, something that wasn't given to me and can't ever be taken away from me.' Her eyes moistened, and she turned away to protect her air of toughness. Daniel, not saying a word, put his arms around her and squeezed. Two droplets fell onto his arm and saturated into the fabric. 'Alright, alright. Enough of the mushy stuff,' Finn said, feigning distress.

'I'm in,' Daniel said before he released her.

'Really?'

'Don't sound so surprised. Someone has to make sure you don't get yourself into too much trouble.'

'Well, that was easy,' Finn genuinely sounded disappointed. 'I had a speech all planned out to sell it to you. I was going to tell you that if you wanted to be a legend, like your dad, you'd have to do what he did; build your reputation by doing quests. And what better place to do that than with The Fellowhood? Among friends.'

'Can a thief really be a hero?' Daniel mused with a giggle.

'Why the vekt not? A thief to one man is a liberator to another,' she pointed out. 'The name LoH will be respected throughout the known and unknown realms.'

'Which will surely bring it to the attention of Eamon and the Syndicate.'

'Not a problem. The leader of the LoH will be a faceless entity, and only you lot will know that it is my brainchild,' she grinned. She really had thought of every eventuality. 'Now, do you think your friend Princess Nyriel would be interested in joining us? Her archaeological knowledge could come in handy.'

'No, doubt about! She'd be over the moon. Her father, on the other hand, not so.'

'Well,' Finn began as she reached over and patted Daniel on the back, 'I'm sure we can talk him around once we remind him who it was that not only slew the Shade but also rescued his daughter from his own treacherous royal bodyguard.'

'Finn, have I ever told you how dangerous you are?'

She laughed. 'No, but go on.'

AS THE FIRST OF ARIEST'S dual suns, the light blue Horinesti, was beginning to set, leaving the lilac Sual alone in the darkening pink sky, the companions saw signs of civilisation, plumes of smoke, visible from up ahead, rose into the sky. A fast-moving river lay ahead of them, halting their progress. Large rocks within it caused foaming white water, suggesting that the current was probably too strong to cross.

'Now what?' Daniel stood and glanced up and down the river. 'I can't see any way of crossing.'

'There are, in both directions, but this is the only way that leads to where we want to go, so we wait.'

'For what?'

'For them.' Finn gestured across the river towards the three men on horseback that were galloping towards them. Just as Finn had said they would, they had arrived at the Tolgarr encampment.

All three were tall with a muscular build, a product of the nomadic hunter-gatherer life their people led. Two of the men had sepia-brown skin, and straight black hair, whilst the rider in the middle had tightly curled black hair with a burnt umber complexion. Their clothes, layers of brightly-coloured silks with intricate weaving, beadwork and precious stones twinkled in the setting sun.

The Tolgarr men dismounted and approached the bankside. The man in the centre studied the caravan whilst his compatriots held their bows by their side, an arrow notched, ready. 'Greetings, strangers,' he yelled across the river in his deep voice. 'If you are looking to cross this river, you have come to the wrong place, but if you tell me where it is you wish to go, I can direct you to the nearest appropriate bridge.'

Finn handed the reins to Daniel and told him and the others to stay in the carriage. She then jumped down, walked to the edge of her side of the river and responded in the Tolgarr native language. 'Stranger? Is that what I am now, Tawani?'

The man scrutinised Finn. 'Who are you? How do you know my name?'

'Come on, Baby Tee. Have I really changed that much? You're the one that's had the growth spurt, not me.'

Tawani thought a moment, then the realisation struck him. 'Finnuala Jesson? Is that really you?'

'Don't call me that!' 'I'll stop calling you that when you stop calling me baby!'

'Ok, baaaaaaby!'

They both burst out laughing. It was a scene that they had replayed many times before when they were younger, and he was a head shorter than Finn as opposed to being the head taller that he now stood.

Still chuckling to himself, the Tolgarrian took something out of the pouch that hung over his shoulder. He blew the dark powder he had taken out then, with his hands held before his face, in a reverent manner, Tawani mouthed some words. As he spoke, both sides of the bank extended outwards until they met each other, creating a wide bridge over the river. Daniel had watched the whole interaction intently, this being the first time he had actually seen shamanistic magic in use.

Once she had led the carriage over, Finn went to her old friend and greeted him in the way of the Tolgarr people; they held each other's opposite forearms, touched foreheads and gave thanks for seeing a loved one again. Then they hugged tightly, the conventional way.

'I can't wait until Crellis sees you!' Tawani laughed.

'How is he?' she asked in common.

'Oh, you'll see,' he grinned mischievously.

'So, when did you get so tall?'

'When did you become a woman?'

'Oi! I've always been a well-refined lady, I'd have you know.'

'Ha! Do all the well-refined ladies in Almedia steal pies and wrestle boys twice their size?'

'I don't remember you complaining about where it came from when you were stuffing your face with it—,'

'It was a very tasty pie, as I recall.'

'—and I had to teach that boy a lesson because I'm the only one allowed to call you Baby Tee.' She smirked.

'You know what? Gulo works under me now,' Tawani's chest swelled with pride.

'Vekt! I didn't notice! Captain of the guard?' She saluted, which he returned. 'You did good Baby Tee.

'There was a moment of silence as the old friends marvelled at the development they'd both made. 'So, what brings you here, Finn.'

'My friend there,' she said, pointing to Daniel, 'is fulfilling a promise he made to Aradia.'

'Aradia? How...? Come on, we'll escort you in,' he said as he remounted his steed. 'I can't wait to see the look on my brother's face when he sees you!'

AS THEY ENTERED THE Tolgarr encampment proper, led by Tawani and one of the guards, having sent the other ahead to announce them, the carriage of the companions drew a lot of attention from the people. Although the Tolgarr were accustomed to seeing regular outsiders, they had been traders; since these nomadic people were known for being excellent fishers, trappers, guides and hunters of the large mammals whose migrations they followed, the Tolgarr had a lot to offer. But they could see that these new people were no traders.

Not all the Tolgarr were bitten by curiosity. However, many continued with their chores, repairing equipment and mending clothes, smoking meats and preserving other foods in preparation for their journey south, which would be upon them in no time. The dwellings of the nomads were round tents covered with skins and felt. Tension bands were used to give the structure strength. There were many such buildings of various sizes and uses; some were warehouses for food, grain or livestock, others for storing weapons and other materials; the majority of them however, were living abodes, giving some idea of the size of the Tolgarr population.

Having all dismounted, Tawani led Finn, Daniel and the others to the largest structure within the encampment, where day to day dealings were over seen by the chief and his dignitaries. By the time the procession reached its destination, they had gathered quite a number of inquisitive citizens who remained outside the huge tent, hoping to hear some of the goings-on and find out who the four strangers were.

'Chief Crellis,' Tawani announced with a deep bow. 'I present to you the strangers I sent word of.'

It had been so long since they had laid eyes on one another, so many years had passed so much experience of life gained. Finn had often wondered how she would react, as well as what her feelings would be, if they ever did meet again; would she be angry and bitter because of the choice he made or would her heart pound so much for her first love that it would burst from her chest.

The man before them was slumped in his throne, head turned to one side listening to one of the four women that flanked him. He nonchalantly looked up at the new people, no doubt more merchants looking to trade. When he saw the purple and violet hair, he immediately sat up and leaned forward, his eyes wide, in an instant, he lost interest in what was being said to him and the people around him. Chief Crellis only had eyes for one person. 'Finn,' he breathed. 'Is it really you?'

Chapter Twenty-Eight
The Thief of Hearts

Finn should have been angry with him. She had given him her heart, and he had taken it only to discard it the moment the throne of the Tolgarr came calling. Finn had been crushed by his decision. So much so that, for many years after, she had sworn off love altogether, finding temporary solace from the pain in the arms of numerous boys and girls alike.

Finn had always been a physically tough girl, but the rejection of love had hardened her emotionally. It wasn't until Daniel came along that she was once more able to truly feel love again. She should have hated him, should have been angry with him... but how could she be when the butterflies in her stomach were starting up again, and he looked the way he did?

His well-muscled physique was more defined than it had been when she had last seen him. Crellis had also shaved off his hair and grown a beard that was neatly trimmed in that time. Finn had to admit that they both suited him, as did the tribal tattoos that adorned his glistening dark skin and marked him out as the chief of the Tolgarr.

He eased out of his throne and walked towards Finn, like a lithe predator. His gaze never left her, his hazel eyes piercing into her as they always had in the past. The moment he stood before her, they greeted each other in the traditional Tolgarr way. As their foreheads touched, Finn distinctly heard him take in-breath.

'Today is truly a blessed day,' Crellis said in a deep voice Finn had yet to hear. 'Finn Jesson walking into my hall was the last thing I expected to see when I woke up this morning. But I must say that it is a very pleasing sight.

So, I was told that someone travelling with you has made a promise to my long-passed grandmother.'

'Hmm?' Finn answered, startled by the question. She hadn't stopped admiring the changes the chief had been through, and him smiling down at her didn't help matters either. 'Oh, right. Yeah, yeah of course,' she stammered and eagerly waved Daniel over, glad for the limelight to be taken off of her; she could feel her face heating up, especially when she realised that she was introducing her first love to her, although unrequited, current love.

'There are actually a couple reasons why we are here, highness,' Daniel said as he retrieved, from his pocket, the peridot crystal Trinity had given to him. This little gem had really been the thing that kickstarted his journey into this world of magic and faeries. It was with this gem that he had first seen a fae, that gnarled faced hobthrust in his school library. Then it had become useful in another way.

Crellis took the offered gem and peered into it. A look of shock swept over his face. 'Is that...?' He glanced up at Daniel and then back to the gem. 'What have you done to my grandmother!'

The guards, upon hearing their chief in an agitated state, immediately drew their weapons and surrounded the group. Finn tried to keep the peace and calm the situation, but it wasn't until Daniel cut in and explained exactly what had transpired within the Shade, that the tension was somewhat alleviated.

Crellis gestured for his head shaman, Milangi, to step forward and he handed the gemstone to him. 'See what you can do about releasing her. For your sake, Daniel Welsh, I hope that my grandmother can verify exactly what you have told me. If I find that Aradia was indeed imprisoned against her will, then you will find that my hospitality will be vastly changed, and not even Finn will be able to stop it.'

After the group were brought to an abode, to wait and relax, the thought that this surprisingly comfortable home could soon be transformed into a prison made Philip decidedly unsettled. 'I am coming to the conclusion, Daniel,' he said, pacing up and down with his arms crossed, 'that deciding to spend the summer with you and your friends may not have been one of my best ideas. Holidays are there for relaxing, sleeping too much, eating too much and having lots of fun! Being hexed, almost kidnapped, fought a spectral banshee, and now I'm a prisoner of the Tolgarr!'

'We're not prisoners,' Daniel reassured him. 'It's just a misunderstanding, and when Aradia is freed, we'll ask her about helping Anjunel.'

'Besides, nobody wanted you here; you all but invited yourself,' Finn added. 'I've had a great time, and it would have been a whole lot better if you weren't here.'

'Of course, you've had a great time. Those bandits were probably friends of yours, and I'm sure your good friend Crellis won't let anything happen to you, no matter what happens to us.'

'What's that supposed to mean?'

'Oh, come on; we all saw the way he was looking at you, touching you. You're the kind of person that would cut a deal for yourself the rest of us stranded!'

'No, just you,' she corrected in such a way that gave him no doubt that her words were the truth.

This was the final straw for the usually cool-headed Philip, and he lunged at Finn, much to the surprise of Daniel, who grabbed hold of his academy mate to save him from Finn rather than the other way around.

'Let him go, Daniel. I've wanted to teach him this lesson for a long time,' she smiled.

Just then, to the relief of Daniel, Tawani knocked and entered. 'Chief Crellis would like to see you.' Daniel released Philip, and both Finn and Anjunel stood, and they all prepared themselves to leave, but the captain of the guard set them straight. 'He has asked to see just Finn.' Philip put on his best I told you so face and retreated to a corner in a huff as Finn reluctantly left with the captain.

As they approached the grand hall once more, Finn asked the burning question, although in the back of her mind, she already had an idea. 'What's this about, Tawani? Has Milangi been able to release Aradia already?' She sounded hopeful.

'No, and I'm sure you know exactly what he wants,' he replied somewhat coolly, something she picked up on.

'Is something wrong?'

'I don't want you getting back with Crellis,' Tawani replied.

'What?' It was as she had feared. He had seen the attraction still there in her eyes. Finn's mind raced to find a way out of the predicament that she was about to walk in to. But then something she hadn't been expecting happened.

'If you were mine, Finn, I would never have left you the way my brother did. I would have chosen you over the throne. I was hoping that I would one day meet again so that you could see the kind of man I have become.'

'And a fine man you have become, Tawani.'

'Fine enough for you?'

'Well, no, because—,'

'You still love Crellis.'

'What? No, because,' Finn felt the ring in her pocket and an idea popped into her head. 'Because I'm married. Yes, I'm married! Married to Daniel! I am married to Daniel.'

'Why didn't you say something earlier? I would have kept my mouth shut,' he said, embarrassed. 'So, you're Finn Welsh, then?'

'No, it's Finn Mondragon, actually.'

'Mondragon? As in...'

'Yup! The great Eric Mondragon is his father,' Finn smiled.

'Well, I guess it would take someone of that status to snag you, Finn.' Tawani opened the door of the great hall and ushered his old friend inside. 'You should know that my brothers' attitude to not getting his way has not lessened with the passage of time.'

SOME OF THE TORCHES that were lit when Finn and the others had been in the hall earlier were now extinguished, making the lighting that was left very atmospheric. She stepped forward, seeing Crellis standing by his throne. 'Do you want me to light some of these torches for you,' she asked as innocently as she could.

'No, I had them put out. This is all the light we need. You look very desirable in this light. Even more so than before.'

'I'm surprised you can see me at all,' she joked.

'Then let me come closer then.'

'That's ok, you don't have to,' she replied, but all too late as his swift strides brought them uncomfortably close to her. She could feel his breath on her face, and she fought to compose herself. Only he and Daniel had ever made her this flustered. 'So, four wives, huh?' She needed to shift his attention off of her.

'And not a single one of them is a patch on you, Finn.'

'Tell me something I don't know.' It was an involuntary brag, things that are like second nature to the thief and come as easily to her as breathing. Playing down her own unique qualities, however, were not. 'My husband is a patch on you, though.'

'You? Finn Jesson is married? I seem to recall you hating the very idea.'

She flashed the ring on her finger. 'It's Finn Mondragon now. Yeah, I wasn't a fan of marriage, but Daniel wooed me, and I couldn't resist,' she explained.

'I could see that there was something between you. I am happy for you.'

The ring suddenly tightened on her finger, momentarily, before returning to normal. She looked quizzically at it for a second.

'Is something wrong?'

'No, no. Just admiring my ring. So, four lovely wives. Wow! If I'd known, I would have sent wedding gifts,' she jested. 'So, any kids?'

'Eleven. Seven girls and four boys.'

'Man, you've been busy.'

'The duty of the chief. But seeing you again, all the feelings that were once there, feelings for you, have come back, stronger than ever.' Crellis suddenly pulled Finn towards him and kissed her hard, which took her breath away as she responded. She hated to admit it, but it was good. Better than what she remembered. But that didn't change the fact that their futures lay in different directions.

'We can't do this,' she gasped, eventually breaking away.

'Come on, Finn. I know you felt it; you want this as much as I do. I know now that I made a mistake all those years ago. I should have asked you to come with me?'

Again, the ring on Finn's finger tightened and then released again.

'Would you have accepted?'

'We'll never know now.'

'But now that Aradia is back, I could step down. We could do what we should have done from the beginning; we could leave together.'

The ring squeezed her finger. 'And what about your wives and children? You chose your people over me before. Why is it so easy to leave them now? What about the duty you spoke of?'

'I love you, Finn and I will have you back, I vow it.'

'But you have your wives, and I have Daniel.'

'Leave him, and we can be together again.'

'I enjoyed the time we had, but that's just it – HAD. I wouldn't leave anyone for you.'

'Very well,' he said resignedly. His mood had changed. A darkness had come over his face. 'If you will not leave him, then I will just have to take what I want and prove that I am the one you should be with. Have you forgotten the ways of the Tolgarr people, Finn? Tell your husband that, in the morning, I will challenge him for the position of your alpha.'

Chapter Twenty-Nine
An Important Lesson Learned

Daniel paced back and forth. He hadn't stopped doing it since Finn returned and told them what had happened with Crellis. It was the last thing that he was expecting to hear, but he didn't know why; this was Finn, after all. 'So, you told him we're married?'

'After everything I told you, after telling you that he's challenged you, that he kissed me, the only thing that's reverberating around your head is the fact that I told him that we're married? It's not as if it's a huge leap from the truth, is it?'

'Finn!'

'What? Come on, Danny, you know that there'll always be a spark between us,' she said with a wink. 'Even Crellis saw it, and I thought that it might dissuade him from his advances, but no.'

'Now I have to fight him for our fake marriage.'

'Think of it as protecting my virtue.'

Daniel scoffed. 'Virtue? I think you lost any you had left a long time ago.'

'Whatever.'

'Besides, I don't want to fight anyone.'

'Don't worry, it's not like it's to the death or anything. Well, not usually. So just rest up, and you'll be fine, Daniel.' Finn stretched out on a bed and patted the space next to her. 'Now,

you should sleep over here, next to me, just in case a guard comes; it wouldn't do for the loving married couple to be seen sleeping separately.'

THE NEXT MORNING ARRIVED with Daniel having had very little sleep. His mind wouldn't settle, and he had tossed and turned most of the time. If Finn hadn't been such a heavy sleeper, Daniel was certain that he would have woken her. Standing at the entrance watching Anjunel go through her morning stretching routine was almost therapeutic to him, even if he didn't participate.

He was feeling just as much pressure as he had during his Adept Standard Exams back at Hartfield Mage Academy. The only difference being that had been a structured exam, whereas what he was about to face this morning was tantamount to a duel. And the idea of that brought back images of his almost disastrous exam duel against Andrew Wilson.

It had gotten out of hand and, if it hadn't been for Gydion's timely return, lives could have been lost. It really brought home the words of the prophecy to Daniel. All the speculation about whether he was the destroyer or if it was his offspring troubled him, more than he allowed others to see.

He wondered what it would be like if everyone knew about Queen Rhiannon's dream and not just the select few that did. Would they fear him, like some at Hartfield did; consider him to be incredibly powerful and just as dangerous.

There was a huge difference between being feared and respected. Now that Daniel was away from the academy environment, he could reflect on what Finn had told him and what he was too blinded to see himself. The students adored him, but as she had said, they did so because they feared him. And that was down to one person.

'Why do you look so worried, Daniel?' Philip said as he joined Daniel in the doorway. 'You don't seriously think that this guy can beat you?'

'He's the chief of his people, that must carry some weight.'

'I'm sure it does, but you're the shining star of Hartfield, my friend.'

'The star that's hated,' revealed Daniel.

'What are you talking about? Don't you remember how they were all cheering your name?'

'Probably because they were scared that I'd do to them what I did to Andrew.'

'And?'

Daniel was shocked by Philip's callous response. 'What do you mean "and"?'

'You need to recognise what world you're in, Daniel. This is the world of magic, and you are a student of the arcane. In this world, the one that has the power has respect. That's how the hierarchy of a magocracy works.'

'A what?'

'It's the rule where those that can dominate over those that can't, as decreed by the elven queen. A magic user has an immediate advantage, and his status is determined by the power he wields. There are some cities on Ariest where this is strictly adhered to. At Hartfield, you are at the top of that tree. They may fear you, but they also undoubtedly respect you.'

Those that can do magic have a higher status than those that don't? He hadn't really seen any evidence to that end. Although, now that he thought about it, he had received looks when people found out that he was a Mage, even when he stood in front of King Noi D'Laani in Pichini Palace, when he was in Murias City. Just because you don't use magic, your standing counts for less, as if you're some sort of lower class. How is that fair? It just didn't sit right with Daniel. And he didn't believe he was the only one. Someone like Sayyidah should love the idea of a magocracy, should be thriving under it, but she believed that people should be allowed to reach their full potential.

Magic for all was not such a crazy idea.

THE GUARDS LED DANIEL and the others to the makeshift arena, which was nothing more than a large rope laid in a circle in a clearing in the back of the Tolgarr encampment. Finn explained that it didn't need to be anything more, as it was only really used for combat training; things like this alpha contest were few and far between.

The whole of the Tolgarr tribe surrounded the ring. Daniel had flashbacks to when he had entered the academy arena, but that day he had people cheering him, today it would just be Finn, Anjunel and Philip, thankfully in that order so that Finn and Philip didn't continue their scuffle from last night.

Suddenly, the Tolgarr began to rhythmically stomp their feet and chant. It was a deafening sound that signalled the arrival of their chief, Crellis. The crowd parted, and he walked imperiously to the ring, led by two guards. He was an imposing figure, making Daniel look no more than a child next to him. That fact was even more evident when they came face to face in the centre of the ring.

With Daniel being a similar height to Finn, when Tawani brought the two combatants together, it really did look like a man versus a boy. He swallowed and looked over at Finn who, smiled broadly and gave him two thumbs up. Daniel wished he could have just an ounce of her attitude; he was sure that she could overcome many an obstacle with just her willpower and unwavering belief in herself.

'This alpha contest,' Tawani shouted, at which point the crowd fell silent. 'This alpha contest is for the hand of Finn Mondragon. She is the betrothed of one and desired by another.' The captain pointed at Daniel then Crellis, respectively. 'As is the custom of our tribe, if one believes they are a better match, they must fight to prove it. As the fourth chief's wife proved herself. The winner while be the first to make his opponent submit, unable to continue or knocked from the ring.'

'I've been wondering why she's been glaring at me,' Finn whispered to Anjunel. 'Don't worry, Madame Chief!' Finn yelled across the ring. 'Me and your husband is never going to happen! I'd bet everything I have on it!' An idea suddenly struck Finn. She scanned the crowd until she found the person she was looking for, the book maker. 'Don't go anywhere; I'll be right back,' she said and disappeared through the crowd.

'If both combatants are ready, you may step back to the ring edge, and the contest will start with my signal.'

Daniel walked slowly back to his friends and tried to figure out what his next course of action should be. He was still reluctant about the whole thing, but he couldn't avoid it now. 'I think I'm just going to walk out of the ring,' Daniel said to no one in particular.

Just then, Finn came barging through the crowd. 'No, you can't do that! If you refuse to fight, you lose your wife.'

'I don't have one.'

'And you never will with that kind of attitude. Now go out there and make me some money,' she said, patting his back.

'What?'

'I said get out there and fight for your wife.'

As Daniel turned around to face Crellis, he recalled all the information he could about shamans. Aradia had told him that they have a larger Essence pool but can only use realmic spells, meaning they take longer to cast but tend to be more powerful. They commune with the spirits and natural elemental energies and, through these powerful mystical links, shape and influence the world around them. When he had read that in the library textbooks, he hadn't thought that he'd be seeing a shaman's magic so up close and personal. He was only supposed to deliver a gem.

'Combatants ready? Fight!'

Daniel's heart was already pounding as he watched Crellis going through the motions of casting a spell. The young Mage immediately threw up his Mage armour, it was something that had become an instinctive action after all the drills he had put himself through, with Sara Yacon's help, after his first day at Hartfield.

Four elliptical shapes of swirling energy appeared around the chief. They rotated around him, and Daniel could see that they were the shaman's elemental totems; fire, water, earth, air.

Every now and then, each totem would attack, a fireball, a lightning bolt, a rock boulder, a jet of water, but Daniel evaded each attack that could and let his armour take the brunt of those that he couldn't. But Daniel still refused to mount any attack, such was his reluctance to fight.

This fact frustrated several people in attendance, each for their own unique reasons, Finn, Philip but more surprisingly, Crellis. The challenge was intended to show Finn that her heart belonged to him, despite her refusal, and he knew just how to do it, once and for all.

Crellis had been secretly training and was well on the way to becoming a summoner, a practitioner of the arcane arts specialised in beckoning a monster from the farthest reaches of the realms to do his bidding. The spell, an entreaty of sorts, was lengthy, but with his totems refreshed and continuing to attack, he was able to complete it unhindered.

Suddenly, there was movement in the crowd and familiar if weak voice could be heard coming from the commotion. Eventually, Milangi pushed a hole through to ring and cleared a way for Aradia. 'Stop this, at once!' But they had arrived too late.

A crackling portal opened before the Tolgarr Chief and rapidly grew in size. And what stepped through was a monstrous, hairy, nose-less, humanoid with iron fangs and muscular limbs, the end of which were powerful, hooked iron claws. Where ever it had been dragged it, it wasn't happy, and it let out a bone-rattling roar.

Chapter Thirty

The Magical Journey

There were audible gasps when the creature with the shaggy, reddish hair had appeared. These quickly turned to panicked screams when it became evident that Chief Crellis was not in total control of his summoned monster. Instead of attacking only Daniel, it leapt into the crowd and attacked everyone nearby.

'What are you doing!' Daniel screamed at Crellis. He couldn't believe the carnage. Bodies were flying everywhere, and try as he might, the Tolgarr Chief couldn't dismiss the animal.

The beast lashed out with its claws, this way and that, taking down a number of Tolgarr. It clamped its vicious fangs into another victim and drank its blood. The chaos was building and it all but saw the end of the alpha contest.

Crellis redirected his totems, having given up on trying to send the animal back, he now focussed on killing it. Daniel may not have wanted to partake in the duel, but there was no way he was about to stand by and let innocent people be mauled to death. He raised his Essence and prepared to take down the raging animal.

'Well, since I won't be making any money on the outcome of that little fight, it would seem like the gods have given me a way to make my money after all,' Finn said as she and the others joined Daniel in the ring. 'If I'm not mistaken, that's an Asanbosam, and those fangs and claws are worth a pretty penny.'

'We're not killing it,' replied Daniel. 'It didn't come here by choice, so why should it pay for someone else's actions? How is it fair that it should be punished for something that was out of its control?' The parallels weren't lost on Daniel. The hidden magical caste system of Ariest had put a blight on this world in his mind.

'Ok, so how are you going to stop it?'

'You stop your boyfriend, and I'll stop the beast.' Daniel ran towards the Asanbosam, grinning as he heard Finn swear and scream that Crellis wasn't her boyfriend.

Tolgarr guards were already in position, some cleared the people whilst others let loose volleys of arrows. Time was running out for Daniel to do something as he saw more shaman on their way to take down the Asanbosam. Fireballs and lightning bolts had stopped hitting the creature. Crellis was laid out at the feet of the ever-reliable Finn. Now Daniel had to do his part.

Seeing the chief out like that reminded Daniel of the night they had spent in the cabin, in particular the scroll that had been used against them. Although that sleep scroll worked differently than the spell he had read in class, Daniel knew that the effect would be exactly the same.

He began to draw upon the Essence reservoir in his chest, allowing the mystical energy to flow down his arms, into his hands as he traced the arcane sigils in the air and recited the necessary words of power. As he completed the spell, Daniel pursed his lips and blew toward the animal. A large billow-ing cloud of sparkling blue vapour left his mouth, completely surrounding the rampaging beast, halting it in its tracks. Seconds later, it toppled heavily to the ground, fast asleep.

WITH THE HELP OF MILANGI, Crellis, sporting a bruised jaw, was eventually able to return the deep sleeping Asanbosam to the jungles from whence it came. Once he had done that, he had to take care of chiefly duties, seeing to the injured and paying respects. Daniel and the others helped where they could, but soon he received a summons from Aradia.

'Firstly,' she said after he had arrived at the hall. 'I want to thank you for your assistance in dealing with that beast. Secondly, I want to thank you for fulfilling your promise to me. And lastly, I want to apologise for my ignorant grandson. It seems that his time as chief has not made him any less impulsive than he was as a child. Perhaps he could learn from you, young Daniel, because it seems as though you are a different boy than when we last spoke; you are becoming a man. Although you seem to be a troubled one.'

Daniel took the opportunity to explain everything that had happened to him since they had last seen each other; from killing the Shade that had entrapped them, to his apparent death at the hands of multiple Shade on Earth. From being told that he was the Mortokai and what that meant to the foreshadowed return of Baelthorn, Sayyidah and the death of Trinity. From the voice, he had heard to his first days at Hartfield Mage Academy. He also explained to her the situation with Anjunel and how Gydion told him that she might be able to help.

'My, my, my,' Aradia said as she poured Daniel and herself another of the fruit herbal beverage they had been drinking, their third since his arrival. She said it was a restorative, used to help her depleted Essence. He didn't know if it worked or not, but Daniel did like the taste of it. 'You have had quite the adventures, haven't you? And Gydion was right, if anyone can help your friend, it'll be me. Although I don't profess to know a lot about Krez physiology, it should be possible to make a sort of synthetic replacement.'

'That's great news!'

'She'd have to remain here, of course, so we can try the samples on her.'

'To be free of the fear she has inside her and the hold of The Quelling, I'm sure that she is willing to do anything.'

'It'll be good to be able to actually do something and catch up on the world since I've been gone. However, if I'd known that harpy Sayyidah was back, I might well have stayed in that gem of yours. Oh, which reminds me.' Aradia tossed the peridot gem to Daniel. 'I thought you might be wanting that back.'

'I wasn't sure if I'd see this again,' said, looking over the perfect gem. 'Well, not in this condition anyway. I've kind of grown attached to it.'

'Perhaps you could fashion it into something. A magic ring perhaps, or a necklace.'

'I can't even conjure up a familiar, and yet you think I can craft enchanted items?'

'Of course, you can! You've come a long way since I first saw you, my boy. Low-level familiars are easy to summon; that's why it is one of the first spells taught, no matter what school of magic you come from. You have to realise that the power of the familiar grows in tandem with that of the caster. So, considering the levels of Essence you possess, I'm not surprised you have had trouble calling it since you never bonded as a child. But there is a way.'

'Really? Tell me how.'

'You must travel to the realm of the familiars, confront and compel it. Do not show fear. Be confident in yourself and who you are.'

Daniel nodded. 'So how do I get to the familiars; realm?'

'The Tolgarr way; you spirit walk.' Aradia spoke some words under her breath before clapping her hands, at which point a smoking brazier appeared in front of Daniel. 'Breathe deeply, my boy. Take it in.'

He looked at her cockeyed for a moment but eventually did as she asked; he put his head into the plumes of smoke and took a deep breath. As Daniel had half expected, nothing happened, and he sat back.

Then the world began to swirl, and he collapsed.

HE FELT LIKE HE WAS falling, only upwards. The sensations he was experiencing was similar to those he had gone through when he had taken the magical journey from Liverpool Street underground station and arrived in Ariest all those months ago.

Images appeared before him only to fly past his vision seconds later. Places he had been and some he hadn't, one looked surprisingly like Egypt. There were faces too, some recognisable, such as Solomon, and others not.

He didn't know exactly how long it took, but in the blink of an eye, Daniel had landed in a heap on a soft tufted hillock. It was night, and a huge full moon shone down on him. There were clusters of wildflowers everywhere, primrose, bluebells, marigold, foxglove, clover, and the herbs made the air wonderfully fragrant. The oak, ash and hawthorn trees that were there were strong and vibrant. It was almost like he had landed in a picture-perfect forest.

'Fisama know you,' said a high-pitched voice. 'You're Sara's friend, Daniel.'

Daniel looked around and saw nothing at first, then a little male figure, with wispy, moth-like wings, slowly materialised in front of Daniel. 'Fisama? What are you doing here?'

'What Fisama doing here? What are you doing here more like? This is where Fisama from; what's your excuse?'

'I was sent here to find my familiar.'

'Sent here? Oh, you seek Gabinestra!'

'Gabi who?'

'Oh, Fisama did it this time,' a female sprite with bright green hair said as she fluttered around Daniel's head.

'Fisama really gone and done it this time, numbskull,' another female sprite said, this one with shocking-pink hair. 'Fisama know outsiders are not allowed unless invited by their familiar.'

'And he doesn't look like Sara to Mitzee.'

'Trixee neither.'

'That's because he's not,' Fisama answered. 'Look, Mitzee, Trixee, Fisama didn't bring him here, Fisama just found him. He said he was sent here. Fisama think he's here for Gabinestra.'

'Another one? Great! There'll be a stench from days. Mitzee be sure to stay away from the mountain this time, so it doesn't get in Mitzee lovely hair,' she said as she affectionately fluffed her green hair.

'Trixee don't know, Mitzee,' the pink-haired sprite responded as she scrutinised Daniel closely. 'There's something about this one.'

'Fisama going to take him there now!' he announced excitedly.

'Just you be quick about it,' Mitzee said. 'If the elders find out, we'll all be in for it.'

'Then we'll have to deal with mum and dad too,' Trixee added.

'We siblings need to stick together,' Fisama replied. 'Fisama won't tell if Mitzee and Trixee won't. Come on, Daniel, let's go.'

THE HIKE THROUGH THE strange land was a short but eye-opening one, and not too arduous either. Even though Fisama had said that they'd be able to make it to their destination without being confronted, that didn't mean they weren't being watched; several times, Daniel had seen bright tiny eyes blinking in the darkness. They passed circles made of darkened moss, walked down narrow pathways until they arrived at where they needed to be.

'This is it,' Fisama said, pointing to a cave entrance.

'Are you sure?' Daniel looked less than convinced. Trees had almost taken over the opening. The roots of the trees on top had sprouted through the roof, weaving around each other to create organic pillars of nature.

The Mage walked closer, with Fisama fluttering beside him, and gazed into the cave, through the gaps and cracks between the roots. Ice-covered the ground, icicles hung from the roof, suggesting that it was a glacier cave, but there were some peculiar scorch marks around the inside of the cave mouth.

After finding a gap large enough got him to squeeze through, Daniel edged his way inside, contorting his body to gain entrance. In the back of his mind, he hoped all this effort would be worth it in the end.

'So, who or what is a Gabinestra?' Daniel asked Fisama as he cleared the last root. He had seen so many different weird and wonderful familiars at Hartfield that he couldn't help but wonder what he'd be getting himself. It was only then that he noticed that Sara's familiar hadn't even followed him in. 'What are you doing back there?'

'Fisama wait over there. Not go inside. Fisama don't want to be collateral.'

'What did you say?' Before he could get an answer, the little fae flew off, leaving Daniel alone. He watched the fast-retreating familiar, then turned and continued down the ice passage.

Something was off, he could feel it, but he couldn't explain it. It wasn't cold, despite slipping on the ice a few times, and putting his hand on the frost-covered walls to steady himself, it wasn't uncomfortable.

Even though the lighting was poor, and it got poorer the further he went, he could still see some of the strange scorch marks similar to the ones he had seen at the entrance. What made them odd was that the marks seemed to be encased in ice, as if the fire had instantly been supercooled.

Daniel rounded a bend and saw a glow up ahead in the distance. He picked up his pace, eager to reach it and see what it was. But almost instantly tripped over something in the dim light. On his hand and knees, he spun around to see what it was and wished he hadn't. They were bodies incredibly burnt by both fire and ice.

The young Mage reeled back in horror, wondering how such a thing could be possible. He clambered to his feet, trying desperately to erase what he had just seen from his mind as he ran and ran until he came to a screeching halt upon entering the glowing chamber. Daniel's jaw dropped at the tremendous sight before him.

The unearthly glow he could see was coming from the bioluminescent aquamarine life that floated in the lake. The moonlight, which shone through the large cracks in the cave roof, high above, gave the algae the energy it needed to give off their eery radiance. But this natural occurrence wasn't the cause of Daniel's sudden palpitations.

A huge, sleek, silvery-white dragon lay curled up in the centre of a lake. Its over lapping scales resembled that of a gleaming armour, and its long tail vibrated like a rattlesnake. He had never thought that he would ever see a dragon, and if he did, he never fathomed how he would react. Of all the impossible, improbable and unbelievable things Daniel had seen since he first arrived in this fantastical world, this was top of the list, by far.

All of a sudden, the dragon got to its feet, reared up and spread its bat-like wings, flapping them a few times, displaying a magnificent, intimidating span. 'Who disturbs the slumber of Gabinestra,' the dragon roared.

Chapter Thirty-One
Gabinestra, The Last Dragon

Each word rattled Daniel's insides as he stood there like a deer in headlights. Surely Aradia must have known what he would face? Why else would she have told him not to show fear? In his mind, he had the thought that he would be facing a bird, a cat, or even a ferret, in fact, any of the multitudes of other creatures that have been spying on him since his arrival here. Then sure, no fear? No problem. But this was a dragon! A big, big, dragon that didn't like to be woken by the sounds of things.

'Be confident in yourself and who you are,' Daniel whispered to himself and let out a deep breath.

Gabinestra scoffed. 'And who is it that you think you are, little man?'

'Think? Well, I know who I am,' answered Daniel, rather more indignantly than he had intended, possibly because she had overheard him. 'You may be an intimidating sight, but I haven't lost all of my faculties. I am Daniel, and I believe that you are my familiar.'

The dragon roared with laughter. 'Another foolish mortal, on another foolish quest.'

'I'm not on any quest.'

'You didn't hear about this place in some legend?'

'Nope. Actually, you should know that I'm not from around here. I'm from a place called Earth.'

'I've heard of it,' she replied, settling down, intrigued by what she was hearing. 'Do continue.'

'On my world, there is no magic, but when I came to Ariest and started to learn magic, I wasn't able to summon a familiar, even though I can do so much more.'

'I see.' Her eyes narrowed. 'A Mage without a familiar?'

'I know. I was sent here to confront and compel my familiar.'

'And what made you come to me?'

'Fisama, the sprite.'

'That meddlesome creature,' she snarled. 'None may compel me save the Mortokai. I must wait for them; that is my penance. All other trespassers must die.'

Without warning, Gabinestra opened her mouth wide, and a glow that began in her stomach rapidly rose through her neck, erupting from her maw. Flame burst forth, bolts of ice spiralling around, aimed directly at Daniel. He had no time to react and was completely engulfed by it.

When the attack ceased, Daniel stood there, panting, heart rate racing, but unharmed.

'My magic is only ineffectual against the Mortokai,' Gabinestra explained. 'Those before claimed to be the one, but I am glad to finally make your acquaintance.'

'You... you tried to kill me!'

'I cannot kill you. My frostfire will not harm you,' she said as she stretched. 'It was a test, nothing more. Only those that make false claims die.'

It was the kind of extreme tactic that Daniel could envisage Finn using. Could he really handle another person like that in his life, he wondered?

'Who is Finn?' asked Gabinestra suddenly.

'You can read my mind?' Daniel exasperated.

'Yes, we can communicate telepathically.'

'So, you could have just looked in my head and seen the truth instead of trying to fry me?'

'Not quite. There is an imbalance within you, which you must address. That is why I could not tell. Just as it is the remit of the Mortokai to keep balance within the realms, you must also keep the balance within yourself.'

'The chaotic magic is so easy to perform.'

'And that is its lure. You humanoids tend to express and cling to your feelings of hatred and negativity with far more relish and belief than you do those of love and positivity. However, do not succumb to either, Daniel. Your humanity is what defines you, not the Mortokai power. Balance is key, it is everything.'

'I must be the Spell Sage as well as the Harbinger.'

'Exactly. But I will help and guide you. I was spared for this reason.'

'Spared from what?'

'Death. I am the last of the Tuatha. I foolishly fought alongside Baelthorn against my brothers and sisters. I saw that it was a lost cause and abandoned them, changed my guise and lived among the humanoids of the new worlds. Until I was summoned by Methys and told that Baelthorn was no more and the Tuatha had decided to leave, but I had to remain, as I had another purpose.'

'Waiting for me,' Daniel replied. Gabinestra nodded. 'But you're not the last dragon. Baelthorn is still alive and intent on destroying the descendants of the Tuatha.'

'So, this is how my repentance is secured,' Gabinestra said wistfully, before determination returned to her voice. 'It is time to go, Daniel.' She lowered herself, allowing Daniel to climb onto her back. Gabinestra flapped her huge and took to the air, flying toward the roof of her cave. She unleashed her frostfire, pulverising the rock and created a large hole for her to pass through into the night sky. 'Your friends will no doubt be worried about you and we must begin your further education immediately, if what you say about Baelthorn is true.'

'What are you talking about? I've only been a few minutes. Why would they be worried?'

'Daniel, you have been sleeping for three weeks.'

DANIEL SUDDENLY SAT up straight in surprise. 'Three weeks?' He glanced around, wide-eyed. He was in a moving carriage. From what he could tell, Anjunel sat one side of him, Aradia the other. 'Has it really been three weeks?'

Aradia nodded. 'You were gone longer than I had anticipated. We couldn't wait any longer for you to wake, so we had to bring you along on our migration.'

'Don't worry about it, I understand. What about the others? Are they here too? And how are you, Anjunel?'

'I am fine. Aradia has made some progress, but she tells me that we have a long way to go. Finn took a horse and went on ahead to Ostina to rendezvous with Grimgaard,' Anjunel answered. 'She was reluctant to leave you but mentioned something about an errand for Gydion. Crellis insisted on going with her. Your friend has taken the carriage with a guard and headed back to Imperial City.'

'Gone back? Wait? If three weeks have passed, that must mean Hartfield will reopen any day now! I need to get back!' As Daniel made to get up from the cot he'd been lying in, he noticed, for the first time, that his clothes had been changed.

'Don't worry,' Aradia began, seeing Daniel start. 'I had a male guard wash and change you when necessary.'

'That was after Finn left,' the elf added. 'Before that, she insisted on doing it.'

Daniel was speechless but not completely surprised by the thief's actions; she was a law unto her own. He made a mental note to talk to her about boundaries the next time he saw her, for right now, though, he needed to get back to the academy.

A teleportation spell would have been just the ticket, but Gydion had warned him against using it until he had taught him the nuances of the spell. He had told Daniel that it was quite easy to find yourself materialising halfway through a wall, as many a student had met their fate before.

Luckily, Daniel had an alternative.

'Now, let's see if that little trip you sent me on was worth it, but first, we'll have to stop.'

Aradia opened the hatch to the carriage driver and told them to pull over as soon as they could, just as Daniel had requested. The driver signalled the other riders, and once the convoy had stopped moving, the three passengers disembarked.

Tall trees surrounding the meadow, butterflies and dragonflies flying here and there. They walked a bit away from the caravan, grass crunching underfoot until Daniel was satisfied. 'Ok, this should be enough.'

'Enough what?' Anjunel said, confused, looking around the meadow seeing nothing but animals and insects.

'Enough space for my familiar,' he answered proudly. 'I did as you said, Aradia. I went there confident in who I was and confronted my familiar. She will be able to get me back to Hartfield before the new term starts.'

Daniel began to focus on the arcane energy of his Personal Essence pool, then to perform the gestures, exactly as he had done on his first day at Hartfield Mage Academy in Penelope Pinnywickle's Summon Familiars class. That day nothing happened. This time he succeeded, although not quite in the manner he had been expecting. Gabinestra sat perched on his shoulder, roughly the size of a small chicken.

'Gabinestra? What's happened to you? Why are you so small?'

'I told you before, Daniel, I am not your familiar, but if you insist on calling me in that manner, then I will give you what you desire.'

'Well,' Aradia searched for the words. 'I am very pleased that you have finally been united with your familiar, Daniel. What a cute drake she is too, but I don't see how she will be able to help you get back in time.'

This slight was too much for the ancient dragon to bear, and she flew down to the ground. Her silver-white scales shimmered from front to back, and she rapidly grew in size until she was once more the impressive sight Daniel had seen.

'Is this the visage of a familiar?' Gabinestra stood tall and proud; the sun gleamed off of her scales. Daniel couldn't help but smile at seeing all the stunned faces in the meadow.

'We meant no disrespect, Great one,' Anjunel said with a bow.

'You count a Krez elf among your friends, Daniel? You accept people for who they are, despite what others think.' She seemed impressed. 'Maybe you can reach neutrality after all. I have much respect for your people and what they have been through, Anjunel Lynsu'unara.'

Daniel was about to ask how she knew the elf's name, then he remembered what had happened in the cave.

It was there in your mind like an open book. Gabinestra said telepathically. *For someone with such a capacity for magic, your fundamentals are
surprisingly lacking. You have your work cut out for you, Daniel, especially
if you are to fulfil the roles set out for you by Methys.*

'*Which is why I need to get back to Hartfield Academy in time, so I can
do just that,*' Daniel replied with a thought.

'Very well, little one. Climb up, and we will be off; it should take no more
than a day or two.'

'I'm sorry for having to leave you, Anju,' Daniel said, hugging the elf,
much to her surprise. 'I'm hoping that Finn and Grimgaard have travelled
back to Imperial City with Sara, and as soon as we can we will come back for
you.'

'I know you will, and thank you for getting me this chance to be free of
the Rising. I owe you a debt.'

'You owe me nothing, Anju, we're friends.'

'Don't worry about her, Daniel,' Aradia said. 'We will take care of your
friend as one of our own. I will send word to you the moment we have been
successful in finding a formula.'

With their final goodbyes said, Daniel climbed onto Gabinestra's back.
The mighty dragon beat her wings, wind and dirt buffeted the onlookers,
and the pair took to the sky, a magnificent sight heading towards Imperial
City.

Chapter Thirty-Two
The New Term Begins

True to her word, two days after leaving the Tolgarr, Gabinestra touched down in Imperial City, specifically the courtyard of Mondragon Estate. She had shrunk in size, to that of a griffin, as she came in to land, so as not to cause distress to those not used to seeing dragons flying over.

Daniel jumped down, allowing Gabinestra to revert to her small size and perch on his shoulder as he looked around at the work completed in his absence. It made an impression on him and was a much-welcomed sight from what it was. Quinn Jesson had done magic of a different sort.

'Come on, Quinn,' pleaded Finn. 'Why not?'

'Because it'll be too much work!' Quinn replied. 'The lower level isn't deep enough, and the excavation work alone would be difficult.'

'What's all the fuss about Finn?' Daniel hadn't been spotted by the bickering pair, but when Finn heard him, she rushed over excitedly. He was just as pleased to be reunited, his questions coming thick and fast. 'So, you made it to Ostia and back? How's Grimgaard? Did you meet with Milos Yacon? Were there zombie frost giants? Have you told Gydion yet?'

'Grimgaard is communicating with him now. Vekt, Daniel! I should kick your behind. I was so worried about you when we couldn't wake you up!' Finn didn't know whether to shake him or squeeze him, so she did both. 'At least it was worth it, I suppose. That *is* a pretty cool drake.'

'Her name is Gabinestra, and she's not a drake.' Daniel moved closer to Finn and added conspiratorially. 'She's a dragon.'

'What? A real dragon? But they've been gone for millennia. You have a dragon as a famil—'

Daniel slapped his hand over her mouth before she could finish.

'I prefer to be known as his companion,' the dragon replied. 'But I suppose I should get used to hearing this until the time when I can fully reveal myself.'

'Why hide at all?'

'Because many humanoids fear change.'

'Sometimes change is necessary,' Daniel said whimsically.

'To some, a returning dragon can only mean that they are there to exert its rule. Especially one that has attempted it in the past.'

'Well, Gabi, you've come to the right person when it comes to keeping secrets. I haven't told anyone that Daniel says my name in his sleep.'

'I do not!'

'Come on, Daniel, we've slept together several times now, so I think that I'm an authority on the subject.'

'What was that?' Quinn had finished taking measurements and had joined the others.

'We just shared a bed,' corrected Daniel. 'Nothing more.'

'Yeah, first as goddess and consort then as husband and wife.'

'What?' Quinn was even more uncomfortable than Daniel was.

'There is a reasonable answer for all of this,' began the young Mage, then he thought for a moment and realised something. 'Actually, no, there isn't. What I do know is that it was all Finn's fault, and she'd be glad to explain everything to you. Right, I need to get my trunk and head to Hartfield.'

'Your trunk? A funny thing happened with that yesterday morning,' explained Finn. 'So, I was woken up by this banging. Not all of us can have the sleep of the dead like Grimgaard. Anyway, I came down, and I saw your trunk charging the doors like a battering ram.'

'You're kidding?'

Finn shook her head. 'Nope, I'm not. When the Archers returned from the fish market, your trunk took the opportunity to escape. Hopefully, Joseph was right. He said that they're enchanted to return to Hartfield in time for the start of term.'

'It would have been nice if someone had told me,' Daniel huffed. 'I'll have to have words with Sara.'

'Speaking of Sara, something happened in Ostia. She—'

'No, time,' Daniel interrupted as he sprinted to the entrance. 'I need to get to the academy, but I'll contact you as soon as I can.'

Finn rolled her eyes and, with a sigh, headed back to the house.

THE BEGINNING OF TERM at Hartfield Mage Academy was a far different experience for Daniel than what he had witnessed at his first appearance at the celebrated school. Then, there had been just a few students milling about the front court of the academic complex. This time round, it was full of students and their families.

Fresh young Adepts were having teary farewells with parents, whilst others tried to put on a tough exterior and resented their parents' incessant pampering, not realising that they would be missing it soon enough. Older students reunited with friends they hadn't seen since before their holidays.

Daniel glanced up at the Hartfield insignia, the triangle with the three circles engraved above the entrance of the venerable building. He knew that it was supposed to represent the reservoirs Essence and the body of the student, but after hearing about the supposed magic caste system, from Philip, he believed that the circles could just as easily represent those that had magic, at the pinnacle and those that didn't at the bottom.

The way people looked at him, both students and parents alike, reminded Daniel of when he was here with Gydion when he had desired the same looks of adoration that the Archmage had received. Now he wasn't so sure he wanted them. Knowing it was down to a hierarchy of magical power instead of any real respect that had been gathered, as it was for his father. He had magic, so they had to hold him in high regard. It didn't feel the same as it would if he had earned it.

'Welcome back to Hartfield, Daniel,' Morgana Goodfellow smiled down at him with her ruby coloured eyes. The proctor wore her jet-black hair in a single long braid, which rested over her shoulder, as she stood with her hands on her hips and surveyed the scene before them. It was hard to tell if the students that passed the pair were dumbstruck by her statuesque beauty and lustrous skin or if they were star struck by the presence of Daniel Welsh, the Shade Slayer. 'You were lucky to miss this carnage last time,' she went on. 'This is my busiest period of the year for me; all these new students trying to test me, trying to see if the stories are real. Then they find out that everything they heard is true when I come down on their ill-discipline like a tonne of bricks.' The gleam in her eyes couldn't be hidden. It was evident that she enjoyed her role as proctor. 'Anyway, shouldn't you be heading off to join your Grade Head.'

'My What?'

'Oh, I forgot, you weren't here last time. Right, as each of the six grades have Alti Vex, they also have a Grade Head. Since you are now Adept Grade II, your Grade Head is Professor Pinnywickle. She's just over there,' the proctor indicated.

In front of the prodigy estate, which was the main building of Hartfield, either side of the stairs which led up to its entrance, were three groups of students. One was very regimented, the young Mages standing quietly in a neat column. At its head stood the no nonsense disciplinarian, Professor Tobias Law. He knew that this was the group of Novice Grade II students when he saw all three Yacon sisters and Philip lined up. He had a momentary urge to rush over and greet them all, but thought better of it.

'Begin the year as you mean to go on,' he said to himself, and that didn't involve getting on the bad side of Professor Law. Daniel continued to pass the remaining Grade Heads; professors Amy McGillicuddy, divination, Valeria Runelara, enchantment, Tremaine, evocation and Fijit Milton, magic 101, until he came to the other Adept Grade II students. There were a few that Daniel remembered from Adept Grade I and some that had failed their Grade II exams and hadn't made it to the Initiate level.

Professor Pinnywickle was already going around the group, testing everyone's ability to summon their familiar. Some were less than enthusiastic about it, saying it was "baby magic" whilst others enthused about showing off their mystic creatures. Daniel was reluctant to participate for his own reasons. He hadn't seen anyone with a drake here, let alone an actual dragon. Revealing Gabinestra now, with everybody in attendance, would elevate his standing within the magic community, something Daniel was loathed to do at present.

'Well, Daniel?' Professor Pinnywickle repeated after still not getting a response from the young man. 'Have you made any headway finding your familiar?'

'Uh...yes...yes I have,' admitted Daniel.

The voice of the ancient dragon suddenly sounded in his mind. *'I feel your reticence about doing this, Daniel, but you must realise that you are above them; you would be above the hierarchy of their magocracy if I was with you or not. These are the facts. You came to me accepting who you were, now you must prove it, be who you are supposed to be. Do not hide because of a flawed system.'*

Reluctantly he closed his eyes and was about to go through the motions of summoning a familiar, but stopped himself and sent a mental call to Gabinestra instead. He felt the sudden weight of the dragon on his shoulder and heard the gasps of his peers. *You're right, Gabinestra, the system is flawed, and as Martin Luther King said, "our lives begin to end the day we become silent about things that matter."*

FOR A NEW STUDENT, the first few days at Hartfield were not particularly strenuous. They consisted of nothing more than introducing yourself to your dorm mates and gauging their personality based on how they decorated their quarter of the room. Next, it was introducing yourself to your Grade Head, selecting the subjects you wished to study and, if you are so inclined, also putting your name forward for Altus Vex consideration. The final round of introductions went to the professors and classmates of all of your chosen subjects, where you would get your timetables and outline of the curriculum.

Those students who were into their second year or further had the added commitment of reuniting with friends, most of whom they hadn't seen since the end of the previous academic year.

'I should be mad at you for not coming to Ostia,' having caught up with him at lunch, Sara rebuked Daniel but still gave him a hug. 'You left me with my sisters for the entire summer.'

'I'm sorry. I really did want to see your village.'

'It's ok, I'll let you off; Finn explained everything. Besides, I don't know how I would have coped with Philip being there too.'

'Was the Lammas festival really that bad?'

'No! Quite the opposite. It was the best ever! Not only did Finn offer me a spot in the Legion of Heroes, which I accepted, I also got to go on a rescue mission with her, Grimgaard, and Crellis. And to top it all off, we kissed.'

'Who?'

'Finn and I.'

'What?' Daniel sputtered his drink.

'It took me by surprise too,' Sara smiled. 'I didn't think she felt the same way, but when Crellis was making advances towards me, she kind of swept in.'

Daniel put his head in his hands and sighed. It was another Finn-measure, an extreme measure that only a thief would consider taking. He assumed that this was what she was trying to tell him before he had left the estate.

There was reason behind her madness, though. Finn was no doubt protecting Sara from her ex, which in itself was an admirable thing. And how was she supposed to know that Sara had a liking for her when he himself didn't know.

'It does create a situation between us, however. You and me,' she explained, seeing Daniel's confusion. 'She told me that you two are married. I hope we can still be friends despite what happened.'

He threw his head back and groaned loudly.

'Finn said that she would talk to you about it.'

'Oh, we are going to talk alright,' he replied through pursed lips.

AFTER LUNCH, DANIEL and Sara went their separate ways, with the witch heading to Abjuration class and Daniel to Enchantment. He walked down the halls to class, blocking out the buzz of Hartfield: the students laughing, footsteps on the wooden floors, heavy doors banging shut. His mind was firmly focussed on one thing, the dilemma of righting the wrongs of the previous generations of Ariest and changing the mindset of the present ones, and if it really was his place to do so., and if he did, would it really make it a better world?

He turned the final corner to where his Enchantment class was held. The crowd of students lessened as they entered the lecture hall. That's when Daniel saw Philip among them. 'What are you doing here?'

'I've been waiting for you, of course. Come on, we have to go.'

'What are you talking about? I've got class.'

'No, you don't; you've been excused.'

'What? How?'

'That doesn't matter. The names of all those that were put forward for Altus Vex is on display in the foyer. Remember those boys you had trouble with last year?'

'You mean Andrew Wilson, Robert Masterson and Edward Sands? How could I forget? What's the problem? '

'They're in it too; one of my lackeys overheard them cooking up something.'

'Wait a minute, you have lackeys? Besides, I might not even draw any of them. I don't see the problem?'

'The thing about the Altus Vex competition is that it's not a tournament; it's a free for all, a battle royal. They'll be allowed to gang up on you.'

'Three on one?'

'No, all on one. They've been talking to the others. They all know you're the strongest, so if they eliminate you, their own chances of success go up.

'Daniel had to admit that it did make tactical sense. A force of superior numbers has been the deciding factor of many a battle throughout history, but crucially, not always. The Battle of Crecy and some seventy years later the Battle of Agincourt were two such occasions where armies outnumbered anywhere from 2:1 to 5:1 came out victorious.

'Maybe you should have a hit. You know, do some Essevate so that you're in tip-top condition.'

The temptation was there, he couldn't deny it. Just to feel those sensations again, the euphoria, the blissful freedom. But Daniel couldn't do it. He had made a promise, and he intended to stick to it, no matter how much he yearned for the elation EV could give him. But the possibility of losing his magic and himself was too high a price to pay. 'I think I'm going to pass. If the Altus Vex battle royal is tomorrow morning, then I'll be fine with some rest.'

Philip could barely hide his disappointment, and he left with a scant goodbye.

'Ah, Mr Welsh,' Professor Runelara said in her melodic elven tone. 'I was told that you would not be joining us today. I am so glad that will not be the case. Take a seat, and I will continue. As I was explaining, enchanting is more than just about exerting magical influence over someone...'

He sat down and took out his notebook. Daniel felt bad for letting down his friend, but he had made a promise to another friend. Someone who, although at times could be a pain, still meant a lot to him. There was no way he would tell Finn any of this, however, her head was big enough as it was.

Chapter Thirty-Three
The Key and What We Do for Love

If the first few days of the first term at Hartfield Mage Academy was not too strenuous for the students, then the first Friday morning of that first week was the complete opposite.

This was the day of the Altus Vex Battle Royals.

Six competitions, level one and two of the Adept, Novice and Initiate grades. There wasn't one for the High Mage Grade as they spent the majority of their time learning under their master.

Similar to the Test of Succession, where you could take your exam whenever you felt ready, if you felt you were capable, a student could compete in the contest for a higher grade, even though they study at a lower one. It wasn't unheard of for a group Altus to be made up entirely of lower grade students.

The academy was a hive of activity, everybody buzzing about, and since they would have no Altus Vex to assist them until next week, it was the professors themselves rushing around making sure that everything was as it should be.

Just like the end-of-year exams, these Mage battle royals were open to the paying public, and as usual it was a sold-out event. Friends and families of the participants were automatically sent complimentary tickets the moment students declared themselves for the position, and there was no way that Finn or Grimgaard were going to miss such an opportunity, they were even able to spring tickets for Quinn and the Archers when they mentioned Daniel's name, with Finn showing off the wedding ring which was becoming a very useful prop.

'These are some really good seats,' Finn said to Grimgaard, a broad grin on her face as she passed down the food she'd bought from the vendor. 'We'll be able to see all the action.'

Grimgaard squinted at Finn. 'What are you on about? Look at this place,' he gestured to the colosseum-like Hartfield arena. The tiered seating was full of fans, people sitting or standing shoulder to shoulder, holding up handmade signs of with the names of students on them. 'this place is designed so that every seat gets a good view.'

'Yeah, well, I'm sure our seats are more comfortable.'

Grimgaard rolled his eyes and lit his pipe, realising that there was no point arguing with the girl, especially over the crowd that was beginning to ramp up and chant as an announcement was made, calling for all grades of Altus Vex contenders to enter the ring.

The students hit the field, some bounding with energy, feeding off the capacity crowd, others with nervous strides, as they realised the mistake, they'd made by putting their name forward.

Despite what Philip had told him about the possibility of his competitors allying against him, Daniel, was still feeling rather good. This was what he had aimed for since his first day at Hartfield when Sara Yacon had told him about it, although it wasn't so much about the prestige and respect that someone in the role garnered. Not anymore. She had said that every Archmage had also been an Altus Vex. If he was to make real change in the future of Ariest, make society fair and equal, he would have to do so from a position of authority. Becoming Altus Vex was a step in that direction.

As the thousands of voices continued the din, their song swelling until the stands almost began to vibrate, Daniel looked around, hoping to see any of his friends, but found none. Now that they were in the same grade, he had half expected Sara to refuse to enter her name for fear of possibly having to face Cara and Mara; despite their differences, they were still sisters at the end of the day. But that didn't explain Philip's absence. What was his excuse for not going for pathetic prefect position again?

Although Daniel hadn't seen any of his schoolmates, he had noticed the royal elf guard in their distinctive armour. They were in greater number than they had been during the exam, no doubt in response to what happened that day.

A hush began to slowly descend over the audience, and Daniel followed the gaze of his compatriots to and saw headmaster Radek Zislaa making his way out. He came to a stop and held up his arms, eventually bringing complete silence to the arena, broken only by the occasional cough.

'I would like to welcome you all to Hartfield Mage Academy and to the annual Altus Vex competition!' The crowd erupted into applause. He put up his hands again and a quiet descended once more. 'For those in attendance for the first time, the rules are very simple; eliminate your opponents by forcing them through the magical barrier surrounding the ring. The final three students left within the ring will become this year's Altus Vex of their chosen grade.' The audience cheered again. 'As is the custom at Hartfield, an honorary guest will get the proceedings underway. It is a pleasure to introduce Grandmaster Kay Haichi.'

A chubby man of medium height walked purposefully out and stood beside the headmaster. The grandmaster stroked his long beard as the fans showed their appreciation for the appearance of such a legend. The journey to and from Kuai Quan Monastery was an arduous one. Situated far to the northeast of Ariest, hidden within the vast Spine of the Goddess mountain range, the pilgrimage to the sacred school was treated as a test of the individual's worthiness to enter its hallowed walls. The people knew this, some more than others. The ones called super fans.

As the audience quietened down, there was one person who continued to clap rapturously. Daniel didn't need to turn around to know that it was Finn, the gun-toting thief that had enough self-confidence to fill half the stadium and her "don't give a damn what people think of me" attitude could fill the other. Daniel smiled; you couldn't help but.

'Thank you,' the grandmaster said. 'Thank you kindly for such a welcome. I am sure that you are all eager and intrigued to see what kind of talent Hartfield is developing, as am I, so shall keep this brief. You students have got big dreams...you want fame, the accolades, the prestige. Well, this is where it begins. Your hard work, dedication, blood, sweat and tears will get you where you want to be. The more of each you are willing to commit to your dreams, the more chance you have of fulfilling them. It won't be easy, but Hartfield will bring the best out of every one of you, if you are willing to make the sacrifices necessary. For some of you, this will be your first battle within this arena, for others this is almost your last. Wherever you are on your journey, don't waste this opportunity to impress and express yourself. Do not let the sacrifices you have made be for nothing. Finally, good luck to all the Altus Vex contestants!'

As the crowd cheered, Daniel stood there in a trance. He barely heard Radek Zislaa call for the Initiate and Novice students to exit the ring. Hardly noticed the magical domed barrier erected over the ring. He scarcely perceived the headmaster shout begin! All because of what Grandmaster Kay Haichi had just said. The more he thought about it the more he was certain that it had to be correct, that he had finally figured out what the theme of the dreams were. Daniel knew the key to reviving Trinity!

'What the vekt is he doing?' Finn said, seeing her friend stock still. 'Was he hit by a spell or something?'

'I don't know, but he'd better snap out of it, or this will be all over before it's even begun,' replied Grimgaard.

A poorly aimed magic missile whizzed pass Daniel and evaporated on the barrier that surrounded them. It was enough to bring him back to his senses. He raised his protective shield and let fly his own attack; each of his missiles struck home. Magic combat was becoming second nature to him.

As he looked across the battle field, he could see that Philip had been right; they were all working together against him. The odds were against him, but Daniel had something they didn't know, tactical combat knowledge.

It wasn't from personal experience but rather the hundreds and hundreds of books he had read. History was a particular favourite, and he had gone through so many texts about battles; the Punic wars, Viking raiders, the victories of Alexander the Great, Bonaparte, Nelson, Shaka Zulu, to name but a few. This was the first time that he was able to use that information and knowledge in a practical way. And he was positive that it would give him victory.

He would use the duplicate spell, something he had always wanted to try, and create mirror images of himself using them as, a shield wall, sacrificing them to protect himself. Then he would target the new students with something big or flashy. Knowing that this was an all-new experience for them, there was a high probability that they would panic, become tense, and as he had learnt from Trinity back on Earth, in what amounted to be his first lesson in magic, tension is a barrier between Mages and their magic.

It was a sound enough tactic that would have quickly reduced their number. It was also something that he wouldn't be able to implement.

Something he had heard in the grandmaster's speech. It seemed inconsequential at the time, but it sparked something. Daniel recalled what Gydion had said about him playing a part in Trinity's return and explicitly what Grand Mage Penwyll had instructed him to do; prove that he understood the key, the theme, that connected her lives, go to the divine tree in the druid grove, and speak what he had learnt to wake her.

He didn't know who he was supposed to prove his understanding to, but there was only one thing that he could think of to do, give up something that he really wanted.

Daniel made a mental call to Gabinestra. The dragon appeared, full-sized in all her glory, having sensed Daniel's urgent need. People were unsure what to think of the sight. A real dragon had not been witnessed on Ariest for millennia, and many believed that it was merely an illusion and applauded. However, the professors of Hartfield knew differently, and headmaster Radek Zislaa slowly got to his feet as she let out a deafening roar. Most of the other students in the ring ran away, eliminating themselves from the competition, the others were too frightened to move.

'I'm sorry that call was so forceful,' Daniel said.

'Well, your secret is out in the open now. Expect your life to change from here on out,' she replied.

'It is what it is. I'll face up to it when we get back.'

Gabinestra lowered her head and allowed Daniel to climb onto her back. 'Where are we going?'

'To the Druid Glade.'

The mighty dragon flapped her powerful wings and took to the air, flying Daniel out of the magical barrier and set a course for the elven druids home.

'Daniel, what have you done?' Grumbled the dwarf as he watched to activity down on the ground. The elven royal guards had congregated together before approaching the headmaster. He could be seen shaking his head before they all left together.

'What has he done? He's only gone and eliminated himself from the vek-ting contest, that's what he's done,' Finn answered as she continued to watch the quickly shrinking form of the dragon. 'And he didn't even offer us a lift.'

'WHEN I HEARD THE GRANDMASTER talk about making sacrifices, something in me just clicked,' Daniel excitedly explained to Gabinestra when she asked about their rapid departure from Hartfield. 'In each of the major lives Trinity has led, it was the only thing that was repeated; making a sacrifice out of love. Against Sayyidah, she gave her life to save mine. In Iron Age Britain, I gave my life so that Aloisia could escape the Romans. In seventeenth century, France we sacrificed our lives for each other.'

'You seem pretty sure of this, Daniel.'

'I am. That's why we need to hurry. I don't know what Tristan is doing to her.'

'We are almost there now.' Gabinestra said as she began her spiral descent.

Daniel could see the druid elves running this way and that far below them. He could imagine that it must have been quite a sight seeing a dragon flying overhead, especially when they were low enough for him to see their faces.

'That's the divine tree there, in the Sacred Grove.'

'Ok, hold on. I'm going down.' She used her wings to buffer her landing, which kicked up small plumes of dirt and sent ripples across the lake to the small island on which the divine tree stood on.

As soon as Daniel jumped down, Archdruid Tavisum arrived with her guards. Upon seeing the dragon, they didn't take up an offensive stance, however, but rather bowed and dropped to a knee. The druids revered nature and the natural world and if there was one creature that they held on a par with the dragon, Green Man, the spirit of the forest, it would be the dragon gods.

'Now, this is how I should have been greeted from the beginning. I hope you are taking notes, little Daniel.'

As Daniel approached the Archdruid, she stood up to greet him warmly. Although their first meeting had been anything but pleasant, she had refused him entry into the Glade because she had believed that he was indeed the destroyer from Queen Rhiannon's dream prophesy, she had grown to respect him especially after Daniel had helped bring the murderer of the Green Man to justice,

'A dragon!' The usually aloof Tavisum was in awe. 'A real dragon! If I were to die tomorrow, I would go happily knowing that my life was complete. What brings you back to the Glade, Daniel?'

'I'm here to revive Trinity.'

Chapter Thirty-Four
The Brothers Mondragon

The last time Daniel had been here in the Druid Glade, the divine tree of the Sacred Grove had died, poisoned by the Undany traitor, Ch'tan. It was withered and blackened, with barely a leaf left on it. Now it was bigger, stronger than it had ever been. It's canopy full and lush with vibrant green leaves. It was alive!

Archdruid Tavisum walked Daniel, with Gabinestra on his shoulder, around the archipelago until they came to a stop at a large flower bulb hanging from the tree. Although he could not see inside of it, a rhythmic glow pulsed within.

'If you are sure you have the answer, Daniel, speak it now.'

He looked at the elf and then at the pod. Taking a deep breath, Daniel spoke in a clear voice, a single word. 'Sacrifice!'

The glow of the bulb pulsed faster and faster until it was a constant bright light, at which point it slowly began to open. The tension built as they both looked on with bated breath. Daniel didn't know what to expect, but, in all fairness, he was expecting more than what actually happened. He realised, judging by Tavisum's reaction, that she was anticipating something more also.

'This is all wrong,' she said in a hushed tone. 'She should be here, waiting for her chosen one to revive her. The Green Woman and the Devine Tree are linked; look how healthy this tree is. Look at the strength of its roots. She has been here, transforming, becoming her transcendent self. Yet, she is not here. Very puzzling.'

'This is what I was afraid of! I'm too late. It must be Tristan. He warned me, but I delayed doing anything. If he's hurt her...'

He reached out and touch the bulb and was instantly transported away.

A NEW MOON SHONE BRIGHTLY overhead as a mist crawled slowly across the ground. He could hear something like crying or sobbing, whispered prayers and people speaking in low voices. But neither he nor Gabinestra could see anyone.

'Well, that's not creepy at all,' Daniel said to the dragon.

'Indeed,' she replied. 'Wherever we are it's magical in nature.'

'Then let's take a closer look.'

He moved forward, twigs snapping and leaves rustling underfoot. Daniel pushed open the iron-wrought gate before him. It creaked in protest and angrily clanged shut behind him as he entered the old neglected cemetery.

Once well-tended lawns were now patchy, and the pathway that wound its way between the graves was cracked with weeds poking through. The headstones were discoloured or vandalised at best, cracked or crumbling at worst.

All of a sudden, they heard what sounded like dirt clattering against a coffin. They both looked around and again saw nobody, except the moonlight now seemed to be concentrated on two marble headstones. He was being directed to them, and Daniel went to take a closer. They were in overlooked by dead trees. He had to brush their twigs and detritus away so that he could read the carving clearly.

"Here lies Eric Mondragon. The legend, the hero, the man that left his own son to die."

Daniel took a step back and looked at it with a creased brow. He glanced over at the second gravestone, cleaned it up and read the inscription.

"Here lies Daniel Welsh Mondragon. The not-quite legend, the wannabe hero. The lesser brother; Daniel the lucky. Daniel the late. Daniel the one ruled by fate."

'What is this madness?'

'What this is, is the path you have decided to take, dear brother.'

The voice was everywhere. 'Tristan! What have you done with Trinity?'

'What have I done? I've done nothing. I told you, she was my bargaining chip to bring you to me. And here you are.'

'Yes, I am and, where are you?'

At that moment, there was a loud creaking of a door opening. Daniel spun around to see a mausoleum behind him with climbing ivy and moss growing in between cracks of the stone. 'that was definitely not there a moment ago,' he said. Gabinestra nodded in agreement. He didn't want to enter, but he knew that he had to if he wanted to find Trinity. Going further into this creepy dreamworld seemed to be the only way to do that.

Burnt out candles, their wax drippings hardened on their sticks adorned the wall along with vases of decomposed flowers. Spiders made elaborate webs in the corners, traps for prey that would never come. A single sarcophagus stood in the centre of the room. As they moved nearer, it was possible to hear the soft sobs of a girl.

'Trinity?' Daniel rushed around the corner of the imposing coffin and found her sitting there, her head in her knees as she cried. 'It's ok, Trinity, I'm here now. I'm going to take you home.' He pushed her thick auburn hair to see her, but when she looked up, he fell backwards and desperately scrambled away. What looked like roots were coming out of her eyes, ears and mouth. She crawled towards him before she collapsed.

Daniel let out a huge sigh of relief, which was premature, to say the least, as the floor beneath him vanish, and he tumbled into the darkness. Gabinestra held onto him with her powerful claws and slowed his descent.

'Are you positive this girl of yours is worth all this effort?'

'What kind of question is that? Of course, she is.'

'She had better be, Daniel. I could be out there flying over Ariest right now. Oh, how I have longed for it. I have been trapped...no, imprisoned in that Familiar realm for far too long waiting for you.'

'That's hardly my fault, but I'll tell you what, when I'm on my next holiday from Hartfield, we'll go together. I still have yet to see all of Ariest.'

'Well, isn't that touching,' Tristan rang out from the shadows. 'A boy and his pet. An uninvited pet, I might add.'

Gabinestra flew from Daniel's shoulder, grew to her medium size and, without so much as a second glance, let loose her frostfire in a sweeping arc in front of them, smothering the unsuspecting Tristan in the dragon's breath attack.

Daniel had to shield his eyes from the intensity of the assault. He felt some remorse as he heard the cries, no matter how insane Tristan had become, at the end of the day, he was still his brother.

The cries of agony suddenly stopped, only to be replaced by that of laughter. 'Well, well, well,' Tristan said from within the flames as the walls around him caught fire. 'Now, isn't this a pleasant surprise.'

'How is that possible, Gab? I thought you said only the Mortokai was immune to your flames?'

'The Mortokai and my... consort.'

'And who's that?'

'Baelthorn. He—he has the blood of Baelthorn in his veins.

'Tristan hand like a maniac as he inspected his scaled arms. 'This just gets better and better! What a coincidence. I should take that lucky part off your gravestone, brother dearest. Coming down here with your little pet dragon thinking that you would reduce me to ash. How did that work out for you?'

The dragon charged at Tristan. 'You will soon discover that a dragon is so much more than just its breath attack, little fool.' With her vicious row of teeth, she snapped at him, but he had already prepared for the attack. As she clamped her fangs into what she thought was the man that had insulted her, twice, Tristan dispersed into mist, then arcane tethers wrapped around her completely as if the dragon were being mummified.

'Now, that we are alone,' Tristan's said from behind Daniel. 'Let us talk about you accepting my gracious offer.'

'Give me Trinity.'

'Are you ready to take your place with me at the top echelon?'

'All I would have to do is perform magic, and I would be up,' Daniel stated flatly. 'You talked about recognition, acclaim, respect. What kind of respect is that when it is not earned? In a society that is unbalanced? I want nothing to do with your plans for false godhood. I want nothing to do with this magocracy. I just want Trinity.'

'But does she still want you?'

'I don't want to listen to any more of your rubbish. You tried to make me turn against my friends, made me question their motives, well not this time! Give me Trinity!'

Tristan saw Daniel clench his fists until they shook and chuckled. 'We've been here before, brother. You have no advantage over me any longer. I am physically stronger than you, more athletic, and with this dragon blood, my magic is just as powerful. And let's not forget, you won't attack first.'

'And I told you, people change!'

With a rapid blur of movement, Daniel's hands completed the somatic of his spell. He spoke the arcane words, and a dark grey cloud swirled into existence above Tristan's head. Daniel had unleashed an Ice Storm.

The temperature dropped and an icy deluge of snow and sleet pelted down. Bursts of magical hailstones bombarded the area, striking Tristan several times. A cold wind whipped up, rapidly chilling the air. Sharpened icicles fired out of the cloud, which were swiftly followed by bolts of chaotic magical energy; all the while Tristan tried to evade the attacks, laughing madly.

'Look at all this destruction you wrought, brother!' He had to yell through the howling winds. 'And you still think you are not the destroyer?'

The intensity of the storm had increased along with Daniel's own anger and frustration. Tristan's incessant goading and him not being able to find Trinity was fuelling the Harbinger. The realisation of it struck Daniel hard.

'You are what they say you are, Daniel! The progeny of the champion shall bring death and destruction. The ghost of the dragon shall change Ariest forever. The Mortokai has come! Your fate is sealed, Daniel! You cannot deny it! Destroy it all! Then you and I can be the heralds of Baelthorn... brothers united, and together we will be the new gods, of a new world.'

'I already told you, I want no part of your plans.'

'*Excellent, Daniel,*' Gabinestra said, projecting into his mind. '*Control of your emotions is the key to becoming the Spell Sage. Balance your emotions. Bring more positivity into your being, more love. Bring parity to the hatred and negative feelings powering your magic.*'

It was easier said than done. The animosity he had towards Tristan was growing so much. He couldn't forget what he did to those innocent people; the smell of their torched bodies would stay with him for a long time. Kidnapping Trinity, making advances towards her, Daniel had no idea what he was doing to her. Not knowing, was worse.

But he had to persevere; he needed to. He made her a promise, she was relying on him. She had chosen him, because she believed in him and because she loved him. Daniel knew how lucky he was to have such people in his life; Trinity and Finn both loved him dearly, and he them, but others too were close to him Aradia, Grimgaard, Anjunel and even Gydion in their own way.

As Daniel's mind filled with images of his loved ones and dear friends, the tumultuous storm above Tristan began to diminish, the bolts of chaos energy vanished, and the winds lessened. As the feelings of joy and positivity permeated Daniel, the destructive magic of the Harbinger was brought under control.

Tristan brushed the snow and ice out of his hair, then his clothes, a look of disappointment and disgust plastered on his face. 'You are such a letdown, Daniel. I have always wanted to know what it was like to have a brother. It could have been great, but you are a failure of a sibling. All this power, yet you are afraid to use it. It is wasted on you! If you will not use it, then I will kill you and drain every last ounce of Essence from your body and leave you as the useless husk you are!'

With his insanity spiralling ever deeper, Tristan used the ball lightning spell and directed the crackling sphere towards Daniel. Sparks of electricity arced from the fast-moving ball connecting it to the walls, floor and ceiling. Gabinestra let out howls of pain as the ball of lightning swept over her.

In barely enough time, Daniel was able to raise his own protection, just as his brother's lightning ball struck him. Hearing the dragon's groans moments before should have prepared the young Mage, but he had no idea of the strength of the attack, and it sent him crashing against the back wall.

As Daniel struggled back to his feet, he could hear Tristan beginning to cast another spell. It was too late to cast a Counter Spell himself, so he racked his brain for some way to interrupt it.

Then an idea popped into his head.

Reaching into his pocket, Daniel pulled out the peridot gem, infused it with some magical Essence and flicked it. With unerring accuracy, it struck his brother in the forehead, halting his spell casting.

Tristan slapped his hands to his head and growled. Before he could do anything else though, Daniel had followed up his initial spell with another one, Longstride, which he used to cover the ground between them in one huge step, and crashed into his enemy.

'Where is she?' Daniel shook Tristan as he shook him. 'What have you done with Trinity?'

Tristan laughed wildly. 'She's not here. She's already dead.'

'What? I'm too late?'

That moment of hesitancy was all the opportunity the battle-hardened Tristan needed to reverse their positions, but he didn't waste time talking and delivered punch after punch to Daniel. 'The truth is,' he explained between each strike, 'I don't know where she is. She was here, in this very chamber. I had planned to kill her in front of you, but I guess I'll have to enjoy that on my own when I find her. And when I finish with you, I'm going to do the same to our father and lay him in that grave, right next to yours.'

'And what about your Mulenaari mother? Aloena, isn't it?' Daniel asked. How do you think she would feel knowing that you had killed the man she had once loved?'

'Shut up!' screamed Tristan. 'Don't you say her name! He left her, just like he left me, and all he gave her was this ring!' Tristan shoved his hand with the bloodstone ring into Daniel's face.

It was a thing of beauty. The platinum band was intricately engraved, and the deep red colour of the stone seemed to swirl within as if it were alive. Gabinestra was just as taken by it as Daniel was.

'You hate him, and yet you still wear his ring?' Daniel questioned. 'Aloena kept it because she had feelings for him. Can't you see that?'

'She'll be just as happy knowing he was dead as I will be ending his life.'

'Then you should end your own life too then. He didn't know who you were. If you had just given your name, dad would have given his and then there would have been no duel. But you were too arrogant and became frustrated when he bested you. You made the test of prowess into a life and death contest, and you lost. Sore loser.'

'Shut up!'

Daniel, who was struggling to stay conscious as Tristan unleashed his fury on him. He could barely keep his eyes open. With each blow he faded a little more.

Suddenly, there was a sound akin to galloping hooves, then a bright green light filled the room.

Chapter Thirty-Five
Trinity's Final Form – The Green Woman

The brightness of the green light grew as the sound of the galloping faded. Tristan rose, shielding his eyes, to see who else had intruded into his play area uninvited. Although Daniel was battered and bruised, he took his chance to scramble away, towards Gabinestra, to see where the light emanated from.

'Are you alright?' he asked the dragon.

'Better than you, I'd imagine,' she replied. 'It has been quite some time since I have had to fight. It would seem that I am a little bit out of practice.'

Through his swollen eyes, levitating in the green haze, Daniel could see the form of a woman, her hair flowing outward as if she were underwater. She slowly looked at each of them before she slowly lowered, and as her foot settled on the ground, small wildflowers sprung up. The green light receded until it was gone, and a naked figure stood there.

'Trinity?' Daniel breathed. Bright green streaks highlighted her auburn hair. Her green eyes were more glistening and luminous than ever. Her floral aroma was more pronounced. It was her! She still had the nose ring in her left nostril and a light dusting of freckles across her nose and cheeks and some on her chest. He turned away, remembering her nakedness.

'Well, so you have come back to me, have you?' Tristan smiled and took a step towards Trinity. 'You realised that my hospitality was rather welcoming after all, huh?'

'I am the Green Woman. I am the embodiment of nature. I am the apotheosis of growth and the unstoppable urge of life to perpetuate itself.'

'That's very nice. I would just like to say that I've never seen you looking so good,' Tristan said with a smirk. 'I always knew you were wasted on Daniel. But we don't need to worry about him anymore.'

'You have violated the one chosen to usher in arrival, my emissary. An action which is also an affront to me.'

'Violated? Darling, I've only just started, and when I'm finished with him, it'll be just you and me.' Tristan reached out and stroked Trinity's arm. There was a slight sound of an electric charge crackling, which brought a smile to Tristan's face.

'You dare to touch a god?'

'For you, I dare anything.'

'Then kiss me.'

'You don't have to ask me twice.'

Tristan put his arms around Trinity and pulled her tight to him. Even though she did not react, watching them was difficult for Daniel to witness, and he turned his head. He felt helpless. How could he sit here and let this happen? The moans of pleasure that his brother letting out rang loudly in his ears.

Then they turned to groans of agony.

Daniel turned back at the sound of his brother's unexpected pain. Trinity's eyes were wide and flashed with lightning, small black storm clouds were in her hair. Their kiss continued but now Tristan was fighting it with all his strength. He used the wall as a brace to help get to his feet.

'No, Daniel,' Gabinestra said. 'I know what you are thinking, but you must remain centred.'

'I have to do something! She's going to kill him! She's not a murderer!'

In his weakened and beaten condition, try as he might, Daniel could do nothing to stop Trinity, as he watched Tristan collapse at her feet, a shrivelled husk. He looked at her aghast and then at what was left of his brother. 'What have you done, Trinity?'

'I was protecting my emissary.'

'Emissary? It's me, Daniel. Don't you recognise me, Trinity?'

'I no longer answer to this name. I am the Green Woman now.'

'Yes, and before that, you were Aloisia and Bianca, but to me, you will always be Trinity, the woman I love.' Daniel reached out his hands to take hers.

Their fingers interlocked, and a flash of remembrance crossed her face, but it was gone in an instant.

She released his hands. 'That woman is dead. Go, return to the woodland elves of the Druid Glade, emissary. Let them, and everyone, know that the Green Woman has been reborn, and I shall come back to the divine tree soon.

IT HAD BEEN SEVERAL days since Daniel, having left the Druid Glade, had returned to Hartfield Mage Academy. When he had told Archdruid Tavisum what had transpired, she immediately set the other elves to work, preparing things for a druid celebration. She had asked Daniel if he wanted to stay, but he had declined the invitation, citing that he needed to return to the academy. That had only been half the truth.

The other half came down to what Trinity had said; that the person he loved was dead. It had taken him a bit of time to reflect and he came to the conclusion that maybe she was right. It may have been Trinity on the outside but inside she was a completely different being, almost as if she were hollow.

He had spoken to Archdruid Tavisum about her change in personality, and she had explained that Trinity was no longer the person he had known. She was now a divine entity who was no longer bound by the constraints of mundane life. Her celestial scope far exceeded the need for such things as love and friendship.

Trinity had a welcoming aura that people gravitated to, but now that was gone, like she was an emotionless shell of the person she once was, and Daniel couldn't bring himself to be around that, let alone celebrate it.

Daniel had felt a growing sense of betrayal festering inside of him. They must have known; Tavisum, Penwyll, even Gydion, they must have known that this would happen when he resurrected Trinity. And yet, not one of them had even mentioned the slightest possibility of it.

He needed to get away to process what had happened, so, he had left the Druid Glade and returned to the academy, to a place that was still abuzz and coming to terms with what had happened at the Altus Vex competition, which Andrew Wilson, Edward Sands and Robert Masterson won. Of course, many had seen the various species of drakes and Wyvern before, but none had seen an honest to goodness dragon. No one had been around long enough to remember a time when the dragon flight filled the skies. No one except maybe the elven royal family.

But Daniel was in trouble, more than he realised. When he had come back, Proctor Morgana Goodfellow had met him and informed him that he could not attend classes and that he was to remain in his dorm room until summoned.

Not only had his dorm mates been moved elsewhere, he wasn't allowed visitors either; magical sentries had been placed on guard at his door. He had heard Sara try to see him a couple times until she had used her influence to be the one to bring Daniel his food.

They were able to talk briefly, and she would let him know if she had heard anything about what was going to happen to him, and keep him informed about Finn and the others. When Daniel asked about Philip, she told him that she had rarely seen him, of her sisters. So much for being good friends, he thought to himself.

The day eventually came when Daniel received his summons to see the headmaster. He dressed in his full uniform and was escorted to Headmaster Zislaa's office by the two guards.

The students in the hallways cleared a path when the escort party was spotted. They stared and whispered as the entourage passed. It wasn't that long ago that they had been laughing at Daniel, then they were cheering his name in awe, and now... now he didn't know what feelings he was getting from them.

DANIEL ENTERED THE headmaster's office, only to find that he wasn't alone. Radek Zislaa sat behind his large desk. There were six plush chairs, three down one wall and two on the other, and the sixth chair was placed in front of the desk. In two of the seats sat soldiers from the elf royal guard. In two seats on the other side sat Proctor Goodfellow and Archmage Gydion.

Seeing his friend and guardian filled Daniel with elation, but when he saw the stern look on his headmaster's own smile vanished.

'Take a seat please, Mr Welsh,' the headmaster said.

Daniel did as he was asked and immediately began nervously kicking the chair's legs with their heels.

'You already know the proctor and the Archmage, of course,' Zislaa said nonchalantly. 'These two gentlemen are headmaster's here representing the elven royal family. Now, I am sure that you know why you are here.'

'I had to go to the Druid Glade—'

'Leaving the school grounds, during term time, without permission is a breach of the school rules, is it not, proctor?'

'It is, headmaster,' Morgana Goodfellow replied.

'Did you obtain permission from a professor to leave, Mr Welsh?'

'No, but—'

'Perhaps you got permission from you, Archmage.'

'No, he did not,' Gydion replied.

Daniel glared at him because he knew exactly why he had to go, and yet he didn't defend him.

'Ordinarily, something like this would have been dealt with by the academy and the proctor, but due to the appearance of a dragon, it has come to the attention of Illandor and the ruling family. These two gentlemen are their representatives. They have expressed concern for what was seen at the contest and have petitioned the academy board to expel you.'

'What? You can't be serious!'

'I am very serious, Mr Welsh. You were to be expelled until the Archmage intervened and appealed on your behalf. The appeal was won, and the expulsion overturned.'

'Yes!' Daniel punched the air.

'However, there was a condition meted out. Namely, you may only perform magic within the walls of Hartfield, during lesson time only. After one year, your performance will be reviewed.' The headmaster placed a golden ornamental bracelet on his desk. 'This circlet was crafted on Illandor and is to ensure that you comply. If you fail to comply, you will be expelled and branded an apostate, a renegade. Do you understand, Mr Welsh?'

Daniel stiffened, a pained look on his face as he looked at each of them with an intense cold stare; even Gydion wasn't spared it. 'I can't believe this! I lose my girlfriend bringing back your nature spirit and this is the thanks I get? I solve your Shade problems, and yet I'm treated like a prisoner. Is this because I was too high up on your little magocracy hierarchy? That's not my fault. Maybe this society needs a revamp. Maybe magocracy rule is not all you people think it is.'

'Don't say another word, Daniel,' said Gydion, his eyes noticing the elves' hands going to their weapons.

'Or what?' Daniel got up forcibly, violently pushing his chair back, its legs scraped across the floor, before he turned to leave the office.

'Mr Welsh,' the headmaster said sternly and tossed the bracelet to Daniel. 'Aren't you forgetting something?'

He caught the bracelet, and in a moment of defiance, flipped them off as he slipped the circlet over his hand.

DANIEL RETURNED TO his dorm room, which becoming more and more like a prison, and slammed his door in a huff. He was incensed, and he could still feel the anger heating his palms. He couldn't believe Gydion just sat there and let it all happen.

At that moment, Daniel's door opened and closed. He almost fell over when he saw Sayyidah standing there in a red frilled off the shoulder dress with a wide black belt. She wore a silver chain headband in her jet-black hair, with a matching necklace and anklets, which connected to toe rings on her bare feet. She jingled lightly as she walked past Daniel and took a seat. 'Good,' she said. 'You have gotten over our initial confrontation.'

'Huh?' It was almost as if Daniel had suddenly come to his senses and was about to cast a spell to entrap the ancient Egyptian mage.

'I would not do that if I were you, beloved.' She pointed at the bracelet on Daniel's wrist, and he stopped in his tracks. 'I am only here to talk, Daniel.'

'We have nothing to talk about.'

'On the contrary, we have so much to discuss, beloved. Our paths are finally joined.'

'Are you insane?'

'On the contrary, I am very sane. Do you want to end the magocracy? Change the society of Ariest?'

Daniel scrutinised the harpy queen to see if what she was saying had the hint of truth. 'I have no intention of starting wars. You're a terrorist. You've killed countless people.'

'One person's terrorist is the next person's freedom fighter. I am sure you have heard that before. Truer words have never been said. You and I are revolutionaries, beloved. You want to end the Mage class system, give magic to all; I want to allow people to become all they can be.'

'How do you know so much about me?'

'It was you that gave me this spark, this drive.'

Daniel slowly sat down, surprised that his want was unnervingly similar to her own. Yet, she was someone that was vilified.

'We have the same enemy, beloved,' she pointed at the bracelet again. 'The same people that try to imprison your magic, the same people that released the prophecy to make you an outcast. The same people that are interfering with the harmonics of magic to control who gets it and who does not. The same people that created the magocracy with themselves perpetually at the top.'

'The elves?'

'Exactly! That is why I had to go to war to bring it down and why I have to bring Baelthorn here.'

'You are insane! You're using a nuke to kill a fly!'

'I do not know what that means, but I do know how to defeat Baelthorn. The Books of Azul, Roj, Clar and Ma'on were created by his brothers to imprison him. If we bring those books together, when the time is right, we can do so again. But you have to make a choice, beloved.' She held out her hand to Daniel. 'Stay here in Hartfield a prisoner, or come with me and change the world.'

'Why do you call me that, "beloved"?'

'Join me, and you will find out.'

Daniel looked deeply into her amber eyes, like two pools of gold, and tentatively reached out his hand. He had been trying to fight against the prophecy for so long, prove that it was wrong, prove that he wasn't the destroyer. Now, for the first time, since he heard it, he was on the verge of accepting his fate. Perhaps it was about him. Perhaps he would change Ariest forever, but one thing was certain, Daniel finally knew his purpose; he was about to do great things. The Mortokai had come.

THE END

Don't miss out!

Visit the website below and you can sign up to receive emails whenever D G Palmer publishes a new book. There's no charge and no obligation.

https://books2read.com/r/B-A-JGOH-RZMOB

BOOKS 2 READ

Connecting independent readers to independent writers.

www.ingramcontent.com/pod-product-compliance
Lightning Source LLC
Chambersburg PA
CBHW050725180626
46814CB00002B/609